"Access to the barn isn't included in your agreement."

Drawing herself up to her full height, Angel somehow managed to look down her nose at him in spite of the fact that he towered over her by a good six inches.

"But that's not what you're worried about, is it, Mr. McBride? You think I'm some sort of loose floozy from L.A. looking for a little dancing between the sheets while I'm stuck here in the boondocks, and I've set my sights on you. Well, you can relax. It's not going to happen. And do you know why? Because I'm not interested.

"Which is a good thing for you, big guy," she taunted softly, thumping him on the chest. "Because if I were, you wouldn't stand a chance."

Dear Reader,

As Silhouette Books' 20th anniversary continues, Intimate Moments continues to bring you six superb titles every month. And certainly this month—when we begin with Suzanne Brockmann's *Get Lucky*—is no exception. This latest entry in her TALL, DARK & DANGEROUS miniseries features ladies' man Lucky O'Donlon, a man who finally meets the woman who is his match—and more.

Linda Turner's *A Ranching Man* is the latest of THOSE MARRYING McBRIDES!, featuring Joe McBride and the damsel in distress who wins his heart. Monica McLean was a favorite with her very first book, and now she's back with *Just a Wedding Away*, an enthralling marriage-of-convenience story. Lauren Nichols introduces an *Accidental Father* who offers the heroine happiness in THE LOVING ARMS OF THE LAW. *Saving Grace* is the newest from prolific RaeAnne Thayne, who's rapidly making a name for herself with readers. And finally, welcome new author Wendy Rosnau. After you read *The Long Hot Summer,* you'll be eager for her to make a return appearance.

And, of course, we hope to see you next month when, once again, Silhouette Intimate Moments brings you six of the best and most exciting romance novels around.

Enjoy!

Leslie J. Wainger
Executive Senior Editor

Please address questions and book requests to:
Silhouette Reader Service
U.S.: 3010 Walden Ave., P.O. Box 1325, Buffalo, NY 14269
Canadian: P.O. Box 609, Fort Erie, Ont. L2A 5X3

LINDA TURNER

A RANCHING MAN

INTIMATE MOMENTS

Published by Silhouette Books

America's Publisher of Contemporary Romance

SILHOUETTE BOOKS

ISBN 0-373-07992-3

A RANCHING MAN

Copyright © 2000 by Linda Turner

This edition published by arrangement with Harlequin Books S.A.

® and TM are trademarks of Harlequin Books S.A., used under license.
Trademarks indicated with ® are registered in the United States Patent
and Trademark Office, the Canadian Trade Marks Office and in other
countries.

Visit us at www.romance.net

Printed in U.S.A.

Books by Linda Turner

LINDA TURNER

began reading romances in high school and began writing them one night when she had nothing else to read. She's been writing ever since. Single and living in Texas, she travels every chance she gets, scouting locales for her books.

Prologue

Engulfed in darkness, the man sat alone in the privacy of his small den and watched, transfixed, as the opening credits of the movie rolled onto his big screen TV. In the background, street shots of New York City flashed lightning quick, then there *she* was, just as he'd known she would be, smiling at him from the television. Angel Wiley. *His* angel. The woman he was born to love.

From the moment he'd seen her in her first movie, she'd lit up the screen with her innocent, virginal beauty. Her part had been a small one that hadn't consisted of more than ten lines, but he'd hung on her every word. And just that easily, he'd fallen in love.

He was a man who believed strongly in destiny, and there was no question in his mind that it was Fate that had led him to see that particular movie that day. Angel Wiley was meant to be his. Deep in his heart, he knew that, accepted it, looked forward to the day he could claim her as his own.

At first, of course, she hadn't known he existed, so he'd had to be content to worship her from afar. He dreamed of her, fantasized about her, and even quit his job and moved to Hollywood so he could be near her. He'd long since given up hope of ever meeting her when Fate once again stepped in and he ran into her quite by accident outside a restaurant in Beverly Hills. It was a meeting he would never forget.

Staring at her image on the TV screen, he smiled dreamily in remembrance. They hadn't had time to speak so much as a word to each other before her friends had swept her away, but no words had been needed. There'd been a spark, a flash of recognition between two souls, and she'd been as aware of it as he had. Nothing had been the same since.

She was all he could think of, but he couldn't just walk up to her and ask her out, not when she was the brightest new star in the Hollywood sky. She was naturally leery of strangers, and as far as she was concerned, that was all that he was to her. He knew differently, of course, but it would take time to convince her that he was the man of her dreams. So he'd had to content himself with following her home that night to get her address. Then he'd begun to gently woo her with cards and candy and flowers.

Just thinking about how delighted she must have been the first time he surprised her with roses made him smile. Although he'd never spoken to her, he knew his angel was a woman who would love flowers. And romantic gestures. She was sweet and loving and innocent and just looking for her knight to come racing up on his charger and sweep her off to happily-ever-after.

And he was her knight. He'd known it the first time he sat in a darkened theater and gazed up at her angelic face. And soon, she would know it, too. When the time was right.

Chapter 1

The woman who opened the door to Angel Wiley's soft knock was tall and spare, with a wrinkled face as stern as a ship captain's. But at the sight of the visitor standing on her front porch, a delighted smile broke across her firm mouth and good humor danced in her sky-blue eyes. "There you are! And looking just as pretty as you do in the movies! Come in, come in, and make yourself at home. We don't stand on ceremony in this neck of the woods— never have. Most folks are just like family." And not giving Angel time to object, she pushed open the screen door, pulled her inside and hugged the stuffing out of her.

Surprised, Angel laughed and returned the hug. She'd long since accepted the fact that because people felt like they knew her from her movies, they felt free to treat her like an old friend. "Mrs. Henderson—"

"Myrtle, dear," the older woman corrected her easily as she released her. "Mrs. Henderson was my mother-in-law, and that woman was meaner than a wet hen. Everybody in the county calls me Myrtle." Glancing past her through the screen door, she frowned in disappointment at the sight of the Ford Taurus sedan sitting at the curb. "Is that your car? I thought you'd have a limo. Garrett Elliot does. I saw him driving around the square just this afternoon."

Angie didn't doubt it. She and her costar had worked together once before, to her regret, and she knew for a fact that Garrett didn't go anywhere without a limo and entourage. Spoiled and insecure, he thrived on the trappings of stardom and the sense of self-importance it gave him. The more looks he drew, even in a backwater little town like Liberty Hill, Colorado, the happier he was.

She, on the other hand, was the exact opposite. She hadn't gone into acting for the fame, but for the work itself. She loved it, loved creating a believable character that came alive on the screen. But the work had its drawbacks, and she hated the notoriety that accompanied success and stripped you of your privacy. Unlike Garrett, she didn't like being stared at, so she kept a low profile whenever possible and tried not to draw attention to herself. Because not everyone who wanted to touch her, hug her, was a harmless fan.

A chill rippled over her at the thought, and it was all she could do not to glance over her shoulder to see if she was being watched from the street through the open front door. This wasn't a sprawling metropolis like L.A., where danger had stalked her without her even being aware of it, she reminded herself. Liberty Hill was hardly more than a village, lost in the mountains of southwestern Colorado. There were no hotels in town, nowhere for a stranger to hide. The studio had made arrangements for the cast to board with the local ranchers and townspeople, then booked every hotel within a sixty-mile radius for the crew during the filming of *Beloved Stranger*. An outsider, left with no place to stay, would stick out like a sore thumb.

When she'd learned the studio had arranged for her to stay in a Victorian mansion that was right in the middle of town and only a block from the sheriff's office, she'd sighed in relief. It had sounded like it was perfect for her.

And at first glance, the old house certainly lived up to its advanced billing. Dripping in gingerbread and charm, it was beautifully preserved and literally right around the corner from the sheriff. A scream would bring him or one of his deputies running to the rescue in a matter of minutes.

But what if she didn't have time to scream? a voice in her head taunted softly. An intruder could slip up on her in the dark silence of the night and she'd never know it until it was too late. All he'd have to do was break one of the ancient window latches or jimmy the lock on the front door, and he'd be inside in a heartbeat. While Myrtle slept peacefully in her bed, he could do God knows what to Angel and be gone before anyone even thought to note the danger.

Stricken, she paled and knew in that instant that she couldn't do it. There was too much at stake. As much as she liked Myrtle and hated to disappoint her, she just couldn't stay there. "Garrett always did like limos. I prefer to drive myself. Mrs. Henderson, about the house—"

"I knew you would love it," she cut in, beaming. "Everyone does. And it's Myrtle, dear. There's no need to stand on ceremony. After all, we're going to be housemates for the next two months, and I want us to be friends."

"Thank you…Myrtle. I appreciate that, but—"

"Think nothing of it, dear. I'm delighted you're here. And you know, of course, that I don't expect you to hole up in your suite the entire time you're here. There's plenty of room for both of us, so please make yourself at home. I heard you like to cook, so I imagine you'd like to look at the kitchen. It's probably not as fancy as what you've got in L.A., but I made sure it was well stocked for you. C'mon. I'll show you around."

She would have given her a guided tour, but Angel couldn't let her, not without feeling like a heel. To let her continue to think she could accept her hospitality would be cruel.

"Myrtle…wait," she said when the older woman started to turn toward the arched doorway at the far end of the entrance hall. "I hate to do this to you after you've gone to so much trouble, but I'm not going to be able to stay with you, after all."

"But the studio's already made the arrangements," she argued, taken aback. "Your rent's been paid, your rooms are ready. All you have to do is move in and unpack." Frowning with a sudden thought, she asked worriedly, "Is it the house? Is it because it's so old? That nice Mr. Douglas from the studio thought you'd be pleased."

"I am. I mean I would be but—"

"You're worried I'll talk your ear off when you try to study your lines at night," she guessed. "Don't be. I'm an old lady, dear," she confided, trying and failing to look feeble. "I don't know if you noticed, but I have a little antique store next door, and it takes all my energy just to stay on top of things there. By the time I get home in the evening, I'm so bushed, I'm lucky if I can stay awake long enough to eat a bowl of cereal during *Entertainment Tonight*."

Fighting a smile, Angel sincerely doubted that. Myrtle might be somewhere in her seventies, but her blue eyes were sharp and full of life, her step lively. She was a long way from being old. "It's not you," she assured her. "It's me. I need to stay in a place that's more…private."

It was a weak excuse, but the only one that Angel was willing to give her. She didn't know Myrtle, didn't know if she could trust her with the truth. She didn't seem the malicious type, but Angel already knew she liked to talk, and that could easily get out of hand. If she inadvertently repeated any of their conversation to any of the reporters that would soon be flooding the area, the news would be all over the papers the next day. She could see the headlines now.

Angel Wiley Threatened By Stalker.

The press would have a field day with that. And so would Garrett. She could hear him now, telling everyone on the set that Angel was so desperate for publicity and her fifteen minutes of fame that she'd do anything to get her name in the paper. Just thinking about it made her cringe.

Not taking her seriously, Myrtle laughed. "This is Liberty Hill, dear, not L.A. You don't have to worry about people peeking in the windows, ogling you. Anyone who goes around sticking their nose where it doesn't belong is asking for a fat lip, and I'll be the first one to give it to them. We respect each other's privacy around here. Or else."

Angel made no attempt to repress a smile. Myrtle looked so fierce, she could just see her taking on the tabloid reporters who regularly parked across the street from her house in West Hollywood and snapped pictures of anything that moved. If they tried that here, they'd be lucky if they still had their hair, let alone their cameras, by the time Myrtle got through with them.

"I'm sure everyone is normally very nice," she agreed. "But we're not talking about neighbors gossiping over the back fence about the county judge and his secretary. Once word gets out that a movie's being shot in the area, fans'll start crawling out of the woodwork. Then the trouble starts.

"Don't get me wrong," she said quickly before Myrtle could misunderstand. "I really do love my fans. Most of them are harmless and wouldn't dream of doing anything more objectionable than asking for a picture or autograph. Those are the nice ones.''

''And the others? The not so nice ones? What do they want?'

''Anything that touches my skin,'' Angel said bluntly. ''They've been known to crawl through a window just to get their hands on a pair of my underwear.''

Her cheeks slightly flushed, Myrtle swallowed. ''I see.''

She didn't. She couldn't fully understand what fame and adoration was like for someone who just wanted to do her job and come home at night and be left alone. The abhorrence of getting filthy letters in the mail from strange men. The fear that pressed in on her in the dark of night when the phone rang and she knew it was *him*—

Shying away from the thought, she stiffened. No! She didn't need to go there for Myrtle to understand that the arrangements the studio had made for her were, unfortunately, unacceptable. ''So you see why I need to stay some place more secluded. Please don't take this wrong—your house is wonderful—but it's right on the street. There isn't even a fence. If I'm going to sleep at all at night, I really need a gated community, some place with a state-of-the-art security system and motion detectors in every room. I'm sure you understand. I guess you could say I'm like Greta Garbo. I just want to be alone.''

It was an outrageous request for the wilds of Colorado, and they both knew it. Liberty Hill didn't even have a movie theater, let alone a gated neighborhood with the kind of security system she described. It was a ranching community, for God's sake! People worked hard for their money and didn't need fancy, high-falutin' houses in town with walls around them to show what they were worth.

Which was more than could be said for a spoiled movie star from Hollywood who thought she was someone special just because she could play make-believe in front of a camera.

Myrtle didn't say the words, but they were there in her eyes, nonetheless, along with a look that told Angel all too clearly that she had read the stories about her in the tabloids and was wondering now if they were true. And it was that that Angel hated the most. The speculation about her character, the doubts total strangers had about her before they even had a chance to meet her, let alone get to know her. Had her overnight success gone to her head? Could she possibly be as spoiled and demanding as everyone said? Did she really insist that the studio fly in fresh strawberries from California every morning for her breakfast and Dom Pérignon champagne directly from France whenever the mood struck her?

No! she wanted to cry, but she never got the chance. There was a sudden bold knocking at the front door, and they both turned to face the visitor who had arrived unnoticed while they talked. Standing on the other side of the screen door and silhouetted by the bright sunlight that streamed onto the front porch behind him, he stood like a dark specter, his face bathed in shadows, his broad shoulders filling the doorway.

He didn't say a word, didn't make a move that was the least bit threatening, but just that quickly, her heart was pounding with the sick fear that had become all too familiar over the course of the last two months. There was no reason to be afraid, she told herself desperately. This wasn't the man who was the cause of her nightmares in the dead of night. It couldn't be. She knew he would eventually follow her from L.A., that it was only a matter of time before he hunted her down in spite of the fact that the studio had been careful to keep under wraps exactly where *Beloved Stranger* was going to be filmed on location. But even he wasn't clever enough to find her just minutes after her arrival in Liberty Hill. Was he?

Still unsure and hating herself for it, she was struggling with the need to run when Myrtle broke into a broad smile of recognition and moved forward to push open the unlocked screen door. "Joe! Come in, dear. I wasn't expecting you until tomorrow."

After working on the sets of two Westerns, Angel had seen her share of wanna-be cowboys, but there was no question that the man who stepped into Myrtle's entrance hall was the real thing. Six foot two, if he was an inch, he looked as tough as a weathered fence post. His jeans and denim shirt were designed for work, not show, and both his scarred boots and battered black cowboy hat had seen their share of use and abuse.

But it was the man himself who bore the stamp of hours spent toiling out on the range in all kinds of weather. His square-cut face was hard and chiseled by the wind, his skin baked and tanned from the sun. Fine lines radiated from the corner of his sharp brown eyes, and although Angel guessed he wasn't much older than his mid-thirties, the temples of his dark brown hair were dusted with gray.

There was, she thought at first, nothing the least bit soft about him. Then Myrtle said, "What are you doing in town in the middle of the day? Oh, I bet you came for Cassie's bed, didn't you? How is the little darlin'?"

"Wild as a March hare," he said with a chuckle. "Zeke swears he's going to be totally white-headed by the time he's forty. Yesterday, he found her trying to ride one of the calves in the barn. She wants to be a bronc rider when she grows up."

A grin broke the stern set of the man's face, stealing Angel's breath right out of her lungs. Transfixed, she couldn't take her eyes off him as Myrtle laughed gaily. "What is she now? Two? Wait 'till she's ten and wanting to drive that great big Suburban truck of his. The poor boy doesn't have a clue what he's in for.''

Suddenly remembering her guest, she exclaimed, ''Oh, lordy, I completely forgot about Angel.'' Turning, she motioned her to join them. ''I'm sorry, dear. I didn't mean to exclude you. It's just that sometimes I get rattling and I completely forget my manners. Have you met Joe yet? No, of course you haven't,'' she retorted, answering her own question with a wry grimace. ''You just got into town, didn't you? This is Joe McBride, my godson. Your movie's being filmed on his family's ranch.''

''Then you must be the one Garrett's staying with,'' Angel told him. Pitying him that, she smiled and held out her hand. ''I'm Angel Wiley. Garrett's costar.''

Between one heartbeat and the next, the good humor in his eyes turned to ice. His gaze dropped to her extended hand, he hesitated, and for one stunned moment, Angel thought he wasn't going to shake her hand! Then he gave a curt nod, closed his fingers over hers for a terse shake, and jerked his hand back as if he couldn't abide the touch of her. Without bothering to say a single word, he turned back to Myrtle. ''I hate to interrupt, but I need to load up the bed and get back to the ranch. I've got a mare that's due to foal any day now, and I don't want to be away from her too long.''

Myrtle shot him a reproving look that would have made a lesser man grovel in apology, but Joe McBride just stared back at her woodenly and didn't so much as blink.

''Well,'' she huffed, scowling in disapproval, ''if you want to act as if you were raised in a barn, then I'm sure there's nothing I can do about it.'' And dismissing him as easily as he had Angel, she turned her attention back to her guest. ''I'm sorry about this, dear, but it looks like I'm going to have to run next door to my shop and take care of a little business. I hope you don't mind. It's only going to take a few minutes. If you'd like, you can go upstairs and check out your suite. You might change your mind about staying here once you see it. It's the first door on the left at the top of the stairs.''

Taken aback by Joe McBride's rude dismissal, Angel nodded stiffly. He'd all but cut her dead, she thought in amazement as the cowboy walked out with Myrtle without sparing her so much as a second glance. Her. Angel Wiley! The winner of last year's People's Choice Award who was, according to *Variety,* one of the brightest new stars to come along in Hollywood in years. Not that she read and believed her own press, she quickly amended. But didn't the man know who she was, for heaven's sake?

Of course he did, her bruised ego snapped in her head. He just wasn't impressed.

That wasn't a reaction she was used to.

She didn't consider herself a conceited woman, and she certainly didn't expect male attention as her due. After all, she wasn't drop-dead gorgeous like Jaclyn Smith, and she didn't have the pouty, sexy beauty of Marilyn Monroe. She was just average, nothing more, like the girl next door.

Or so she had always thought. But with the release of *Heart's Desire,* her first movie, three years ago, men had been making complete fools of themselves over her. She generally only had to smile at one to knock him out of his shoes. And even the more confident ones tended to stumble over their tongues when they got a chance to talk to her.

Joe McBride had done neither.

She should have been relieved. She didn't want any male attention, fawning or otherwise, and if she had any sense, she'd be thanking her guardian angels for making sure that the oh-so-annoying cowboy wasn't the least bit interested in her.

Instead, she wanted to throw something at the darn man's head.

So he wasn't a fan, she thought irritably. So what? She wasn't one of those insecure actresses who needed everyone to love her. People had different tastes—she accepted that. But was a little common courtesy too much to ask for?

She told herself to forget him and his rudeness. She had too many other problems to spend her time worrying about a long, tall drink of water like Joe McBride. But instead of going upstairs to check out the suite Myrtle had prepared for her, she stepped into the front parlor and moved to a window that overlooked the antique shop next door.

Joe strode out of Myrtle's shop just as Angel pulled aside the lace panel that covered the window, and guiltily, she stepped back out of sight. But she needn't have worried that he'd catch her watching him. He never even looked her way. With Myrtle scurrying along beside him, trying to help, he carried the solid wood antique twin bed and set it in the bed of his pickup as easily as if it weighed no more than a feather. When Myrtle scolded him, he only grinned and gave her a bear hug that completely lifted her off her feet.

Seeing them together, their faces alight with affection, Angel couldn't get over the change in the man. Which one was the real Joe McBride? The cold, arrogant one who had barely been civil to her? Or the charming cowboy with the slashing dimples who swept an old woman off her feet just to make her laugh?

Watching his truck head west out of town with the antique bed secured in the back, Angel was still asking herself that same question a few minutes later when Myrtle returned. "Oh, there you are," she said with a pleased smile when she spied Angel in the front parlor. "Did you check out your suite?"

"No, I really didn't see the point—"

"Don't say no yet," she cut in. "Think about it while we have tea."

Angel didn't want her to go to any bother, but she was learning that Myrtle was a force to be reckoned with when she was determined to have her way about something. "It's no trouble," she assured her and escorted her into the large, old-fashioned kitchen.

"When I was a girl, I was raised to entertain guests in the front parlor," she confided with twinkling eyes as she expertly prepared the tea. "My mother always said anything else just wasn't proper. Obviously, I was a sad disappointment to her. I like to break the rules." Grinning, she joined Angel at the round oak table that looked like it was at least as old as its owner and offered her homemade lemon cookies to go with her tea. "So what did you think of Joe? I hope he didn't offend you. In spite of his dreadful behavior, he really is a wonderful boy."

With a weathered face like his and disillusioned eyes that had seen more of life than he wanted, Joe was a long way from being a boy. And from what Angel had seen of him, there was nothing the least bit wonderful about the man. Still, Myrtle seemed to be more than a little fond of him so she wisely kept those thoughts to herself.

"Maybe he was just having a bad day," she said diplomatically, accepting a cookie. "It happens to the best of us."

"No, it's more than that, I'm sorry to say." Sobering, she stirred cream into her tea. "He and his wife, Belinda, divorced four years ago, and it hit him hard. The poor boy was nuts about her, but she was a city girl, and living on a ranch was downright foreign to her. Can you imagine? She didn't even know the difference between a bull and a steer when she came here!"

Struggling not to smile, Angel had no intention of admitting her own ignorance. "You don't encounter many bulls in the city."

"No, I guess not," the older woman chuckled. "But it was more than that. She missed her friends and shopping malls and all the noise of Denver." She shook her head, as if for the life of her, she couldn't understand the fascination. "Anyway, I thought she was adjusting, and so did a lot of other people. Then six months after their wedding, when Joe was busy with the spring roundup, she packed up her clothes one day, left him a note saying she couldn't take it anymore, and ran back to Denver. Joe hasn't had anything good to say about women since.

"Not that that excuses rudeness," she added quickly in case Angel got the wrong impression. "His mother, Sara, is my best friend and I know for a fact that he was raised better than that. He's just got some baggage he's got to deal with. We all do. But I'll tell you one thing, he's a good man. He might not sit next to you or any other single woman in church if he could find a way to avoid it, but if you were in trouble, he'd be the first one there to help you. The McBrides are all like that. They'd give you the shirt off their back if you needed it."

Her teacup lifted halfway to her mouth, Angel slowly set it back down as an idea began to take shape in her head. "They sound like a good family. Just how big is their ranch?"

"Oh, Lord, big enough to get lost in if you don't know where you're going. The place is huge. Janey, the oldest daughter, lives with Sara in the old homestead, and that's three miles from the ranch entrance. The rest of the kids have their own homes scattered about the place, and all of them are miles apart."

"And Joe? How far is his house from the main entrance?"

Her mouth pursed, Myrtle considered the distance.

"Maybe two miles, more or less. Merry has her veterinary office and house near the front gate, then you have to pass Joe's before you get to the homestead. So yeah, I'd say it's about two miles. Why?"

"It's not a gated community, but it sounds like the next best thing," she said honestly. "It's miles off the road, so I wouldn't have to worry about anyone invading my privacy." Or getting to her without someone on the ranch spying them first. Security would already be increased because the film was being shot there, and anyone who didn't belong there would never get past the front gate, let alone two miles down a private road to Joe's house.

"But Garrett Elliot's staying there," Myrtle argued with a frown. "And to put it bluntly, dear, I don't think Joe would be at all pleased to have a woman in his house. If you're really determined not to stay here, why don't you let me call Sara and see if she can put you up?" she suggested earnestly. "I know several of the other women cast members were assigned to her place, and of course, Janey's there, but they might be able to squeeze you in. It'll be crowded, and you won't have the privacy you would have here, but you won't have to worry about any fans peeping in the window at you. If anyone even thinks about approaching the homestead—or any of the kids' houses, for that matter—you can see them coming from a mile away."

Touched, Angel knew it couldn't have been easy for Myrtle to make the offer, especially since she'd so obviously been looking forward to having her stay with her. And if she'd just been worried about a curious fan or two, Sara McBride's home with its house full of women would have, no doubt, been safe enough, Angel acknowledged silently. But the man who had made the last few months a living nightmare for her was far more dangerous than a curious fan. If she was going to sleep at night, she needed

someone hard and tough to protect her, someone who
wasn't the least bit interested in her as a woman.

She needed Joe McBride.

The decision made, she sat back with a sigh of relief.
For the first time in weeks, the sick, hollow fear in her
stomach eased, and she knew she was doing the right thing.
"It's very kind of you to make the offer, Myrtle, but I really
do think it would be best if I stayed with Joe."

"But what about Garrett? Joe only has three bedrooms,
and Garrett reserved two of them so he could use one as
an office."

Not the least bit worried, Angel said confidently, "I'll
take care of Garrett."

And she'd see that he got no more than he deserved.
After all, he was the one who'd gone to the tabloids during
the making of *Wild Texas Love* last year and claimed that
her success had gone to her head, that she acted the star
and disrupted shooting on the set whenever she didn't get
her way. She hadn't, of course, but he hadn't cared about
the truth. He'd only wanted to get back at her for refusing
to sleep with him.

She'd never pulled rank in her life, but she was going to
now. Because she had to. One phone call to Will Douglas,
the producer, was all it would take, and she would be in at
Joe McBride's, and Garrett would be out. A vindictive
woman would have seen that he was given lodging in some
dusty old attic on the other side of the county, but that
wasn't her way. No, she was much nicer than that. She'd
make sure he had a comfortable place to stay…right in the
middle of town. If he didn't like little old ladies who had
a tendency to speak their minds, then he'd just have to learn
a little patience or rumors would soon be flying about him.

Revenge. How sweet it was!

Grinning mischievously, she observed Myrtle with twinkling blue eyes. "How would you like *Garrett* to stay with you?"

Hot and dirty and out of sorts, Joe headed for home just as the sun was sinking below the sharp ridge of mountains to the west. After checking on his pregnant mare, he'd spent the afternoon clearing brush and decaying logs out of the creek bed in Coyote Canyon, trying to improve the flow of the spring-fed creek for his thirsty cattle. And all he had to show for it was an aching back and a trickle of water that wasn't going to last the summer if they didn't get some rain soon.

But that had nothing to do with his foul mood.

Dragging red dust behind his pickup as he raced across the ranch on one of the dozens of gravel roads that crisscrossed the property, he came over a rise and scowled at the eighteen wheelers lined up like ducks in a row under the pines off to his left. There were no logos on the trucks, nothing to signify where they were from, but everyone within a hundred-mile radius knew what was in their trailers. Cameras, lights, sound equipment. Everything needed to make a movie.

Hollywood had come to the ranch, and he didn't like it.

His mouth compressing into a flat line, he jerked his eyes back to the road and reminded himself that he'd do well not to look a gift horse in the mouth. With cattle prices at an all-time low, the cost of feed up because of a drought that looked like it was going to last into the next century, and money tighter than it had been in decades, the ranch had been in serious financial trouble when Gold Coast Studios literally came knocking at the front door. The studio suits had wanted to use the ranch as the location for the filming of its next big blockbuster, and they'd been willing to pay an obscene amount of money to do it.

Even then, his first instinct had been to tell them no and

shut the door in their faces. He wanted nothing to do with the artificial world of movies and the people who made them. He didn't want strangers poking their noses into every nook and cranny of the ranch like they owned the place, scaring the cattle and making general nuisances of themselves. He didn't want to be bothered, dammit!

But business was business, and the ranch was a family operation. He couldn't make a unilateral decision based on his personal feelings. So in a family meeting with his mother, brother and sisters, the matter was presented and discussed. And to no one's surprise, it was decided that, considering the ranch's current financial troubles, they really had no choice but to accept the studio's offer.

The next day, he'd signed a contract giving Gold Coast Studios unlimited access to the ranch for the making of *Beloved Stranger*. Because of the shortage of available housing in town, he'd also given in to the pressure applied by his mother and sisters and agreed to rent out rooms to several cast members at the homestead and at his house. So for the next two months, the cast and crew could go just about anywhere they liked on the property.

Common sense told him he'd done the right thing, but that didn't make him like the situation any better. He'd been running the ranch for the last seventeen years, ever since his father died the summer after he'd graduated from high school, and the land was as much a part of him as the color of his eyes. His brother and sisters had all gone on to college and important careers, but he'd given that up without a single regret. Because it was the ranch that he loved—the vastness of its high mountain meadows, the solitude of its canyons, the beauty of a lone hawk soaring on thermals high over land that belonged to his family as far as the eye could see.

And when he drove over ranch roads that he knew like the lines on the back of his hand, it was deer and elk he expected to see when he caught sight of something moving through the trees, not cameramen and set designers getting ready for the first day of shooting on Monday.

He supposed he would, with time, grow used to the sight of strangers on the ranch, but he didn't think he would ever come to accept the idea of one in his home. Especially one like Garrett Elliot. The man was a jerk, a self-inflated, pompous fool who'd moved in yesterday while he was out, and taken over the house with an arrogance that still infuriated Joe. Elliot had actually had the audacity to claim the master bedroom for himself for the duration of his stay!

Who the hell did the man think he was? Joe fumed. Just because he was a big shot in Hollywood didn't mean he could waltz into his house and start taking over like he owned the place. As far as Joe was concerned, he was nothing but a boarder. And he'd had no trouble telling him that. He'd then given him two options. He could either take the two smaller rooms, one of which he could use as an office, or find himself a hotel. And the closest hotel with rooms still available was seventy-five miles away. Not a stupid man, Elliot had sulked off to the two smaller rooms and been thankful to have them.

But they'd taken an instant dislike to each other on sight, and Joe didn't fool himself into thinking that was going to change. He had no use for a man who thought he was entitled to special privileges because of his position in life. The next two months were, he thought grimly, going to be long ones.

He didn't, at least, have to treat the jerk like a guest. That wasn't part of the deal. He wasn't running a motel. Elliot had to pick up after himself and cook his own meals. Joe doubted that he even knew how to turn on the stove, but he wasn't sticking around to find out. Just as soon as he took a shower and washed off the ranch's red dirt, he was heading into town to have dinner at Ed's Diner. Chili sounded good. And chocolate cream pie. Nobody made chocolate cream pie better than Ed.

Already savoring the taste of it, he spied his house in the distance as the last streaks of red left from the setting sun turned to magenta, then darkening shades of violet. Every light in the house was on, not to mention the floodlights that illuminated the front and backyards. It was barely dark, and the place was lit up like a Christmas tree.

Swearing softly, Joe increased his speed. He could see right now that he and Elliot were going to have to have another talk. The studio might have paid a decent sum for him to stay there for the next two months, but that didn't mean Joe was going to stand by and let him drive up his utility bill just because he missed the bright lights of L.A.

He had a scathing lecture all worked out in his head. Then he braked to a stop behind a red Ford Taurus sedan in his driveway and his mind went blank at the sight of the woman pulling something from the trunk of the car. Angel Wiley. He'd barely spared her a glance at Myrtle's that afternoon, but he'd still have known her on the dark side of the moon. Just like every other man in America.

Not that he was a fan. He didn't give a rat's ass that she was Hollywood's latest sweetheart. But like it or not, she wasn't the kind of woman any man with blood in his veins could easily ignore. And for the life of him, Joe didn't know why. She wasn't drop-dead gorgeous. She was too cute, too wholesome with her wavy, sun-streaked blond hair, freckles and sparkling blue eyes. To add insult to injury, her smile was crooked, and she had dimples, for God's sake. Granted, she was tall and willowy and had legs that went on forever, but she couldn't, under any circumstances, ever hope to be called voluptuous. Still, there was something about her, an air of innocent sexuality, that was incredibly appealing.

Furious with himself for even noticing, he wondered

what the hell she was doing there. Then his gaze shifted from her to the suitcase in her hand, then to his open front door. And it hit him. She was moving in!

Muttering a curse, he slammed out of his pickup and strode toward her, his long legs quickly eating up the distance between them. "What the hell do you think you're doing?"

Her heart thumping crazily, Angel didn't so much as flinch. Myrtle had warned her he wouldn't be happy about the change in plans, but that wasn't something she could be concerned with at the moment. She needed a safe haven, and like it or not, his house was it. Nothing else mattered.

Still, she wasn't nearly as cool as she pretended when she looked down her slender nose at him and met his hostile gaze with a delicately arched brow. "I would have thought it was obvious. I'm moving in, of course."

"The hell you are!" he growled. "Put that damn suitcase back in your car and get out of here. You're trespassing on private property."

There'd been a time when that would have been enough to send her packing. Unlike Joe McBride, she didn't have an ounce of anger in her. She didn't like confrontations, didn't like fights. Given the chance, she avoided them at every turn. But this was one she couldn't back down from. Not when not only her safety, but her daughter's, was at stake.

Standing her ground, she faced him squarely. "I hate to be the one to disillusion you, Mr. McBride, but I have every right to be here. You signed a contract with the studio—"

"My contract is with an actor," he cut in coldly. *"An actor,"* he stressed. "Sharing my house with a woman was never part of the agreement. Especially a spoiled prima donna who thinks she's God's gift to the rest of the world."

Angel felt her cheeks burn and knew she looked guilty as sin. Damn Garrett! Was there anyone who hadn't heard and believed the lies he'd told about her? "Your contract is for a cast member," she said stiffly. "If you don't believe me, you can talk to Will. I'm sure he'll be happy to answer any questions you may have."

She didn't give him time to object, but simply punched in a number on her cell phone and handed the phone to Joe. Stony-faced, he was left with no choice but to speak to the producer. "Douglas, we've got a problem," he snarled. "I don't care what the damn contract says. I'm not sharing my house with a woman!"

Chapter 2

It was a fight he couldn't win, and he was smart enough to know it. But he didn't have to like it. Seething, he told Will Douglas what he thought of a contract that gave a man no say in who was or wasn't allowed in his own home. When he finally turned back to Angel and tossed her the phone, his brown eyes were nearly black with angry promise.

"You win this one, Cinderella. You get to stay, and there's not a damn thing I can do about it. But I wouldn't start celebrating too soon if I were you. You're not going to like it here. I'll make sure of it." And without another word, he brushed past her and stormed into the house, leaving her standing in the driveway.

His mother—and Myrtle—would have chewed his butt out for not at least carrying in her luggage for her, but she wasn't a guest, dammit! Guests didn't go behind your back to force their way into your home, then thumb their nose at you when you objected. She'd stepped over the line, and as far as he was concerned, the last thing she was entitled to was hospitality. Let her carry in her own damn bags!

But as much as he wanted to ignore her, he found to his disgust that he couldn't when she followed him inside dragging a suitcase that had to be as big as a packing crate. It was on rollers, but difficult to maneuver, and must have easily weighed half as much as she did. Still, she didn't ask for any help. Her chin set at a proud angle—as if *she* were the injured party! he thought incredulously—she tugged and pulled, straining with every step, and finally got the suitcase over to the bottom of the stairs.

Delicate color singed her cheeks, and try though he might, Joe couldn't take his eyes off her. Damn her, who the hell did she think she was fooling? There was no way she was going to be able to carry that damn suitcase upstairs and they both knew it. It was too heavy, and she was too slight. The sheer weight of it would drag her back down again. It'd be just his luck that she'd hurt herself, and she was just the type of woman who would revel in that. He could see it now. Laid up in bed like a princess with a sprained toe, she'd expect him to come running every time she crooked her little finger.

The hell he would!

Muttering a curse, he strode over to her, ignored her gasp, and took the suitcase from her as easily as if it weighed no more than a feather pillow. "I'll take it up for you...*this* time," he said coldly. "But don't make the mistake of thinking you're going to be waited on around here, sister. This is a working ranch and everyone carries their own weight." His jaw like granite, he effortlessly carried her bag up the stairs, leaving her to follow or not.

Don't make the mistake of thinking you're going to be waited on around here, sister, she mimicked silently, glaring at his ramrod straight back. Irritating man! Myrtle had warned her he wouldn't make this easy for her—she should have listened. But after everything she'd said about his family, Angel had hoped that he'd at least give her a chance. She should have known better. The ink on his divorce might have dried four years ago, but according to Myrtle, he still avoided women like the plague. The last thing he would want was one living with him.

She could have told him he had nothing to fear from her. She wasn't staying there because she was interested in him in any way, shape or form. He was too hard, too intense, too full of anger, and any woman who got in his way was going to get blasted. She just needed some place safe and off the beaten track for her and her daughter to stay, and his place qualified on both counts.

Still, his criticism stung. Did he think just because she had a glamorous career that seemed to require nothing more of her than she smile and play make-believe in front of a camera that her life had always been so easy? Her father owned a small café in New Mexico and had never cleared in a year what she made in a week. Her mother had died when she was eight, she'd been busing tables when she was ten, waiting them when she was fourteen. Joe McBride didn't have to tell her what it was like to work hard—she'd been doing it all her life.

Resentment glittering in her eyes, she followed him upstairs. Besides the bathroom, there were three rooms—the master bedroom and two smaller bedrooms, one of which contained a single bed and a small desk that Garrett would have no doubt had to make do with as an office. The second was obviously the guest room. Simply furnished with a vanity-style dresser and an old-fashioned spool bed that was covered with a white chenille bedspread, it was modest and unadorned but for the lace half panels at the room's two windows. It was here that Joe set her suitcase.

Stepping over the threshold, Angel took one look at the plain, unpretentious lines of the room and felt the tension that had knotted her nerve endings for the last two months ease. If this was the room Joe had given Garrett, she could just imagine what her costar must have thought when he laid eyes on it. He would have hated it. It was too small, too simple, and didn't even have a television or phone. She'd done him a favor by having him moved to Myrtle's.

She, on the other hand, found in its very simplicity a peacefulness that seemed to call to her very soul. Not only would she and Emma be safe here, she realized with a quiet sigh of relief, but she would find a haven from the tiring rat race that her life had become in L.A.

Joe, obviously finding criticism in her silence, snapped, "I warned you this was no fancy hotel. What you see is what you get. Take it or leave it."

There was no question that he was hoping she'd leave it, but she wasn't that stupid. "I'll take it," she said softly.

A muscle clenched in his jaw. "Then I'll tell you the same thing I told Elliot. There's no maid service, room service, or peons to do your laundry. You cook for yourself, pick up after yourself, and do your share of the cleaning. Since there's only one full bath and we have to share the kitchen, I've come up with a schedule so that neither of us inconveniences the other. It's posted on the refrigerator. I suggest you stick to it."

Or else. The words weren't spoken, but Angel heard them nonetheless. If she'd wanted to irritate him, she could have told him that there was nothing about sticking to a schedule in the contract he had with the studio. She could make mincemeat of his schedule and there wasn't a damn thing he could do about it. But she'd riled him enough for one day. And though he didn't know it, he was giving her and her daughter a sanctuary that was invaluable. For no other reason than that, she'd do whatever she could to make sure she intruded on his home life as little as possible.

"I'm sure that won't be a problem," she assured him quietly. "You won't even know I'm here."

He didn't even bother to dignify that with an answer, but he didn't have to. His snort of contempt told her exactly what he thought of that.

Joe carefully wiped down the newly sanded twin bed he'd bought for his favorite—and only—niece, Cassie, his brow furrowed with a scowl. So he wouldn't even know she was there, would he? he fumed, hardly noticing the beauty of the antique wood beneath his hands. Yeah, right! Oh, his unwanted houseguest had kept out of his way, he had to give her that. In the week since she'd moved in, filming had started on *Beloved Stranger,* and he'd barely seen her except in passing. He should have been happy he wasn't running into her every time he turned around. But a man didn't have to trip over a woman for her to nag him to death. Angel Wiley could do it without saying a single word.

With a muttered curse, he wondered if she had a clue just how impossible she was to ignore. Her food was in the refrigerator alongside his, her damp towel hanging on the towel rack next to his in the bathroom, her clothes in the washing machine when he wanted to do laundry. Then there was her scent. Good God, he thought with a groan. Why couldn't it have been bold and blatantly sexy, just the kind of scent he'd never liked on a woman? Then she would have given him just one more reason to resent her presence in his house.

But the lady didn't do the expected, dammit! Her fragrance was light and delicate and softly enticing. And like a promise whispered on the wind, it lingered on the air and wrapped around him every time he stepped through the front door. But it was the nights that were the worst, when he was asleep and her perfume drifted past his defenses to invade his dreams. He never remembered what he dreamed and didn't want to, but he woke up restless and on edge. And it was all her fault.

In self-defense, he avoided her and the house every chance he got. The summer days were long, thankfully, and the ranch overrun with a film crew that had little experience with cattle, so he found plenty to keep him busy. There were downed fences to repair, strays to round up, and the herd to be moved when it was needed for filming.

He couldn't, however, work around the clock. Eventually, he ran out of daylight and was forced to go home to find the lights on and the infuriating Ms. Wiley already home herself. Normally, he would have cleaned up, then scrounged around in the kitchen for something hot and filling. But not with her in the house. He didn't want to see her, to talk to her, to have any more to do with her than he had to. So every night, he grabbed a cold sandwich from the kitchen, then retreated to his workshop in the barn.

It was his last sanctuary, his woodworking shop, and the one place of his that his houseguest had yet to invade. Here, working on Cassie's bed, the smell of sawdust and varnish thick in the air, he didn't have to think about that damn perfume of hers, didn't have to think of her. And he intended to keep it that way.

Finishing off the last of his sandwich, he ran his hands over the headboard and found it as smooth as a baby's bottom. When he'd picked the bed up at Myrtle's, it had been covered in so many coats of paint that it had been impossible to tell the kind of wood it was made of. It had taken him four days to strip away a lifetime of paint with paint remover, but he was finally down to the bare wood. And it was beautiful.

Elizabeth and Zeke were going to love it. They didn't know that he'd bought an antique, but he'd wanted to give Cassie something special. She was the first baby born into the McBride family in over three decades and he'd wanted her to have something special that could be handed down for generations to come. It had taken Myrtle a while to find what he was looking for, but this was it. After another light sanding, staining and a coat of varnish, it would be beautiful.

"Excuse me. I don't mean to intrude, but there's no hot water—"

Swearing, Joe whirled to find Angel standing at the entrance to his workshop just like she had every right to be there. Too late, he wished he'd locked the door. Because the lady looked too damn good. So much for the rumor mill, he thought sarcastically. Gossip abounded about the ranch now that it had been overrun by the Hollywood crowd, and from what he'd heard, the glamour queen had had a rough day playing the part of a widow trying to break a stallion on the ranch she'd inherited from her deceased husband.

She hadn't done the actual work, of course, but even then, a certain amount of real physical labor was required in order for her to look like she knew what she was doing. Supposedly, she'd thrown herself into the scene—and gotten more than she bargained for when the horse she was working with got out of hand and pulled her off her feet into the dirt.

He nearly rolled his eyes at that. Yeah, right. The studio's publicity department might get her adoring fans to swallow that bunch of malarkey, but anyone who'd been jerked around by a stubborn horse knew better. If a soft city slicker like Angel Wiley had really been pulled off her feet, she'd be laid up in bed right now whining about her sore muscles, not standing there in his workshop looking as fresh as a ray of sunshine in a simple yellow cotton blouse and jeans that clung in all the right places.

Irritated that he'd noticed the enticing curve of her hips and thighs, he growled, ''What do you want?''

Not surprised by his coldness—he hadn't said two words to her after their initial confrontation when she'd moved in—Angel didn't so much as blink. She was just too tired. Every bone in her body ached from her battle on the set earlier that afternoon with the horse from hell, and all she wanted to do was soak in a hot tub, then go to bed. But there was no hot water, and she absolutely refused to go to bed without a bath first.

If she'd known where the hot water heater was, she would have checked the pilot light herself—even if she was too stiff to sink down on her knees to do it—but she didn't. Which left her with no choice but to beard the lion in his den in the barn. And there was no question that it was his den. He'd hidden out for hours there every night that week, not returning to the house until well after she turned out the light in her room.

More than once, she'd been tempted to follow him just to see what he did out there every night. But she'd already intruded on his privacy more than he liked, and the peacefulness of their coexistence was fragile at best. He still didn't want her there and didn't insult her by pretending that he did. And he had no idea how much she respected him for that. He was a rarity in her world, where people played nicey-nice just so they could get close to her. His rudeness could be off-putting at times, but he didn't play games. She knew where she stood with him, and that was a welcome relief.

''I was going to take a bath, but there's no hot water,'' she began, only to gasp in delight when her glance slid past him to the antique bed he'd obviously been working on. ''Is that the bed you bought from Myrtle?'' she asked in surprise. ''The one for your niece? My God, it's beautiful!''

If she hadn't recognized the angels carved into the bed's

headboard, she never would have thought it was the same bed she'd seen Joe carry out of Myrtle's shop last week. Then, it had been ugly and scarred and nearly black with paint. She wouldn't even have looked twice at it. But now…it was gorgeous!

Eager to examine it closer, she stepped across the threshold into the workshop, but that was as far as she got. She never saw him move, but suddenly he was right in front of her, blocking her path, and so close she could almost feel the hard wall of his chest against hers. Startled, she looked up and found herself caught in the trap of his narrowed, dark brown eyes. And for no reason at all, her heart began to thump.

"The barn isn't included in the agreement with the studio."

She knew that and wouldn't have had a problem with it—if the glint in his eyes and the low rumble of his voice hadn't dared her to even think about taking another step. Between one heartbeat and the next, she'd had enough…enough of his hostility when she'd done nothing except have the misfortune to be a single female…enough of his flinty looks and distrust. So he'd been hurt by a woman. She could sympathize with that. But he wasn't the only one who'd ever had the misfortune to be hurt by love. And she wasn't the one who'd hurt him!

Drawing herself up to her full five foot seven inches, she somehow managed to look down her nose at him in spite of the fact that he towered over her by a good six or more inches. "I wasn't going to contaminate the place, just look at the bed. But that's not what you're worried about, is it, Mr. McBride? You're afraid I'm going to trip you and beat you to the ground.

"Oh, don't bother to deny it," she said quickly when his brows snapped together in a fierce scowl that would have intimidated a lesser woman. "You think I'm some sort of loose floozy from L.A. looking for a little dancing between the sheets while I'm stuck here in the boondocks, and I've set my sights on you. Well, just for the record, you can relax. It's not going to happen. And do you know why? Because I'm not interested. Which is a good thing for you, big guy,'' she taunted softly, thumping him on the chest. "Because if I was, you wouldn't stand a chance."

Dismissing him with a toss of her head, she turned and walked out. And never knew that she left him standing there staring after her like a man who had just been hit by a two-by-four.

Tiny's Pool Hall was the only place in town that came close to passing for a bar, and it was a poor substitute. Granted, there was a jukebox in the corner, and smoke hung like a cloud overhead, rising unrestricted to the bare rafters, but the only alcoholic beverage sold was beer, and that was limited to three per customer. The locals knew the rules and had long since accepted the fact that Tiny was never going to let anyone leave his place drunk, but the Hollywood crowd was something else. Packed shoulder to shoulder in the humble establishment and looking for action, they grumbled and whined about everything from the size of the minuscule dance floor, where couples were packed together like sardines, to the fact that the beer wasn't imported. But no one left. Because unless someone wanted to check out Ed's Diner down the street and get something to eat, Tiny's was the only hot spot in town open after eight o'clock.

Seated alone at a rough-hewn table far in the back, Joe nursed a beer and never noticed the interested looks he was getting from some of the female cast members of *Beloved Stranger*. Instead, his gaze was focused inward, on the film's star and the cocky, knowing little smile she'd given him right before she'd lifted that pert nose of hers into the air and sailed out of his workshop like a princess decked out in a tiara.

So she thought he wouldn't stand a chance if she decided she wanted him, did she? he fumed. That he had no choice in the matter? Like bloody hell! He'd gone after her to tell her he had no intention of dropping at her feet like the rest of the men in the country, but by the time he'd reached the house, she'd already gone upstairs. Just the idea of confronting her in her bedroom had been enough to send him packing. He'd only taken time to relight the pilot light on the hot water heater, then he'd gotten the hell out of there.

He hadn't been able to go back to the barn, not without envisioning Ms. Tinseltown there, so muttering curses, he'd headed into town to Tiny's for a beer and a game or two of pool. That should have been enough to push the lady from his mind, but half the population of L.A. seemed to be crammed into the pool hall, and everywhere he looked were reminders of Angel. The blonde on the dance floor wore her hair like Angel's; the brunette at the bar had her smile. It was enough to drive a man to drink.

He had to admit he'd thought about it—having his three-beer limit at Tiny's, then stopping at the Quick Stop on the edge of town and picking up a six-pack to take home. Maybe then he'd be able to forget at least for a little while that he not only shared his home with Hollywood's newest sweetheart, but that he slept right across the hall from her night after night after night. And he didn't like it, dammit! He didn't care how much she stayed out of his hair, he didn't want her there.

He just wanted to be left alone in his own home. To be able to fall into bed at the end of a long, hard day and actually fall asleep instead of lying there half the night, staring at the ceiling and fighting the seductive allure of that damn scent of hers. And when he finally did sleep, to be able to control the hot, erotic dreams he had of the woman. Was that too damn much to ask?

Images from last night's dream swirled before his mind's eye, teasing him, tempting him, driving him crazy. Grinding a curse between his clenched teeth, he started to signal Tiny for another beer. But he hadn't gotten drunk over a woman since Belinda had walked out on him, and he wasn't about to start now. Throwing down a generous tip on the table, he pushed to his feet and walked out, the hard don't-mess-with-me glint in his eyes just daring anyone to get in his way. No one did.

When he got back to the ranch and saw that the light in Angel's bedroom was still on, he didn't even turn into his driveway, but continued on past it and drove straight to his brother's. It wasn't until he braked to a stop in Zeke's driveway and saw that the house was shrouded in darkness that he glanced at his watch and realized it was nearly twelve. Damn! He should have known Zeke and Elizabeth would be asleep. With a two-year-old in the house, their day started early.

Which left him with nowhere to go but home. And it was a sorry state of affairs when a man didn't want to go home.

Scowling at the thought, he just sat there with the motor running and never noticed a light flare on in the living room or Zeke step out onto the porch. Dressed in nothing but jeans, he called out teasingly, "Are you going to sit there all night or come inside?"

He swore softly. "I just wanted to talk, but I didn't realize it was so late. Go on back to bed before Elizabeth wakes up. I'll see you tomorrow."

If it had been anyone but his brother sitting in his driveway wanting to visit, Zeke would have sent them packing. But Joe didn't make a habit of showing up on his doorstep at that hour of the night without a damn good reason. Something was obviously troubling him.

"You're here," he retorted. "We might as well talk now. Come on up on the porch while I get us a beer."

Not giving him a chance to argue, he turned and went back into the house for the beers. When he came back outside, it was to find Joe prowling the length of the porch and back. Arching a brow in surprise, Zeke handed him his beer. It wasn't like Joe to be restless. The only time Zeke had ever seen him let his emotions get the best of him was when it came to family…or a woman. And since there were no family emergencies that he knew about, it had to be a woman eating at him.

It was about damn time.

Grinning, he sank down into his favorite porch rocker and watched with amusement as Joe set his beer down on the porch railing without even tasting it. "Sorry I couldn't help you with moving the cattle today, but I couldn't put off picking up that maimed mamma wolf and her pups north of Denver. The locals were in an uproar and pressuring the sheriff to put them all down, even the pups."

"Idiots," Joe growled in disgust. "You get them settled okay?"

Zeke nodded. He and Elizabeth had opened a wildlife refuge for injured animals on the ranch after they were married, and now they got rescue calls from all over the West. "Merry had to amputate the mother's shattered front leg," he said regretfully, remembering how she'd agonized over the decision but done the only humane thing she could. "So she'll spend the rest of her life with us, but Elizabeth's hoping the pups'll be able to be released back into the wild eventually."

"If anyone can pull that off, Elizabeth can."

Zeke had to agree. A wolf biologist, his Lizzie had pulled off a miracle or two in the past, and she'd do it again.

Taking a swig of his beer, he stretched out his legs and asked casually, "Everything going okay around here?"

Joe shrugged. "Well enough. You've always got some jackass spooking the cattle, but other than that, I guess things are going as well as can be expected."

"And your houseguest?" he prodded, his blue eyes twinkling with devilment. "How's she working out?"

In the time it took to blink, Joe stiffened like a poker and it was all Zeke could do not to laugh. "She's not a guest, she's a renter, and she does whatever she damn well pleases," he snapped. "And don't get that look in your eye. I know what you're thinking and you're barking up the wrong tree. I haven't looked twice at the woman."

"Oh, really? So she has nothing to do with this foul mood you're in?"

"Of course not!"

"You just showed up here at midnight to shoot the breeze? Is that what you're telling me?"

"Pretty much," he retorted, stung. "And to let you know that Cassie's bed will be ready the day after tomorrow. I thought Lizzie would want to know."

That information could have been passed along in a phone call at a more reasonable hour and they both knew it. "Nice try," Zeke drawled, making no attempt to hold back a grin. "But I'm not buying it, big brother. I know you better than that. And from where I'm sitting, I'd say Miss Angel Wiley has you rattled, and I think it's great. It's about time someone shook you up."

"I'm not shook up, dammit!"

"No? Then why are you acting like an old bear with a sore paw? Something's needling you, and if it's not a problem with the ranch, then it's got to be a woman. Namely the one you're living with—"

"I'm not living with her! She's renting a couple of rooms, for God's sake."

"Same thing," Zeke said, dismissing that argument with a wave of his hand. "Bottom line is half the men in the country would kill to be in your shoes. I haven't met her face-to-face, but I've seen her movies, and she's an incredibly attractive woman. So have you kissed her yet?"

His teeth clenching on an oath, Joe gave serious consideration to killing him. But Elizabeth loved him, though God knew why, and Cassie was entitled to grow up with a father…even if he was as irritating as hell. "I'm not even going to bother to answer that," he growled. "There's no reasoning with you tonight. I'm going home."

Storming past him out to his pickup, he never saw Zeke's grin of delight. He knew he was letting him push his buttons, but he couldn't stop himself when his brother called after him, "Tell Angel hi!" Shooting him a rude hand gesture, he drove away in a cloud of dust, cursing all the way.

In the deep silence of the night, a door slowly eased open downstairs, and Angel came awake with a start. Disoriented, she frowned at her shadowy surroundings, trying to get her bearings, when she heard it again. The quiet tread of a footfall somewhere downstairs. Her heart slamming against her ribs, she froze and tried to convince herself it was just Joe.

But in the six days she'd lived in his home, she'd come to recognize the sound of his step, and even in the dead of night, he never moved quite so stealthily. And when she soundlessly slipped from her bed to look out her bedroom window, Joe's truck wasn't parked in its customary spot in the front driveway. He'd left soon after they'd spoken in the barn, and he obviously hadn't returned.

The fear hit her then, low and hard and all the more terrifying because over the last week she had foolishly begun to think she'd found a safe place to bring Emma. Idiot! She should have known better. Every time she'd changed her phone number, hadn't her stalker discovered the new one within a matter of days? And in spite of a state-of-the-art security system, hadn't he managed to find a way into her house twice to leave gifts for her? The police had warned her he was exceptionally clever—

A nearly soundless step on the stairs had her thoughts grinding to a halt and her heart jumping into her throat. He was coming for her, just as he'd promised. Dear God, she had to do something!

Panic clawed at her. Every instinct she had urged her to run for her life, but she could hear him on the stairs, climbing steadily, and soon he would be at the top. Her eyes wide, she looked wildly around in the darkness of her room for some kind of weapon, but the room was simply furnished. Then she spied the vase sitting on the dresser. Grabbing it, her heart thundering in her ears, she tiptoed out into the hall to lie in wait for the man who had made the last two months of her life a living nightmare.

From where I'm sitting, I'd say Miss Angel Wiley has you shook up.

Zeke's words still ringing in his ears, taunting him, Joe swore under his breath and carefully made his way up the stairs in the darkness. Nobody had him shook up, especially Miss Hollywood. If he was restless and on edge, it was just because he didn't like being forced to share his house with a woman. Any woman. Angel could have been eighty-six and as pious as a nun, and he would have still felt the same way.

Lost in his furious thoughts, he was halfway up the stairs when he suddenly noticed a slight movement in the shadows at the top landing. His step never faltered, but every muscle in his body tensed. He never locked his doors, had never felt the need. The house couldn't even be seen from the highway, and crime was rare in Liberty Hill. But then again, so were strangers…at least they had been until Hollywood came to town.

Too late, he remembered Angel sleeping upstairs, unaware that someone had broken in. Was she safe? Fury flashed in his eyes at the thought that someone might have harmed her. She might drive him nuts, but by God, no one was going to hurt her while he was around. Braced for a fight, he reached the top of the stairs.

He had no time to think after that, only react. The intruder moved in the shadows off to his left, and suddenly something came flying at him in the dark. Cursing, he dodged it just before it could connect with his head and heard it crash against the wall behind him. Furious, he hit the hall light switch almost at the same instant he launched himself at his attacker. It wasn't until his arms closed around a struggling, squirming woman that he realized it was Angel.

"What the devil!"

"Joe!"

"You were expecting Jack the Ripper?" he snapped, furious now that he knew she was safe. "Of course it's me! Dammit, what were you doing hiding in the dark like that? I could have hurt you!"

"Me? You were the one sneaking around like a thief! When I heard someone moving around downstairs and I saw your truck wasn't here, I thought someone had broken in. Why didn't you turn on a light, for God's sake?"

"Because I don't need a light to see where I'm going in my own home! And I didn't park out front because my truck is low on gas, so I left it by the gas tank so I could fill it up in the morning."

Still holding her close, Joe glared at her and only just then noticed that she was wearing nothing but a pale blue nightgown. Made of cotton and designed more for comfort than seduction, it was hardly the type of nightwear you'd expect Hollywood's latest sweetheart to wear to bed, but there was something about its very simplicity that would have tempted a saint. And God knew, he was no saint.

Stunned, he knew right then he should have released her and gotten the hell away from her. But with a will of their own, his fingers tightened on her arms, drawing her closer, and there didn't seem to be a damn thing he could do about it. He watched her eyes flare with awareness, and suddenly the air between them was thick with a tension that had nothing to do with anger. His gaze dropped to her mouth, and just like every other man in America who'd sat in a darkened theater and watched her on the big screen, he found himself wondering what she tasted like. Right or wrong, he had to find out.

In the bright glare of the hall light, she read the intention in his eyes and stiffened like a board. "No."

"Yes," he growled, and covered her mouth with his.

The second his lips touched hers, he knew it was a mistake. The sweetest things always were. Like an addiction that called to a man's very soul, her soft, generous mouth trembled under his, innocently teasing, tempting, until the need to taste became a need for more. His head clouded, and with a low groan, he gathered her closer and took the kiss deeper.

Her senses reeling, Angel clung to him and tried to tell herself this couldn't be happening. Not with Joe McBride. He didn't like her, had made it clear from the moment he'd laid eyes on her that he didn't want anything to do with her. And the feeling was mutual. She wasn't any crazier about him. He was cold and distant and whenever the opportunity presented itself, he went out of his way to make her feel unwelcome. If anyone had told her he was a sensuous man who could turn her knees to butter with just one kiss, she would have called them a liar. She would have been wrong.

And it was that, more than anything, that abruptly brought her to her senses. The last time she'd let herself be taken in by a man's kisses, she'd been wrong about him, too. She'd been young and naive and so damn trusting that just thinking about it made her wince. She'd actually thought she'd found her prince. Instead, she'd been taken in by a toad. She'd promised herself then that she'd never make that kind of mistake again, and that wasn't a promise she intended to break.

Furious with herself for letting him tempt her even for a second, she abruptly broke free of his arms and quickly sidestepped him when he instinctively reached for her again. Her blue eyes sparking fire, she snapped, "I don't know what you think is going on here, cowboy, but somebody read the script wrong, and it's not me. Back off!"

The taste of her still on his tongue, infuriating him, Joe rasped, "You're the one who came at me in the dark dressed in nothing but a skimpy gown. I only took you up on your invitation, sweetheart."

She gasped, outraged. "I already told you I thought you were an intruder! What was I supposed to do? Stop to change while someone was sneaking up the stairs to rape me? I don't think so!"

She was right, of course. He was being completely unreasonable, and that only angered him more. He'd taken advantage of the situation, of a guest in his home, and he'd never done that in his life. But, dammit, he wasn't made of stone! What man wouldn't lose his head when he found Angel Wiley in his arms and dressed for bed?

"Next time, throw on a robe before you leave your room," he retorted coldly.

"I should have known you'd find a way to make this my fault," she tossed back. "That's just like a man. Always blame the woman. Well, for your information, Mr. Mc-

Bride, this never would have happened if you hadn't sneaked into the house like a thief in the night!''

"So now it's my fault for being considerate? I didn't want to wake you, dammit!''

"Well, you did!''

"Well, excuse me for breathing. Next time, I'll come stomping in so you'll be sure to know it's me. Will that make you happy?''

"As a clam.''

"Fine!''

Seething, they glared at each other like two eight-year-olds facing off in the playground across a line drawn in the dirt. It was a fight neither of them could win. Frustrated, Joe swore and turned to storm into his bedroom. A split second after he slammed his door, he heard the echo of Angel's across the hall.

Tearing off his clothes, he let them lay where they fell and crawled into bed, determined to forget the entire incident and go right to sleep. But long after the dust settled in the hall and the silence of the night crept back into the house, sleep eluded him. Because every time he closed his eyes, he could see the awareness in Angel's eyes right before he kissed her, taste the sweetness of her on his tongue, feel the soft, enticing curve of her breasts pressed against his chest as he'd wrapped her close in his arms. Furious with her, he tried to convince himself it had been too long since he'd had a woman, that he would have reacted the same to any female who appeared before him in her nightgown, but his body wasn't buying it. There was only one woman he ached for tonight, dammit, and like it or not, that was Angel Wiley.

Chapter 3

After kissing Joe McBride, locking lips with Garrett Elliot was like kissing a snake. Angel hated it—and despised him—but there was no getting around it. Garrett played her love interest in the movie, and when the script called for a kissing scene, she had no choice but to step into his arms.

She liked to think she was a professional and a damn good actress. She didn't so much as cringe when Garrett made one little mistake after another and the director called for the scene to be reshot time and time again. Instead, she prided herself on never breaking out of character. Her face alight with the love her character felt for the man she adored, she lifted her mouth to Garrett's and melted into his arms. No one but she and Garrett knew that her skin crawled every time he touched her.

It had always been that way between them, from the day they'd met on the set for the first time last year during the making of *Wild Texas Love*. One of the most sought after leading men in Hollywood, he'd had a reputation for sweeping his leading ladies off to his bed...until he'd worked with her. She'd turned him down flat, and he'd never forgiven her for that.

If she hadn't been so desperate to get out of L.A. for a while, she never would have agreed to work with him again. He'd made her pay in the past by spreading outrageous lies about her and earning her an unfair reputation, and now he was making her pay again by deliberately blowing one take after another so she would be forced to kiss him again and again until he thought she had suffered enough.

She could have told him that that point had long since come and gone, but she'd be damned if she'd give the worm the satisfaction. So she hid her distaste deep inside, where no one could see, and told herself the man she was kissing wasn't Garrett, but his character, Sebastian. When she closed her eyes, she *almost* believed it.

She might not have completely convinced herself, but the director, obviously bought it. "Cut!" Charles yelled. "That's a take."

Relieved, Angel jerked out of Garrett's arms and whirled away, her only thought to get back to her dressing room where she could wash away his touch. She'd barely taken three steps when she found herself face-to-face with Joe.

After the heated words they'd exchanged last night and a kiss that she hadn't been able to put out of her mind, she'd left the house that morning still feeling like the injured party. She'd promised herself that it would be a cold day in hell before she spoke to him again, but she'd forgotten she would have to spend the morning kissing the devil.

"I didn't know you were on the set," she said stiffly. "How long have you been here?"

"Long enough. I've been waiting to talk to Charles."

Behind her, Garrett said something crude to one of the

crew and didn't care who heard. Her face expressionless, she thought she hid her distaste well, but Joe shot a sharp glance at the other man, then brought his gaze back to her and studied her through narrowed eyes that saw far too much. "Are you all right?"

She started to say no, that kissing Garrett always made her feel slimy, only to remember what Myrtle had told her about the McBrides. An old-fashioned family raised on values that had unfortunately gone out of style in today's world, they were protective of friends and family and anyone in need of help. As much as Joe might dislike the idea of her living in his house, she couldn't imagine him standing idly by and doing nothing if he suspected Garrett had taken advantage of her or any other woman. He'd confront him. And while she had to admit that she would like nothing more than to see Garrett have to answer to someone who wouldn't hesitate to knock him on his ass, he was her problem to deal with and she'd handle it—without ending up on the cover of the tabloids again.

Drawing on all her skills as an actress, she laughed gaily. "Are you kidding? I just spent most of the morning kissing the number one heartthrob in America. Why wouldn't I be all right?"

She would have sworn her smile was carefree and deserving of an Academy Award, her tone right on target, but Joe was shrewder than she'd given him credit for. For what seemed like an eternity, he just stared at her with those razor-sharp brown eyes of his, probing to her very soul. Returning his gaze unblinkingly, she didn't so much as twitch an eyelash, but whatever he saw in her eyes did nothing to soften the rigid set of his square jaw.

"If he does anything that makes you feel uncomfortable," he growled, "I want to hear about it. Understood?"

She understood all right—if he and Garrett locked horns, *she* would be the one who would be blamed! And that left her with no choice but to make excuses for her costar. "Garrett's a jerk, but he's not usually as obnoxious as he was this morning. I guess he was paying me back for getting him moved to Myrtle's. He'll be fine once he cools down."

"I don't care if you had him moved to Mars, that's no excuse for that kind of behavior. If he doesn't want a lesson in manners, he'd better toss the attitude and clean up his act." Shooting Garrett one last warning glare, he strode off to meet with the director.

Staring after him, Angel sighed in relief. Not because a potential fight between the two men had been averted, but because Joe McBride was turning out to be everything she'd thought he would be. If he was willing to take Garrett to task for his juvenile behavior, she could just imagine what he would do to a man who threatened not only her, but her daughter.

"Mommy!" With a shriek of delight, Emma was out of the studio limo and racing up Joe's front walk toward Angel as fast as her dimpled little legs would carry her.

Tears welling in her eyes, Angel met her halfway and scooped her up into a bear hug, clutching her close. *Mine,* she thought with a sob. Every time she touched her golden curls, looked into dancing blue eyes that were the image of her own, it still amazed her that God had blessed her with this precious three-year-old bundle of energy and unconditional love.

Lord, she'd missed her! She'd wanted to send for her days ago, right after she'd moved into Joe's, but she'd had to force herself to be patient, to make sure she was doing the right thing and could really trust Joe McBride before she brought her daughter into his home. Yesterday morning on the set, when he'd told her he wanted to know if Garrett stepped over the line, he'd convinced her that he wasn't a

man who would tolerate anyone abusing the females under
his care. She didn't care what he thought of her—her
daughter would be safe with him and that was all that mattered.

From the second she'd found out she was pregnant with
her, nothing had ever mattered but her baby. She couldn't,
unfortunately, say the same thing about Kurt Austin,
Emma's father. The director of her first movie, older and
much more experienced than she, he'd made it clear right
from the beginning that all he wanted from her was a nice,
quiet little affair while they were making the movie. But
she was in love for the first time in her life and sure that
what they had would last a lifetime. She'd been wrong. It
ended the day she told him she was pregnant and he coolly
suggested she get an abortion.

Alone and pregnant and twenty-one, she'd wanted to go
home to New Mexico then, to her father and the security
of the home where she'd grown up, to have her baby. But
her father was a hard, conservative religious man who'd
never understood her love for acting. He'd disowned her
when she ran away to Hollywood, and she couldn't bring
herself to turn to him for help when she was in trouble. So
she'd retreated to a small town in California where no one
knew her and had Emma away from the glitter and glamour
and gossip of L.A.

She was hers, no one else's, and somehow, she'd been
able to keep her daughter's existence a well-guarded secret
from most of the world. She knew that couldn't last—the
more famous she became, the more diligently the press dug
into her past—but for now, it wasn't the press she was
worried about. It was a single man, a psychopath who
stalked her, a crazed fan who thought he was in love with
her and threatened to stop at nothing to be with her. He'd
already broken into her home, already left notes warning
her that when she finally committed herself to him, there

would be no place in their life for another man's child. If Angel couldn't get rid of her, he could.

It was because of him that she'd agreed to work with Garrett again in spite of the fact that she despised him. It was because of him, this man who seemed to know her every move regardless of the security measures she took to protect herself and her daughter, that she'd jumped at the chance to get out of L.A. *He* was the reason she'd pulled whatever strings she had to so she and Emma could stay with Joe.

She should have explained the situation to Joe, should have warned him that there was a very good chance that her stalker would follow her to Colorado and cause trouble when he discovered her whereabouts. But Joe had been so set against her, so determined that she wasn't spending so much as a single night under his roof, that she'd been afraid to chance telling him that two other females would be invading his space once she was sure it would be safe for them to do so. Because *that* wasn't part of his contract with the studio. The agreement was that he would rent a bedroom and office to one actor; there'd been no mention of a three-year-old and her nanny tagging along.

He would, no doubt, be livid, she thought as she nuzzled Emma's neck and made her giggle. But if he was the man she thought he was, he would never direct his anger at an innocent child. If she was wrong, the three of them would be out on the street by nightfall.

"That's my girl," she said huskily, tightening her arms around her. "Did you have a good trip? Did Laura pack your teddy and blanky?"

"And Miss Annabelle and my bunny angel, too!" Dimples flashing and her eyes dancing, she pulled back. "They rode all the way with me." And taking off like a shot, she raced back to the limo to collect her favorite toys.

Laughing, Angel rose to her feet, love squeezing her

heart as she watched her daughter struggle to hold a ragged, overgrown teddy bear and a doll that was as big as she was. "God, I've missed her. And you, too," she added, giving Laura an affectionate hug.

Thirty years her senior, Laura Carson had applied for the job of nanny when Emma was barely six months old and Angel's skyrocketing career had begun to make it impossible for her to continue to care for the baby alone. Inexperienced, filled with guilt at the idea of leaving her child with a stranger, she hadn't liked any of the women she'd interviewed until she'd met Laura. She was older than the other applicants, wiser and more settled, with a glint of patient humor in her gray eyes that had instantly appealed to Angel. She'd hired her on the spot and never regretted it.

"We've missed you, too," the older woman said as she returned her hug. "Emma was so excited about seeing you that she was practically bouncing off the ceiling last night."

Her smile fading, she glanced past Angel to the house and the open range that surrounded it for a thousand yards in every direction. There wasn't another sign of civilization for as far as the eye could see. "When you said this place was secluded, you weren't kidding. You could see anyone coming from a long way off. You had any visitors?"

Not pretending to misunderstand, Angel said, "No, thank God. It's been very quiet. How about you? Anyone drop by unexpectedly at the house?"

"No, but the mailman delivered a package the day before yesterday," she said in a quiet voice that wouldn't carry to Emma's sharp ears. "I didn't open it, but it was postmarked L.A. and addressed the same as before."

To my darling Angel. All too easily, Angel could see the rough scrawl on the packages that had been delivered to her house time and again over the course of the last two months. The gifts were always the same—revealing lingerie, nightgowns and teddies and intimate apparel that a stranger, a pervert, had not only bought specifically for her, but in his twisted mind, she knew he'd pictured her wearing it. Just thinking about it turned her stomach.

"You sent it to the police?"

Laura nodded. "Unfortunately, it was the same as the others—wiped clean of fingerprints and mailed in a plain cardboard box that looked like a thousand others that go through the post office every day. There's no way to trace who sent it."

"When was it mailed?"

"Two days after you left town. *From* L.A.," she stressed. "It looks like your plan worked. The sleazeball doesn't even know you've left town."

Relieved, Angel didn't know whether to cry or laugh. Thank God, thank God! When she'd decided to accept the role of Grace in *Beloved Stranger,* her biggest worry had been how she was going to get out of L.A. with Emma and Laura without her stalker following them. She'd known it was only a matter of time before he discovered where she was, but before he did, she intended to have her daughter ensconced somewhere where he couldn't get to her.

Tricking him hadn't been easy. He knew where she worked and lived and she couldn't just walk out her front door with Emma without him following them. So she had her agent circulate the rumor to the press that she was laid up at home with a viral infection. While her stalker thought she was too sick to leave her bed, she'd slipped out of her house in the dark of night and caught a late flight to Tucson. From there, she'd rented a car and driven to Liberty Hill without her tormentor ever knowing she'd left town. Then, just yesterday, she'd notified Laura it was time to make a move.

"You're sure you weren't followed?" she asked worriedly. "We started shooting on Monday. He's bound to have heard by now that I'm here on location. He must have been watching the house all week, waiting for you to leave with Emma so he could follow you.''

''If he did, all he saw was the two of us going to Disneyland in the limo.''

''The driver was able to drop you at the front gate without any problems? What about Tammy?'' she asked, referring to Laura's sister, Tammy, who had worked at the park for years. ''Did she have any trouble getting you in?''

All too aware of the terror that Angel had lived in for the past few months, Laura sympathized with her fear of something going wrong. ''Everything went like clockwork,'' she reassured her. ''Tammy was waiting for us and already had our entrance passes. If your stalker was following us, he got held up at the regular ticket booth and had to stand in line just like everybody else. By the time he paid and got in the park, we'd already left through a fire exit in the Fantasyland section, where another limo was waiting for us.''

Her gray eyes lighting on Emma, who had found the porch swing on the front porch and was swinging her menagerie of toys, she laughed softly. ''For a minute there, though, I was sure we were toast. I warned Emma we were just going to take a quick walk through the park, that we'd come back another time and stay the whole day. I thought she understood she wasn't going to get to ride any rides. Boy, was I wrong! When she realized we were leaving, she let out a cry that could have been heard on the other side of the park. I thought security was going to stop me for child abuse.''

''Oh, Laura, she didn't!''

Chuckling, she said, ''Oh, yes, she did. Luckily, we were only two steps from the fire exit when she started pitching a fit. I scooped her up, dropped her into the limo, and we took off for the airport. She finally calmed down when I reminded her that we were going to be staying on a ranch with you and she might get to ride a pony.''

It was a logical promise to make to a child, but one Angel wasn't sure they could deliver on. ''That could be a problem,'' she said with a grimace. ''I didn't tell the man we're staying with—Joe McBride—that you were coming. He's not going to be happy about it.''

''Oh, Angel, you didn't! Why?''

''Because he doesn't even want me here. He's divorced and has nothing good to say about women. If I'd told him my daughter and her nanny were going to be joining me, he'd have tossed me out on my ear.''

''But he can still do that. Then what are we going to do?''

''He won't,'' Angel assured her, love misting her eyes as they rested on her daughter. ''Not after he sees Emma. He may be a hard man, but he's not cruel. He would never turn his back on a child in trouble.'' Not if he was the man she thought he was.

Praying she hadn't misjudged him, she flashed a confident smile. ''It's all going to work out fine. Let's get your things out of the car and get you two settled inside. If we're going to keep the peace with Joe, there's a schedule you need to know about.''

He hadn't been able to think of anything but her all day. The feel of her in his arms the other night. The quick, infuriating spurt of jealousy that hit him when he found her locked in Garrett Elliot's arms on the set. The rage that washed over him when he saw the relief and revulsion she hadn't quite been able to hide when the director called ''Cut!'' and she could finally step away from her costar. He'd wanted to flatten Elliot then. And carry Angel off somewhere where no one could ever touch her again.

She had him tied in knots—because of a kiss that never

should have happened, dammit!—and he didn't like it. She was a boarder in his home, nothing more, and had no right to push her way into his thoughts whenever the mood struck her. He didn't want to care what she did or who she did it with as long as she left him the hell alone. But he couldn't shake the image of her face when she'd pulled out of Elliot's arms. What had the bastard done to her?

The question nagged at him long after he left the set to repair a downed fence near the ranch entrance that some drunk had knocked down, and the more he thought about it, the more tempted he was to hunt down Elliot and demand some answers from the jerk. When he saw the crew leaving at the end of the day, he climbed into his pickup and automatically turned toward town...and Myrtle's, to talk to the jackass.

Suddenly realizing what he was doing, he swore and slammed on his brakes. What the hell was he doing? Angel Wiley didn't need him to fight her battles. In fact, he'd never seen a woman less in need of protection. If she could stand up to him when he'd threatened to throw her out of his house and try to bash his head in when she thought he was a thief in the night, she could handle Elliot with one hand tied behind her back. She didn't need him, she didn't need anyone.

Turning around, he drove home in a foul mood that didn't lighten much when he saw Zeke's Suburban in his driveway. He was in no mood for company, but then he saw Elizabeth and his niece, Cassie, in the vehicle, and waved. "What's up?" he asked his brother as Zeke stepped from his Suburban.

Zeke took one look at the hard line of his jaw and said, "Uh-oh, rough day, huh? We dropped by for Cassie's bed, but we can get it tomorrow."

Cassie let out a wail from inside the truck at that, and Joe couldn't help but grin. One of the few people who could tease him into a smile when he was in a bear of a mood, Cassendra Ann McBride was two years old and dimple cute, not to mention just a tad willful. And he was crazy about her. When she wrapped her arms around his neck and gave him a baby soft kiss, he just turned to putty and so did everyone else in the family.

Humor glinting in his eyes, he told Zeke, "You don't really think you're going to be able to leave here without it, do you?"

"Pweeze, Uncle Joe," a pitiful voice called from the back seat. "Can I have my bed?"

Seated in the front passenger seat, Elizabeth laughed. "Don't let her con you, Joe. She can sleep in her old crib one more night if you don't want to mess with this now."

"Mama!"

"And disappoint my favorite niece?" he said, chuckling at Cassie's indignant tone. "I don't think so." Opening the back door, he unbuckled her car seat and held out his hands to her. "How about a piggyback ride to the barn, your highness?" With a squeal of delight, she launched herself into his arms.

Cassie was delighted with her first *big girl* bed, and Elizabeth was thrilled. "It's beautiful, Joe. Just perfect. Where in the world did you find it?"

"It belonged to an old friend of Myrtle's in Gunnison," he said as he helped Zeke carry the refinished bed out to the Suburban and load it in the back. "Myrtle's been trying to buy it off of her for years, but she couldn't bring herself to let it go, then a couple of weeks ago, she suddenly decided it was time to get rid of it. The second Myrtle described it to me, with the angels on it and everything, I knew it was perfect for Cassie."

"It's going to take more than a couple of wooden angels to watch over her," Zeke retorted, grinning broadly. "Last night after I put her to bed, I heard a noise in the hall and found her trying to slide down the banister. If she'd have been a couple of inches taller, she'd have managed it, too! I'm telling you, the kid's fearless. I don't know where she gets it from."

Joe choked on a laugh. "Are you kidding?! If I remember correctly, you were climbing on calves, trying to be a bronc rider, when you were three, and you jumped out of the hayloft when you were five and broke your arm. And Lizzie works with wolves, for God's sake! Where do you think she gets it from?"

"He's got a point, sweetheart," Elizabeth said dryly, her blue eyes sparkling with laughter. "You might as well face it, she's going to make both of us gray before our time."

Zeke groaned. "Maybe should lock her in her room until she's thirty-five," he began, only to break off as Angel came around the side of the house with an older woman and a little girl who wasn't much bigger than Cassie. "Looks like your houseguest has company," he told Joe quietly, glancing past him to the two women.

Surprised, Joe turned just as the two little girls spied each other. Cassie immediately took a step toward the newcomers, only to remember at the last moment that she wasn't supposed to speak to strangers. Hesitating, she glanced up at her parents and silently asked permission to make a new friend.

Pleased, Elizabeth smiled. "It's okay. Go ahead."

She didn't have to tell her twice. Cassie took off like a shot, as did the other little girl, and the adults were left to follow.

Angel watched Joe and the couple with him draw near and wanted to sink right through the ground. Too late, she questioned the wisdom of not telling him in advance that he was about to have two more houseguests. She'd thought it was for the best at the time she'd made the decision, but now, she realized it was outrageously rude. And there was nothing she could do about it but smile and make the introductions in front of strangers.

Tension knotting her stomach, she said stiffly, "Joe, this is my daughter, Emma, and her nanny, Laura Carson. Laura, this is Joe McBride, our host."

Our host. Not a slow man, there was no doubt that he caught that little tidbit of information. His eyes narrowed on her dangerously, promising her she had some serious explaining to do, but before he could say so much as a word, Laura held out her hand to him and gave him her calm, unruffled smile.

"You have a beautiful place here, Mr. McBride. I hope you don't mind us showing up on your doorstep unannounced."

Considering her own rude behavior, Angel wouldn't have blamed him if he'd been less than gracious, but he shook Laura's hand politely and said coolly, "I'm getting used to it. Ms. Wiley likes to surprise me."

He introduced both women to his brother and sister-in-law, who, unlike Joe, seemed delighted with the turn of events. Grinning broadly, Zeke told Angel, "Personally, I think it's great. He's alone too much, and all he does is work. A few surprises is just what a man needs to make life interesting again. Don't you think so, Joe?"

Biting back a smile when her brother-in-law just glared at Zeke, Elizabeth shot her husband a reproving look. "Behave yourself. Joe's content with his life or he'd change it." Turning her back on the two men, she drew Angel's attention to where Cassie and Emma were playing on the porch. "It looks like our daughters have made friends," she said with a smile. "I hope you'll let Emma come to the house someday and play. You and Laura are welcome,

too, of course," she added quickly. "We just live another
five miles down the road. Joe can give you directions."

If anyone in L.A. had issued such an invitation, Angel
would have immediately suspected that they were using her
daughter to get to her. But Elizabeth McBride had a look
of pure love on her face when she looked at her daughter,
and there wasn't a doubt in Angel's mind that she'd only
thought of her as Emma's mom, not Angel Wiley the movie
star, when she invited her over. She wanted a playmate for
her daughter, nothing more, and had no idea how rare that
was in Angel's world.

"I'd like that," she said softly. "I'll give you a call the
next time I have an afternoon off."

"Good. We can visit while the kids play."

Angel would have enjoyed visiting with her more right
then, but it was getting late, and she had Emma to get
settled and lines to study before she could call it a day. "I
hate to break this up, but it's getting late and Emma's had
a long day. She needs her bath and some time to get used
to everything before I put her to bed."

Understanding all too well, Elizabeth didn't have a problem with that. "And we've still got to put Cassie's bed
together tonight or we'll never hear the end of it. She's
been talking all day about sleeping in the bed Uncle Joe
bought for her."

Within moments, the children were rounded up, good-
nights were said, and Zeke and Elizabeth were backing out
of the driveway with a yawning Cassie strapped into her
car seat in the back seat. Seeing the look of grim resolve
on Joe's unsmiling face, Laura quickly hustled Emma inside with the announcement, "Emma and I will start un-
packing our things." And all too soon, Angel found herself
alone with Joe.

He was, she knew, going to rake her over the coals and
she couldn't say she blamed him. After the hospitality he'd

given her, keeping him in the dark about Emma and Laura was inexcusable. "I apologize for springing Emma and Laura on you with no warning," she said before he could tell her they would have to start looking for somewhere else to live in the morning. "You have every right to be angry. I should have told you. But the timing never seemed appropriate and you weren't exactly approachable. You didn't want me here—you still don't. If you didn't have a contract with the studio, I wouldn't be here now."

He didn't deny it. "I don't like being tricked."

"I can understand that," she replied. "If it's any consolation, the switch with Garrett had nothing to do with you personally. I just needed somewhere more private to stay than Myrtle's." And safer—but that wasn't something she could tell him when she was already skating on thin ice. If he knew that she was hiding from a monster who would in all likelihood follow her to the ranch and cause trouble, she wouldn't blame him for throwing her out. He had a family of his own—a niece who wasn't even as old as Emma—to protect.

"I realize that your contract with the studio is for only one person," she continued, "but I hope you'll overlook that and let the three of us stay. I know Emma can be a handful—what three-year-old isn't?—but if you're worried about her taking over the house and driving you crazy, don't be. Laura and I will pick up after her, and I'll do everything I can to see that she stays out of your way."

Far from impressed, Joe just stared at her. He wasn't worried about Emma—she was a cute little thing, and he liked kids. He'd never take his irritation with her mother out on her. Angel, however, was another matter. She might have stuck to the rules he'd laid down the day she moved in, but his opinion of her hadn't changed one iota. She was a star, pampered and spoiled and carted around on a feather pillow by the studio. She had a car, but as far as he knew, she hadn't driven it since the day she moved in. Why should she when she had a limo to pick her up every day and take her anywhere she wanted to go?

And she wanted him to believe she would pick up after her daughter and see to her needs? he thought with a snort. Yeah, right. The woman didn't even do her own nails. If the truth was told, it was the nanny, not Angel, who would be doing all the work.

That, however, was none of his business as long as *she* stuck to the original rules of their agreement. He wouldn't, of course, ever throw her and her daughter and Laura out— he wasn't that kind of man. But that was something he had no intention of telling her. Not when she already thought she only had to crook her finger and smile to have the rest of the world fall at her feet.

"You stick to your end of the deal, and I have no complaint," he said curtly.

Expecting a simple thank-you, he was surprised when a relief completely out of proportion to the situation flared in her eyes. Confused, he frowned, his eyes searching hers, but in the time it took to blink, her expression was free of any emotion but appreciation. "Thank you," she said huskily. "You won't regret this."

He regretted it the minute she hurried into the house, then later still, when he was in his study working and feminine laughter drifted down the stairs from the bathroom upstairs as Angel bathed Emma. Focusing on trying to balance the ranch books, he deliberately ignored the sound and added a column of numbers for the third time. And for the third time, he came up with a different total.

"Damn!" Scowling, he started over again, this time determined to get it right, but he couldn't concentrate for the sound of water splashing upstairs and childish giggles that made him want to smile. He found himself listening for

Angel's laughter as she murmured to her daughter, and that only irritated him all the more.

"She's doing this for your benefit," he muttered to himself. "She wants you to think that she takes care of Emma just like any other mother. So why does she have a nanny, huh? She's a movie star, for God's sakes! She doesn't have time to take care of a three-year-old. Poor Emma's probably lucky if she gets home in time at night to tuck her in."

But even as he grumbled to himself, poor Emma didn't sound like a child who'd had little or nothing to do with her mother. She laughed and played with her, and from the sound of a sudden laughing shriek from her mother, felt comfortable enough with her to douse her with bathwater. There was no question that they shared a deep love for each other.

And that didn't fit at all with his image of Angel Wiley.

Not liking the direction his thoughts were taking, he scowled and told himself not to be taken in by the woman. So she wasn't completely self-centered—she had a loving relationship with her daughter. That didn't make her a saint by a long shot. She was still spoiled and demanding and stubbornly determined to have things her way, come hell or high water.

So if he knew that, why the devil did he still have this crazy need to kiss her again?

He'd been working too hard, he told himself desperately, glaring at the paperwork that littered his desk. That was the only explanation. Maybe it was time he got away from everything for a while, took a weekend off and went back-packing up in the mountains. He needed some time to himself to get his head on straight, to—

A sound behind him had him pivoting in his office chair to find Emma standing in the doorway and dressed for bed in baby-doll pajamas. Her golden curls were still damp and fell in ringlets around her face, her rounded cheeks pink from the warmth of her bath. She grinned at him like they were coconspirators, and it was easy to see that the little imp was going to be a heartbreaker when she grew up.

Not the least bit shy, she announced, "I'm s'posed to go to bed. Mommy said so. But I want to play a game on the 'puter."

Joe's mouth curled into a grin. "I'm sorry, sweetheart, but I don't have any games on my computer. I only use it for work. But I've got some candy. Will your mother mind if you have some before you go to bed?"

He started to pull open his desk drawer, but Angel hurried in at that moment, flushed and damp from her own bath. Joe took one look at her and felt his mouth go dry. She wore the same gown she had the night she'd nearly brained him in the upstair's hallway, this time with a modest robe that concealed her every curve. With her face free of makeup and her hair wild from a hasty blow-dry, she shouldn't have been the least bit seductive. But she looked warm and soft and damn inviting, and for the moment, all he could think about was getting his hands on her.

"I'm sorry!" she said breathlessly, snatching Emma's hand and holding it firmly. "I hope she didn't disturb you. I was turning back the bed while Laura took a shower, and she got away from me. It won't happen again," she assured him, and gave her daughter a stern look that promised her she would hear about this later.

Far from concerned, Emma only grinned. "Mr. Joe said I could have some candy."

"A sucker," he clarified. "If it's all right with your mother. She's in charge and we don't want to get in trouble."

Not the least disturbed at that, Emma said decisively, "I want a red one."

Fighting a grin, Joe arched a brow at Angel. "It's your call, Mama. What's it going to be?"

She should have said no. It was bedtime, and Emma had had a long day. But there was a twinkle in Joe's eyes that had never been directed her way before. Dazed, she felt the punch of it all the way to her toes and had no memory of telling Emma she could have a sucker. But the next thing she knew, her daughter was sweetly thanking Joe for the candy, then taking her hand and climbing the stairs with her to bed.

An hour later, long after Emma was asleep next to her and Angel sat propped up against her pillows, trying in vain to study her lines, images of Joe haunted her. All she could think of was the unexpected sparkle of laughter in his eyes when he looked at her over Emma's head, the way the hard lines of his face softened when she thanked him with a kiss on the cheek for the candy, the way her own heart had lurched in her breast when he'd kissed her.

She had to stop this, she told herself sternly. Every man she'd ever let into her life had hurt her—Emma's father, Garrett, her own father when he disowned her for following her dreams. And then there was the psycho who stalked her, who claimed to love her at the same time he threatened her daughter's life. She didn't want any more pain, any more betrayal. She'd had enough to last her a lifetime.

But when the shower started in the bathroom across the hall, she couldn't think of anything but Joe standing under the hot spray of water, his body lean and rugged and far too tempting. Her heart started to pound, and that's when she knew she could no longer deny the truth. Like it or not, she was attracted to Joe McBride.

Chapter 4

It was the smell of frying bacon that woke him. Stirring, Joe rolled over to look at the clock on the nightstand and frowned. It was barely six in the morning. Who the devil was cooking at that hour of the morning?

Laura, he thought. It had to be. After living with Angel for the past week, he knew she never crawled out of bed before she had to. The studio sent a limo for her at five after six, and he never heard her stir before five. She was usually still combing her hair when she ran outside, and she never bothered with breakfast. He'd assumed she was either watching her weight or ate on the set, but now he had to wonder. Maybe she was just too lazy to get up early to cook breakfast for herself. But Laura was here now, and paid to be at her beck and call. She could slave over a hot stove at the crack of dawn while Miss Hollywood managed to catch a few extra minutes of her beauty sleep, then hand her a breakfast sandwich as she ran out the door to catch her ride.

Irritation flared in his eyes at the thought of Angel lounging in bed while a woman nearly old enough to be her mother waited on her. And to think that last night he'd actually fallen for her devoted mother routine and begun to wonder if he'd been mistaken about her! What a sucker. How many times did he have to be taken in by her before he remembered who and what she was? A woman who made a living pretending to be something she wasn't. And she was damn good at it. He'd do well to remember that.

Furious with himself for letting her fool him even once, he rose from bed and dressed, his mood foul as he headed downstairs. He needed coffee, the stronger the better, and not any made by Angel Wiley's hired help. The poor woman already had Angel to wait on, then Emma to care for and chase after all day. He could damn well make his own coffee.

His face set in harsh lines, he stepped into the kitchen expecting to see Laura at the stove preparing some fancy egg dish to go with the bacon for Angel's breakfast. But the woman puttering around his kitchen was Angel, not her nanny. Dressed in her gown and robe, her hair neatly combed and pulled back from her freshly washed face, she appeared to know exactly what she was doing. Cracking a half dozen eggs into a bowl, she briskly whipped them, then poured them into a hot skillet and began to scramble them.

Surprised, Joe scowled, not sure he believed what he was seeing; and that was how she caught him. He would have sworn he hadn't made a sound, but suddenly, she whirled, her blue eyes wide in a face that had gone white.

"Oh!" she laughed shakily, pressing a hand to her heart as she recognized him. "It's you. I thought—" She hesitated, only to grimace at herself and wave off whatever she was going to say. "Never mind. I wasn't expecting anyone else to be up this early. I hope I didn't wake you."

She had, of course, but he only said, "I've got to drive into Colorado Springs for an auction and thought I'd get an early start."

His dark brows knit in a frown, he studied her searchingly. For a second, when she'd first spun to face him, her eyes were shadowed with what looked like fear. Why, dammit? Why was she so jumpy? What—or *who*—had put that look of terror in her eyes?

He didn't like the idea of any woman being terrorized and was tempted to ask her what had her so skittish, but she didn't give him the chance. "I know this isn't the time we agreed that I could use the kitchen," she said stiffly, "but Emma usually gets up with the chickens, and I like to cook breakfast for her whenever I don't have to be on the set early. I hope that isn't going to be a problem. If you need the stove—"

"No." It wasn't his agreed upon time to cook, either, so he could hardly complain that she was invading his space. And if she was playing the dutiful mother for his sake, it didn't matter. Emma was the one who benefited, and only a jerk would deny a little girl the chance to have breakfast with her mother.

"I just want some coffee," he growled. "Go on with what you're doing. You won't get in my way."

She shouldn't have. When he'd had the house built, he'd made sure the kitchen was large and old-fashioned, like the one in his mother's house. With so much counter space, they both should have been able to work without going anywhere near each other.

But when she turned her attention back to her eggs, then made toast, all without saying a word, his attention was on anything but what he was doing. He put too much coffee into the coffeemaker, then almost forgot to add the water. Behind him, he could hear Angel retrieving plates and fought the need to turn and watch her. No, he told himself fiercely. He wouldn't go there. He wouldn't ogle her in her nightclothes and watch the knee-length gown and robe she wore ride up the back of her thighs as she reached into the cabinet above her.

But he wanted to, dear God. He wanted to.

Swearing softly under his breath, he glared at the coffee machine, willing it to hurry up and do its job so he could get the hell out of there. Time, however, seemed to drag. Finally, the scent of brewing coffee filled the room, and with a sigh of relief, he turned toward the cabinet that held the thick, diner-style mugs he liked to drink coffee out of. At almost the same instant, Angel turned toward the refrigerator for Emma's favorite jam and they collided in the middle of the kitchen floor.

Lightning quick, Joe caught her before he could knock her off her feet. His hands closed around her upper arms to steady her, and between one heartbeat and the next, they were kissing close. And neither of them had a clue how it happened. Stunned, they froze, hardly daring to move, let alone breathe.

Let go of her. Now!

The voice of reason barked out the command in his head, but he couldn't bring himself to follow the order. Not when she was this close and he could see in her eyes the memory of a kiss neither of them had been able to forget. Under his hands, her skin was smooth as silk and so soft that he couldn't stop touching her. With a will of their own, his fingers stroked her, caressed her, heated her blood and his.

And with no conscious thought on his part, he drew her closer, then closer still, until he felt the brush of her breasts against his chest and his body tighten with desire. Just a kiss, he promised himself. That was all he wanted. Just one more kiss to see if he'd imagined the sweetness of the first one. After all, what could it hurt? The rest of the household was asleep; there was no one to see. And they both wanted it. He could see the need in her eyes, feel it in the pounding of her heart—

"Mommy?"

Emma's sleepy call caught them both off guard, and for a second, they froze, then they were springing apart like two teenagers caught necking on the front porch. Heat climbing into her cheeks, her eyes avoiding Joe's, Angel whirled to where Emma stood in the kitchen doorway, sleepily rubbing her eyes and trailing her dearly loved blanky behind her.

Her heart still pounding crazily, Angel reached her in two strides and scooped her up. "Good morning, sleepy-head," she said huskily, forcing a smile as she nuzzled her. "I thought you were going to sleep all morning. Are you hungry? Breakfast is just about ready. I made your favorite—bacon and scrambled eggs and toast. How about some milk to go with it?"

She knew she was chattering, but she couldn't seem to help herself. Behind her, she heard Joe pour his coffee, but he didn't stick around to drink it. Yanking open the back door, he strode out onto the porch without saying a word.

Still feeling as if she'd almost stepped off the side of a cliff, Angel didn't know how she got through the ritual of breakfast without spilling or dropping something. Her fingers weren't quite steady, and even though she never glanced toward the back door, her attention was continually distracted by the man on the porch. Was he as shaken as she? Or relieved that Emma had stepped into the kitchen when she had? Would he have kissed her again if she hadn't? Would she have let him?

No! she wanted to cry. But even as she tried to convince herself that she never would have allowed herself to be tempted into making that mistake a second time, she couldn't quite believe it. Not when just thinking about it made her go weak at the knees.

"I'm sorry I overslept!" Laura said breathlessly as she rushed into the kitchen buttoning the cuffs of her denim blouse. "You should have woke me. What time did little bit get you up? I didn't hear either one of you."

"I wanted to let you sleep late," Angel told her as she set Emma's breakfast in front of her. "And my alarm clock here actually didn't wake up until six-fifteen."

Proud of herself, Emma grinned. "I scared Mommy and Mr. Joe."

Hot color warming her cheeks, Angel couldn't deny it. "You certainly did, sweetheart. I almost jumped out of my shoes. Eat your breakfast now before it gets cold."

Turning away to pour Laura and her some coffee, she would have sworn her innocent tone was just right to fool even the sharpest ear. But Laura was nobody's fool. When Angel turned to hand her a steaming mug, the older woman's gray eyes twinkled knowingly behind the lenses of her glasses.

"So Mr. McBride's an early riser, too, is he?" she teased. "Isn't that interesting? What did the two of you talk about while you were all alone in here? The cooking schedule?"

The heat deepening in her cheeks, Angel didn't know if she wanted to laugh or strangle her. "As a matter of fact, we did, Miss Nosey. Do you have a problem with that?"

"Not at all," she chuckled. "And evidently you don't either since you're not grumbling about the poor man. Does this mean the two of you have made peace?"

Angel wouldn't have said that—not when there wasn't anything the least bit peaceful about the emotions the man stirred in her just by walking into a room—but they weren't enemies either. "Let's just say we're working on it," she replied simply. "Now that we've got that settled, I suggest we eat. The limo'll be here at eight to pick me up."

* * *

"Bye, Mommy! See you later!"

Her smile wide and her blue eyes bright with excitement, Emma gave Angel a big hug and a smack on the cheek, then darted off with Laura to visit the new foals and their mamas in the corral attached to the barn. Watching Emma's curls bounce as she danced beside Laura in the morning sunshine, Angel felt her eyes mist with tears. Lord, she loved her! And time was passing so quickly. It seemed like only yesterday that she'd brought her home from the hospital. She'd had no experience with babies, had no one she felt she could turn to for advice. She'd been so scared that something would happen to Emma that she'd sat by her crib every night for that entire first week, watching her breathe. And now she was three. Soon she would be in school, and before Angel was ready for it, she'd be grown and married and have children of her own.

She'd given her love and happiness and, thanks to the success of her movies, had the funds to make sure that she never lacked for anything. But there was one thing that money couldn't buy, one thing that she wanted more than anything for her daughter, and that was family. And the one man who could help Angel give her that wanted nothing to do with her. Her father, Emma's grandfather.

Call him.

Not for the first time since she'd arrived in Colorado, her heart urged Angel to try to contact her father. He was so close, just three hundred miles away in New Mexico, and she needed to find a way to make peace with him. She owed Emma that, owed her the legacy of her family and a grandfather, who knew nothing of her existence. And she owed herself. James Wiley was a hard man, but there'd never been any doubt in Angel's mind that he loved her and she wanted him in her life again.

Call him, her heart coaxed again. You know you want to.

She couldn't deny it. It had been years since they'd spoken, even longer since she'd felt his arms wrap around her and hold her tight. Surely if he knew about Emma, about the loving, responsible way she was raising his granddaughter, he would forgive her for turning her back on everything he held dear to chase a dream he couldn't understand. All she had to do was take a chance and call him.

A glance at her watch warned her she had only fifteen minutes before she had to be on the set, but she didn't care. Hurrying into the kitchen, she picked up the phone and dialed the number she still knew by heart.

"Wiley's Diner."

Her father's gruff voice barked impatiently in her ear, and she almost laughed aloud at the familiar tone. He would be right in the middle of the breakfast rush and in no mood to be tied up on the phone, but she wasn't about to hang up now that she'd worked up the courage to call him.

Tears misting her eyes, she swallowed the lump in her throat and said huskily, "Hi, Daddy. It's me."

For a moment, there was nothing but a sharp intake of breath, and she could almost see the surprise on his face. Then, without a word, he quietly hung up.

Later, Angel couldn't have said how long she just stood there with the phone still to her ear, the dial tone buzzing mockingly. They must have been accidentally disconnected, she told herself, and wanted desperately to believe it. But this was no accident, and she knew it. He'd deliberately hung up on her. He couldn't have hurt her more if he'd reached through the phone and slapped her.

With trembling fingers, she returned the phone to its cradle, and it was then that the anger set in. Damn him! He could hold on to his grudge with her for the rest of his life if he wanted to, she thought furiously, but by God, he wasn't going to dismiss his granddaughter so easily! She'd make sure of it.

Her blue eyes dark with outrage, she sat down at the kitchen table and quickly wrote him a letter, telling him about Emma. She was, she knew, giving him all the ammunition he needed to condemn her for leading a fast and loose life, not to mention what he would consider an immoral one for having a baby out of wedlock, but she didn't care. Before the week was over, he would not only know that he had a granddaughter, but he would also have her picture. Pulling one from her wallet, she folded the letter around it and slipped it into the envelope. If he could ignore Emma after that, he wasn't the man she thought he was.

She was still fuming when she finally reached the set, and not surprisingly, the day went downhill from there. Nothing seemed to go right. Props were missing, a generator blew, shutting down everything for an hour, and one of the trained horses turned stubborn during the shooting of a vital scene and nearly destroyed a set. And when shooting finally did resume, Angel kept blowing her lines.

Frustrated, she apologized and tried to focus, but she couldn't forget the sound of her father hanging up on her. And then there was Garrett. He knew something was wrong—she could see the glint of wicked satisfaction in his eyes—and he took advantage of every opportunity to push her buttons. He threw off her timing, came in too fast with his lines, scratched himself whenever Charles wasn't looking. She knew exactly what he was doing, but try though she might, she couldn't get her rhythm. And he loved it.

Finally, Charles had enough. "Cut, dammit! What's wrong with you people today? Can't anybody hit their mark? Or is that too much to ask of professionals making more money than God?" Glaring at the cast and crew alike, he threw down his script in disgust. "To hell with it. Everybody break for lunch and be back here at one. And you'd damn well better be ready to work."

No one asked what would happen if they weren't. Like chastised school kids let out for recess, they all scattered.

Her stomach turning at the thought of food, Angel cut across the pasture to the motor home the studio had reserved for her as a dressing room, her only thought to lie down for a while and forget the world. Just an hour, she thought, rubbing at the headache that throbbed at her temple. That's all she needed. Maybe then she could forget this morning ever happened.

But when she stepped into the motor home, all thought of sleep vanished at the sight of the bouquet of roses sitting on her dressing table. Yellow roses. Big, beautiful yellow roses that were only just beginning to open. Roses that any woman would have loved to have. Yellow roses like the ones her stalker had been sending her every week for the last two months to show how much he cared.

There was no card, but she didn't need one to know that they were from him. Horrified, she felt her blood run cold even as she told herself not to panic. She'd known it was only a matter of time before word got out that she was on location in Colorado. The studio couldn't keep a lid on that kind of information indefinitely when so many people knew about it. Just because her stalker knew where she was didn't mean he had necessarily followed her. He could have easily ordered the flowers from L.A. and had them delivered to the set.

Just to be sure, though, she made a few calls, first to Myrtle to get the name of the local florist, then to Becca Ryan, the florist, herself. "Oh, Ms. Wiley," the florist gushed as soon as Angel identified herself, "I do hope you liked the roses! I had them brought in from Colorado Springs this morning especially for you."

"They're beautiful," Angel assured her and meant it. But they were from a man who wanted her daughter dead so he could have Angel all to himself, and that made them vile. "There was no card, Mrs. Ryan, and I was just wondering who sent them. If you could just look up the order for me so I could send a thank-you card, I would really appreciate it."

"But that's why there was no card," the other woman explained. "Whoever ordered them didn't give his name, but he must be crazy about you. A dozen roses don't come cheap, especially when they have to be brought in fresh the same day of delivery."

"Then maybe you could describe him—"

"Oh, but he didn't actually come into the shop. Didn't I tell you? The order was through the mail and accompanied by a money order. Here—let me see—I think I still have the envelope..." Trailing off, she shuffled through some papers. "Here it is! But there's no return address or name," she said in disappointment. "What a shame. It's postmarked L.A. three days ago, though, if that's any help."

Just like the others, Angel thought with a sigh of relief. From the moment her stalker had first become obsessed with her and started sending her flowers, he'd religiously used the same m.o. The order was always placed through the mail with a money order that couldn't be traced back to him.

"I imagine this kind of thing happens to you all the time, but I just think it's so romantic!" Becca Ryan said dreamily. "Just think—a secret admirer. It must be wonderful to be a movie star."

Angel wanted to tell her that glitter and fame and money weren't everything, but Becca Ryan would never understand. To her and the rest of the world, her life seemed touched by magic. No one wanted to hear about the dark side of that magic and the dregs of humanity it attracted. They didn't want to know about the fear that set her heart beating every time her phone rang or the paranoia that gripped her the second Emma was out of her sight.

And then there were the questions that haunted her whenever she found herself surrounded by a crowd. What did the face of a stalker look like? Was he old, young, average-looking or handsome as the devil? Was there something in his eyes that hinted that he had long since lost touch with reality or did he look as safe and normal as a Methodist minister?

She had no answers, only questions, and Becca Ryan couldn't help her with those. So she told her what she wanted to hear. "Yes, it is wonderful sometimes, Mrs. Ryan, but I really don't consider myself a movie star. I'm just a working mother who happens to act." Changing subjects, she said, "Would you mind doing me a favor? If any more orders like this one come in for me, would you please send them to the local hospital? I'm sure the patients there would enjoy them."

"Oh, yes, of course. How sweet of you!"

Feeling like a fraud, Angel thanked her for all her help, then hung up and tried to find comfort in the fact that just three days ago, her stalker was in L.A. There was no reason to believe that he'd followed her to Colorado since then. But she had no proof that he hadn't, either. And that was what scared her the most—not knowing where he was.

Picking up the phone, she quickly dialed the number to Joe's house to inform Laura of the latest developments, only to frown as the phone rang and rang before she remembered that Joe didn't believe in such modern inventions as the answering machine. Swearing softly, she called Laura on her cell phone and waited impatiently for her to answer.

When she got Laura's voice mail, she assured herself

there was no cause for concern. Laura and Emma were probably out exploring the ranch, and Laura had just left her phone at the house or in the car. She'd just page her. Laura never went anywhere without her beeper and knew to call her as soon as she could get to a phone.

Long minutes passed after she punched in her pager number, however, and the phone never rang. Watching the clock, Angel frowned. Just because Laura hadn't returned her call didn't mean that there was a problem, she reasoned. There were remote areas of the country where cell phones didn't work—for all she knew, this could be one of them. Or maybe the battery was low in Laura's pager and she hadn't even gotten the message to call.

"It could happen," she said aloud, and knew even as she said it, that it hadn't. Laura was too conscientious to let the battery die in her pager. She knew how important it was to Angel to be able to contact her at all times about Emma. If she wasn't able to answer her page, there had to be another explanation.

The stalker had somehow gotten his hands on her and Emma.

The thought snuck up on her from behind and stopped her heart dead in her chest. Stiffening, she immediately tried to dismiss it. No. He couldn't have. She knew for a fact he'd been in L.A. just three days ago. Even if he'd left that same day for Liberty Hill, it wasn't common knowledge where she was staying—the studio had made sure of that. And even if he'd heard gossip in town and discovered she was at Joe's with Emma, he couldn't have just driven onto the ranch like he owned the place. Security was everywhere—at the front gate and checkpoints throughout the ranch. Anyone who didn't have the proper credential was immediately stopped and escorted off the property, or arrested if they insisted on trespassing.

But even the best security could be breached, the voice

in her head cautioned. And the man who stalked her like a lion on the prowl in search of his next meal was no lightweight. He was sharp and cunning and diabolical. He let nothing get in his way. He'd gotten past security at the studio and in her own home with an ease that was frightening, then had the nerve to leave her taunting notes that promised her it was only a matter of time before they were together. Outwitting a few guards would be a piece of cake for a man like him.

How could she be sure that he hadn't already done it? That he hadn't found a way to fool the guards? That he wasn't somewhere on the ranch right this minute...with Emma?

Stark terror seized her at the thought, and with a strangled cry, she grabbed the phone and called for a limo. A split second later, she ran for the door, uncaring that she had to be back on the set in less than twenty minutes. Emma was missing and she had to find her. Nothing else mattered.

The new foal was only hours old and still not steady on his spindly legs as he explored the stall he shared with his mother. Leaning against the stall door, his arms crossed over the top, Joe admired his black and white coat with a grin. There was something about a paint that he'd always loved, and this one was going to be a beauty. He couldn't wait to see him grown and racing across one of the high mountain pastures with his mane streaming out behind him.

Behind him, the barn door opened suddenly, shattering the silence that engulfed the barn. Surprised, Joe turned just in time to see Emma and Laura step inside and had to fight a smile. Clinging to the nanny's hand, Emma peered wide-eyed into the soft musty shadows, so excited she was almost hopping.

"Are there horses in here, Auntie Laura?" she asked in a loud whisper. "Do you think we can ride them?"

"Not today, sweetheart," Laura replied with a smile. "We're just exploring, remember? And we don't touch or ride anything without first making sure it's okay with your mother and Mr. McBride. We're visitors and—" Suddenly spotting Joe standing in the shadows at the far end of the barn, she stopped in her tracks. "Oh, Mr. McBride, I didn't realize you were in here. I hope we're not intruding. Emma wanted to see what was in here…"

"Then she'll want to see the newest baby," he cut in smoothly. Grinning at the little girl at her side, he said, "Whatdaya say, Emma? You want to take a look at him? I was hoping maybe you could help me name him."

Emma didn't have to be asked twice. Her blue eyes sparkling, she dropped Laura's hand and made a beeline straight for Joe. "Can I really, Mr. Joe? I can really name him? Right now?"

"Right this minute," he assured her, and stepped back so she could see the new foal and his mother through the slats of the stall gate.

With a squeal of delight, Emma immediately poked her pert nose through the slats. "Oh, look at the baby! Can I touch him? Please, Mr. Joe? Please? *Pleeease?*"

Cute as a button, she looked up at him with pleading eyes and just that easily, broke the hard shell around Joe's heart. Lord, she was a little scamp, he thought, fighting a grin. If she was this engaging at three, what was she going to be like at sixteen?

Chuckling, he said, "I think that can be arranged. If it's okay with your auntie Laura." At the nanny's nod, he added, "But you have to let me hold you. His mama doesn't know you, and we don't want to scare her. Okay?"

Without a word, Emma held up her hands.

* * *

Tires squealing, the limo driver, urged on by Angel, slammed to a stop in Joe's driveway. Before he could even think about unbuckling his seat belt and getting out to open her door for her, Angel was out of the car and running toward the house. It was unlocked, thank God, or she was sure she would have kicked the door in. Panic driving her, she ran inside, fear clutching at her throat. They had to be here, she told herself, swallowing a sob as she frantically searched the downstairs, then bolted upstairs. They had to be!

"Emma!? Laura!?" she screamed. "I know you're here. Answer me, dammit!"

But the house was empty and silent as a tomb.

Her heart slamming against her ribs, she ran back outside and looked wildly around, but there wasn't another human being in sight for as far as the eye could see. Then she spied Joe's truck parked beside the barn, and it was like an answer to her prayers. He might not like her, but there wasn't a doubt in her mind that he would help her find her daughter. Her breath tearing through her lungs, she stumbled toward the barn.

Darkness hit her the second she ran inside, blinding her, and for what seemed like an eternity, she just stood there, unable to see a thing. Then, without warning, her eyes cleared, and the first thing she saw was Joe at the other end of the barn…holding Emma.

"Emma! Oh, dear God, thank you!"

Then she was running, sobbing, and reaching for her daughter, clutching her tight. Tears streaming down her face, she never saw Joe's puzzled frown or the worry in Laura's eyes. Thinking they were playing some kind of new game, Emma giggled and gave her a fierce squeeze. Only then did the fear gripping Angel's heart like a vise start to ease.

"I touched the baby horse, Mommy," Emma said excitedly as she pulled back to give Angel a wide grin. "Mr. Joe letted me. He said it was okay if he holded me." Suddenly noticing Angel's tears, she screwed her little face up in a frown. "Why are you crying? Do you have something in your eye?"

Sniffing, Angel forced a weak smile. "I guess so, sweetheart. So you got to touch the baby horse, did you?"

"And name him, too," Joe added somberly as Emma wiggled to get down, then darted back to the stall to talk babytalk to the foal through the stall door. "We've decided on Spotty."

Swallowing the lump in her throat, she said huskily, "I see."

"Angel, what's wrong?" Laura asked worriedly in a low tone that didn't carry to Emma. "You're trembling! And you looked scared to death when you came rushing in here. Has—"

"We'll talk about it later," she said quickly, cutting her off before she could mention her stalker in front of Joe and Emma. "Right now, I want to know where your pager is. When I paged you and you didn't answer, I thought something had happened to you and Emma."

Stricken, the older woman paled guiltily. "Oh, God, I'm sorry! I didn't think I would need it here at the house, with the phone and everything."

"I called the house. No one answered."

"You can't hear it from out here," Joe said quietly, watching her through narrowed eyes. "I've been meaning to have an extension installed, but I haven't gotten around to it."

Another woman might have thankfully latched onto the excuse, but Laura was having none of it. "If I'd had my pager with me the way I was supposed to, it wouldn't have mattered that I couldn't hear the phone. I'm sorry," she solemnly told Angel. "It won't happen again. From now on, I'll take the cell phone and beeper with me everywhere. If you'll excuse me, I'll get them now. Emma,'' she called, ''it's time to go inside now. Give Mommy a kiss so we can go back to the house.''

Emma wanted to protest, but one look at Laura's somber face, not to mention her mother's, and she grudgingly did as she was told. She kissed her mother, then surprised Joe with a hug before forlornly letting Laura lead her out of the barn. If her bottom lip had stuck out any farther, she would have tripped over it.

As soon as the door shut behind them, Angel turned back to face Joe and realized too late that she should have taken her own leave when the opportunity presented itself. Watching her like a hawk with eyes that missed little, he said, ''Now that the munchkin is out of earshot, why don't you tell me what's really going on here? I may look dumb as a post, but believe it or not, not a hell of a lot gets past me. You didn't race halfway across this ranch like a mad-woman because Laura didn't answer your page. You were scared to death, and I want to know why.''

Chapter 5

"It was nothing."

"Don't give me that," he growled. "I know fear when I see it. You were white as a ghost when you ran in here. Why? What did you think had happened to Emma?"

She didn't want to tell him, didn't want to talk about it, didn't want to even think about the monster who took such enjoyment out of threatening her and her daughter. But one look at the determined glint in Joe's eye, and she knew he wasn't going to let this go. He wanted an answer and he was prepared to keep her there all day if he had to to get it.

"Several months ago, I started getting letters at the studio from a fan," she finally admitted stiffly. Her gaze focused inward, she stared unseeingly at the dust particles that floated on the beam of sunlight that streamed in through the barn's open door. "They were sweet and touching and just like hundreds of others I receive every week. I didn't think anything of them…until I started getting more personal letters at home."

"How did he get your address?"

Not surprised that he had guessed the letters were from a man, she shrugged. "I don't know. The studio doesn't give out that kind of information, and even though I'm buying the house, it's not in my name. But somehow he discovered where I lived and began to send me flowers and small gifts. I didn't realize he was watching me, though, until he called one night and told me everything I'd done that day. It was creepy."

It was warm in the barn, but she shivered, hugging herself, and Joe swore silently, enraged. The bastard was stalking her, not to mention doing a damn good job of terrorizing her. "You went to the police with this?"

She nodded. "Not that it did much good. I had kept everything. All the letters and gifts and cards, even the wrapping paper. I was sure there had to be something that the police could use to identify this guy, but he was too clever. There were no fingerprints, no credit card numbers, nothing. He paid for everything with money orders through the mail, and nothing could be traced back to him. Every lead to a dead end."

"So the police just let it go?" he demanded incredulously.

"There was nothing else they could do. Oh, they kept the case open, but until he made a mistake, there wasn't much they could do. So I told myself that I had to expect this, that this was one of the side effects of fame, and I just had to get used to it. Then he threatened Emma."

She told him then about the son of a bitch's plans for her, how he had no intention of sharing her with another man's child, and Joe's blood ran cold just listening to her. The pervert wasn't just sick, he was dangerous, and Joe could understand why she'd taken the role in *Beloved Stranger* just to get her and her daughter out of L.A. She had to have been terrified.

Which brought him back to his original question. "But what happened *today?* Why did you think Emma was in danger? You're stalker's back in L.A.—"

"Yellow roses were delivered to my dressing room today," she replied. "There was no card, but there never is. He knew I would know they were from him."

"You think he's in Liberty Hill?"

"He wasn't three days ago when he mailed the order for the flowers from L.A. But he obviously knows I'm here. If he's not here yet, he soon will be."

Joe didn't need to hear anymore. "C'mon," he told her, heading for the house. "I'm calling Nick."

"Who?"

"Nick Kincaid. The sheriff."

Readily admitting she was guilty of stereotyping, Angel expected Nick Kincaid to be a laid-back, doughnut-eating small town peace officer who moved at a snail's pace. He wasn't. Less than thirty minutes after Joe called him, he pulled up in the drive in his black-and-white patrol car. If he spent his days eating sweets, you couldn't tell it. Tall and lean, with an angular face that could have been carved from stone, he greeted Joe with a smile, but his brown eyes were sharp and perceptive. Shaking his hand as Joe made the introductions, Angel imagined he'd only have to give a suspect one hard flinty look to make him squirm.

All business, he said, "Joe said you were having problems with a stalker, Ms. Wiley. Why don't you tell me about it?"

Taking a seat in Joe's study, where the three of them had retired to discuss the problem out of earshot of Emma, she patiently went over the story again, leaving out nothing. "I don't know if he's left L.A. yet, if he even has the means to follow me here," she concluded, "but I wouldn't put anything past him. He scares me. If something happened to Emma…''

She couldn't finish the thought, and unfortunately, just as she'd suspected, there was little Nick could do to reassure her. ''I wish I could tell you that the jerk's not going to get anywhere near you on my watch,'' he said grimly. ''Normally, I could. There's usually not much going on here, and strangers have a tendency to stick out. But we're flooded with outsiders right now. And I'm not just talking about the Hollywood crowd. Ever since the word got out that you and Garrett Elliot were here making a movie, people have been coming in by the truckload.''

He sounded more than a little disgusted, and Angel couldn't say she blamed him. Just last week, Liberty Hill had been a nice quiet little town, but that had changed virtually overnight. Reporters were now camped out at the entrance to the ranch and souvenir hawkers were on every corner in town. Then there were the fans and groupies and autograph seekers who'd descended on the town out of nowhere to try to get a glimpse of some real live movie stars. The place was a zoo.

''Don't get me wrong,'' Nick hastily assured her. ''I'm not complaining. I'm just trying to make you understand the magnitude of conducting an investigation under such conditions. Think about it. Since your stalker is from L.A., the only sure fact we have is that he isn't one of the locals. With the town crawling with strangers, that leaves a hell of a lot of possible suspects. Anyone of them could be your stalker.''

Scowling, Joe swore. ''Dammit, Nick, I called you out here to help her, not scare her to death!''

''And that's what I'm doing,'' he retorted. ''This isn't L.A., Joe. I don't have the manpower to surround her and her daughter with bodyguards. I'll do everything within my power to keep her safe, but I'm going to need her help.''

"Tell me what to do," she told him. "The bastard who wants my daughter dead has made good on every promise he's made me so far, and that scares me to death. He laughed when I had the security system beefed up in my house and promised me he could get past it. A week later, he sent me a pair of my own underwear in the mail."

Just the thought of it still sickened her. "He's not going to hurt Emma," she said fiercely. "I could send her back to L.A., or to New York, but he would find her. And just the thought of sending her away makes me cringe. No one will protect her like I will. So tell me what to do—I'll do it."

"Keep your eyes open for suspicious characters," Nick said flatly. "I know there are a lot of fruitloops in town right now, but this guy's not going to be that obvious. He'll try to blend in with the crowds, so watch the people around you. Whenever you're out in public, stay close to someone you know and trust. Don't go anywhere by yourself. And for God's sake, don't keep this a secret from your friends and co-workers. The more people who watch for this guy, the better chance we've got of catching him."

It seemed like so little—keep your eyes open and don't go anywhere alone. But short of locking her and Emma up in the jail, Angel knew there was little more the sheriff could do until the stalker made some kind of mistake that would hopefully lead to his arrest.

Rising to her feet, she held out her hand and gave him the smile that had men all over the world dreaming about her. "I appreciate your help. I may be overreacting—for all we know, he's still in California—but I can't take any chances with my daughter's life."

"Or your own," he replied somberly. "Don't forget that this guy's main objective isn't your daughter, but you. *You're* the one he wants, so be careful. If anyone comes near you and makes you the least bit uncomfortable, don't worry about looking foolish—scream your head off. And if you get any more gifts, I want to know about it.''

"You'll be the first person I call," she promised. "Now if you'll excuse me, I need to call my producer about this and talk to Laura.''

She hurried out of the study, and without a word, Joe shut the door behind her. When he turned back to Nick, his face was set in grim lines. "Just how dangerous is this bastard?"

Not one to beat about the bush, Nick said, "I wish I could say the jerk's all talk and gets off by just scaring her, but at this point, there's no way to know for sure. He's a sick puppy, and God knows what's going on inside his head. It would be a mistake to underestimate him.''

Joe had no intention of doing any such thing. As far as he was concerned, he didn't care if the guy was nothing but all talk, he'd threatened a woman and a little girl and that made him lower than dirt. If he tried to come near either one of them, he'd personally make him wish he'd never been born.

"I'll notify Zeke and the ranch hands and let them know what's going on so they can keep an eye open for anyone wandering around where they don't belong.''

"Which, from what I've seen, is half the cast and crew of the movie," Nick retorted. "You've got your work cut out for you.''

He wasn't telling Joe anything he didn't know. Every time he turned around on his own ranch, he was running into a stranger. Since they'd gotten past security at the front gate, he'd naturally assumed that they were with the studio and had a right to be there, but now he wasn't so sure. The eastern boundary of the ranch was fronted for miles by a well-traveled country road. An electric fence marked the property line and should have been more than enough to discourage any trespassers, but Angel's stalker wasn't your average curiosity seeker. This was a man who'd disarmed her security system and broke into her house without anyone being the wiser. An electric fence would present no obstacle for him.

And that scared the hell out of Joe. Not because he was attracted to the lady, he told himself quickly. All right, so there was something about her that made her impossible to ignore, but he still would have worried about her if she'd been ninety-two and hadn't had a tooth in her head. She and her daughter were guests in his home, dammit, and she had a right to feel safe there. Anyone who threatened them or even thought about hurting them was going to have to get past him first to do it.

Thanking Nick for his help, he walked outside with him and watched him drive away, then circled the house, his narrowed eyes scanning the surrounding countryside for any sign of an intruder. Only when he was sure nothing moved in any direction for as far as the eye could see did he go back inside.

Emma was in the middle of her lunch and chatting happily to her mother and Laura about the new baby horse when Joe stepped into the kitchen. The two women hovered close, like they expected her to disappear any second, and Joe couldn't say he blamed them. She was a baby, for God's sake! A harmless child. Just the thought of anyone trying to hurt her infuriated him. And he barely knew her. What must it have been like for Angel over the past two months, knowing there was someone out there who wanted her daughter dead?

For the first time, he understood why she'd pulled whatever strings she had to to stay with him instead of Myrtle Henderson. As crazy as he was about Myrtle, she was still an old woman who'd lived in Liberty Hill all her life and didn't have a clue just how dangerous the world could be. Half the time, she didn't even lock her door at night. Angel would have been a basket case if she'd had to stay there with Emma.

So she'd come to him. And what had he done? he thought in disgust. Given her nothing but a hard time. Granted, she hadn't bothered to explain to him why she needed a more secure place to stay, but that didn't excuse his own behavior. He'd treated her like dirt and believed all the bad press about her simply because she was too pretty for his peace of mind.

That was going to change.

She looked up then from her conversation with Emma to find him watching her. "If you have a minute, I need to talk to you," he said and stepped back so she could precede him to his study.

She should have told him she had to return to work, but thanks to Will, she didn't have to be back on the set for the rest of the day. She hadn't asked for the time off, but Will had children of his own. Once he'd learned her stalker now knew where she was in Colorado, he'd been insistent that she take whatever time she needed to see to Emma's safety.

As for Angel's own safety, the studio had always contended that the best way to deal with stalkers was to keep a lid on the story so that it wouldn't end up in the tabloids and encourage other weirdos to do the same thing. After she'd told Will about her discussion with Nick, however, he'd been forced to admit that the only person they were protecting with their silence was the stalker. The more people who knew there was someone out there terrorizing her, not to mention threatening to harm an innocent child, the less chance he would have of getting anywhere near Angel and Emma. Besides beefing up security, he'd promised to alert the entire cast and crew to be on the lookout for anyone who looked the slightest bit suspicious.

As much as she took comfort in that, however, she knew

it was Joe McBride she would turn to in the event of an emergency. He might not like her and she wouldn't blame him if he resented her for bringing her problems to his doorstep, but he would never turn his back on her or Emma if they needed his help. When it came to a crisis, he'd be rock-steady and there for her. And that gave her a tremendous sense of security.

Stepping into his study, she turned to face him. "I want to thank you for calling the sheriff. I know I should have told you about this the first day I moved in, but I didn't know you and I wasn't sure how you would react."

"I wasn't exactly in the best of moods," he admitted. "Coming home to find you moving in was a shock. I wasn't very diplomatic."

He'd been downright rude, but she hadn't handled the situation all that well either. "I wasn't exactly Miss Manners myself."

"Then why don't we start over?" he suggested. "Ditch the schedule, forget everything that was said that day, and start over?" Giving her that rare smile of his, the one that always made her heart knock sideways in her breast, he held out his hand to her and smiled down into her eyes. "Welcome to my home, Ms. Wiley," he said huskily. "I'm Joe McBride. It's nice to finally meet you."

She should have laughed, should have played along with him and let the moment slip by without making a big deal of it. But caught in the trap of his eyes, she couldn't seem to think. In slow motion, she placed her hand in his and felt his fingers close around hers. In the time it took to draw her next breath, the fire that always sparked to life whenever they made the mistake of touching was there between them, heating their blood and setting their hearts hammering crazily.

"It's nice to meet you, too," she whispered softly.

Staring down at her, Joe knew he could have her in his

arms with just a tug of his hand. That's all it would take. One tug and she would lift her mouth to his and he could lose himself in the taste of her again. Since he'd walked out of the kitchen that morning, he'd thought of nothing but her all day, and it was driving him crazy. He didn't want to want her, didn't want to ache for her, but damn her, she tempted him past bearing! And it had to stop! He had to get her out of his head, and if the only way to do that was to kiss her until he satisfied this damn craving he had for her, then by God, he'd do it.

His eyes dark with purpose, he tightened his fingers around hers and started to draw her toward him when he suddenly realized what he was doing. Stiffening, he clenched his teeth on an oath. What the hell was wrong with him? Had he lost his mind? He'd kissed the lady exactly twice—and had a hard time forgetting it. A third time, and he just might get so wrapped up in her that he forgot Belinda, forgot how a city woman could fall into your arms one moment, then stab you in the back on her way out the door the next. Was that what he wanted?

Swallowing a curse, he dropped her hand and stepped back like a man who'd suddenly found himself standing at the edge of a cliff without knowing how he'd gotten there. "I meant what I said about the schedule," he said roughly. "Forget it. And I don't expect you to keep Emma penned up in your rooms either. I may need to shut myself up in my study on the nights when I have to catch up on paperwork, but other than that, the three of you are free to use whatever rooms you like, whenever you like."

Her eyes searched his, but she was as businesslike as he when she nodded. "Thank you. But I should warn you that you might live to regret that. Emma can be a handful."

"She's a sweetheart." The quick smile that curled one corner of his mouth died at the thought of anyone even thinking about harming her. "I know you're worried and I don't blame you, but this really is the safest place you could be right now. Think about it. The house sits in the middle of an open valley. Only a moron would try to grab you or Emma here, especially during the day. The nearest tree's over a half mile away. If anyone even thinks about making a move in this direction, the guards'll spot him the second he steps out in the open."

"What about at night?"

"Extra guards'll be posted," he assured her. "And the house does have a security system. I know the bastard tracking you didn't have any trouble getting past the one at your place in L.A., but this one should at least slow him down.

"And then there's Buster. One of my sister, Merry's, German shepherds," he explained when she arched a brow at him. "She's got three of them, and Buster's the best of the lot. I'll go pick him up this afternoon and bring him over to meet you and Emma. He's small for a shepherd, but you won't find a better watchdog anywhere. If anyone even thinks about coming near you with him around, they'll live to regret it."

That sounded good, but Angel wasn't so sure that having a strange dog around was a good idea. The only dogs Emma had ever been around were two golden retrievers that belonged to Angel's best friend, Debbie. Patient and loving, they didn't snarl or bark or do anything more sinister than lick Emma until she giggled in delight. If she made the mistake of thinking she could hang on Buster the same way she did Debbie's dogs, she could get seriously hurt.

"I don't know," she began with a frown. "The only dogs Emma's ever been around were used to children."

"Then she and Buster will get along just fine," he assured her. "Just wait. You'll see."

* * *

Just as Joe promised, Emma and Buster took an instant liking to each other later that afternoon. Within minutes of meeting, they were fast friends. Amazed, Angel watched the German shepherd play catch with her daughter and couldn't believe the dog was as protective as Joe had claimed. With his tongue lolling and his tail wagging happily, he looked like a big overgrown puppy…until he caught the sound of a vehicle coming down the ranch road that passed in front of Joe's house. Growling low in his throat, the hair at the back of his neck rising in fury, he darted around Emma to place himself between her and the road and any possible approaching danger.

The truck that raced passed the house belonged to the studio and had every right to be there, but Buster didn't relax his guard until it was long out of sight. Only when he was satisfied that the danger was past did he trot back to Emma with a satisfied doggy grin on his face.

If Angel hadn't seen it with her own eyes, she never would have believed it. "Did you give him some kind of command? You must have. He doesn't even know Emma. Why would he be so protective of her if he wasn't trained to do so?"

"Because he knows by my acceptance of you that you're both supposed to be here," he replied simply. "And he's very territorial. That makes you his to protect for as long as you're here."

"But I'm going to be here for at least two months! I can't ask your sister to let me keep her dog all that time."

"You didn't," he reminded her. "I did. And she was happy to do it. If someone was threatening Cassie and you had a dog that could protect her, you'd do the same thing, wouldn't you?"

Angel couldn't deny it. It was well known in Hollywood that she'd do anything to help a child in trouble. She gave generously to children's charities, donating both her money and time when she could. Giving, however, was one thing, taking another. She didn't accept favors from just anyone— not in L.A., not without suspecting their motives. But this wasn't California, and Merry wasn't just anyone. She was a McBride. That was all Angel needed to know.

"Yes, I would," she said honestly. "I was just surprised that she made such an offer when she hasn't even met me yet. I would have never asked such a thing of her—"

"Which is exactly why she made the offer," he replied. "I told her what was going on and she wanted to help. Merry's like that. She'd give the shirt off her back to someone in trouble. And I don't like the idea of depending on just guards to protect you," he added with a frown. "You saw what happened with that studio truck. Buster heard it coming long before we did. If anyone even thinks about sneaking up on you or Emma, they'll have to go through Buster first."

He had a point, one that Angel took comfort in later that evening after it grew dark and Joe left to attend a meeting of the Cattleman's Association at the VFW hall in town. The house security alarm was set, the guards provided by the studio were armed with not only guns, but radios to summon help in case it was needed, and Buster was out there in the dark somewhere close by, watching and listening for anything that moved. For the first time in a very long time, Angel felt like she and Emma were finally safe.

Relieved, she bathed Emma and put her to bed while Laura washed the supper dishes, then turned in early herself. By nine, Angel virtually had the house to herself. Joe had told her he wouldn't be back until eleven, and she planned to be in bed long before then. Changing into her nightclothes, she grabbed her script and went back downstairs to study her lines in the family room.

Concentrating shouldn't have been a problem. The night was quiet, and outside, Buster didn't so much as whimper.

Sinking into Joe's favorite overstuffed chair, she sighed in contentment and opened her script. She'd barely read two lines when somewhere in the house, something creaked.

"It's just the house settling," she muttered when her heart jumped in her breast. "Quit acting like a fraidy cat."

Still, her pulse continued to race. Irritated, she tried to drag her attention back to the script, but she was fighting a losing battle. Instead of focusing on the words on the page in front of her, she found herself holding her breath and listening to the eerie, nearly silent groans and moans of the house and wondering what—or who—was causing them.

Disgusted with herself, she snatched up the remote control to the TV, turned to a sports channel, and pumped up the volume. She didn't care two cents about any kind of sports, but the noise blocked out everything else and helped her concentrate. Determinedly, she turned back to her script.

When Joe quietly let himself in the house and quickly reset the alarm, he frowned at the sound of a soccer game blaring from the TV in the family room. He wouldn't have thought either Angel or Laura were the type to be interested in sports, especially at eleven o'clock at night. Not when both women had to be up early, one to be on the set and the other to care for Emma, who invariably rose at the crack of dawn.

Wondering what the devil was going on, he stepped into the family room, only to stop short at the sight of Angel curled up in his favorite chair. Dressed for bed, her script lying forgotten in her lap, she was sound asleep. With her hair in a halo of golden curls and her cheeks slightly flushed with sleep, she looked as innocent as the angels she was named after.

Transfixed, Joe couldn't take his eyes off her. He didn't know how she did it. Every time he saw her, she was more beautiful than before. And harder to resist. It just wasn't fair, dammit!

Walk away, a voice in his head commanded. While you still can.

But it was already too late for that. Long after his meeting was over, he'd sat in Ed's Diner drinking coffee and finding excuses not to go home. And every excuse had begun and ended with Angel. Again and again, he went over all the reasons why he couldn't want her. It changed nothing. And he didn't have a clue what he was going to do about it.

Considering that, he shouldn't have gone anywhere near her. But she was slumped to the side, her head at an awkward angle. If she stayed that way all night, she'd wake up with a hell of a crick in her neck in the morning. Just thinking about it had him moving toward her. Just this once, he'd carry her upstairs and put her to bed. What would it hurt? She was asleep, and she'd never even know it until morning.

The second he scooped her up from the chair and she nestled her head against his shoulder, he realized his mistake. He never should have touched her. Not tonight. Not when he'd been thinking of her all evening and wondering what it would be like to take her to bed. Now he knew.

A smart man would have immediately deposited her back in the chair and got the hell out of there before she could wake up. But he couldn't bring himself to let her go when she lay so sweet and trusting in his arms. Just a few more minutes, he promised himself. That's all it would take to carry her to her room. Unable to resist, he started up the stairs.

Later, he couldn't say when he first realized that she was awake. She didn't move so much as a muscle as he climbed the stairs, but when he reached the upstairs' landing and glanced down at her to make sure she was still asleep, she was staring back at him with blue eyes that were dark and slumberous and sexy as hell. He felt the punch of them all the way to his toes.

He sucked in a sharp breath, only to unwittingly draw in the warm, intoxicating scent of her. Need tightened in his gut like a fist. Put her down! he told himself. Now! But even as he bent to do so in the hallway outside her bedroom door, he knew that he'd waited too long. Surrounded by shadows, with everyone else in the house asleep, it was just the two of them alone in the dark. And he wanted her more than he'd ever wanted a woman in his life. There was no way he could step away from her now.

"Joe, what—"

"You fell asleep downstairs while you were studying your script," he whispered in a gravelly voice. "I was just carrying you up to bed."

Giving in to the need to touch, he lifted a hand to gently brush her hair back from her face and very nearly groaned aloud. How could he have forgotten how soft her skin was? How delicate she was? How kissable? He watched her eyes go wide, her lips part, and could no more resist her than a wild creature could resist the call of its mate. Backing her up against the door to her room, he leaned down and hungrily covered her mouth with his.

Her mind still fuzzy with sleep, Angel couldn't summon a single defense against the heat that flooded through her in a rush. Moaning low in her throat, she melted against him, her arms tight around his neck, and gloried in the feel of his lean, hard body pressed to hers. How long had she been aching for him to hold her again like he would never let her go? To kiss her like he was starving for the taste of her? His tongue rubbed over hers, teasing and seducing, driving her slowly out of her mind, and all she could do was cling to him, lost in the taste and feel and wonder of him.

One kiss led to another, and still, it wasn't enough. She wanted more and couldn't even say the words, but somehow, he knew where she needed to be touched, caressed. Wrenching his mouth from hers, he nipped at her ear, then kissed the sensitive column of her neck, and every bone in her body just seemed to melt. Before she could do anything but gasp, his hands were roaming over her in sensuous exploration, sliding under her gown to caress her hips, her back, the fullness of her breasts. Her breath catching in her throat, she cried out softly as his thumb tenderly brushed her nipple. With nothing more than that gentle touch, he made her burn.

Whimpering, she would have given him anything then, she wanted him that much. And it was that that finally brought her to her senses. Dear God, what was she doing? She wasn't one of those Hollywood starlets who jumped from man to man, bed to bed. She didn't *do* that kind of thing! The one time she'd made the mistake of letting her emotions rule her head, she'd fallen for a man who'd wanted nothing to do with the child they'd created together.

Joe would never do such a thing—if she knew nothing else about him, she knew that he was a man who loved children and family. Still, she couldn't continue to fall into his arms without risking her heart and soul. Her heart was, she knew, tougher than she'd ever thought—it would, with time, mend if broken. Her soul was another matter. It was tender and all too vulnerable. Especially to a man like Joe McBride. He was the stuff her dreams were made of—a man of principles and values, of family and tradition who worked close to the earth and knew what life was all about. He was nothing like the men in her world…and everything she couldn't have. If she continued to give into this aching need he'd stirred in her, he could shatter her soul.

She pushed out of his arms because she had to, because if she didn't do it now, she would be lost. But it wasn't easy. Standing stiff and proud before him, all she wanted to do was cry; but she didn't dare. If she gave into the emotions tearing at her just once, she'd end up in tears in his arms.

"Don't," she said quickly when he automatically reached for her again. "Please, don't."

There was something in her voice, a hint of panic, that penetrated the desire clouding Joe's brain as nothing else could. There was no question that she didn't want him to touch her. Standing stiffly before him, her eyes wary and hot color stinging her cheeks, she looked like she'd bolt if he made so much as one wrong move. Why? What the hell just happened?

Concerned, he frowned. "What is it? What's wrong?"

"What's wrong?" she choked, keeping her voice down so it wouldn't wake Emma or Laura. "You kissed me!"

To deny it would have been ridiculous. "You're damn straight I did! And you kissed me back. So what's wrong with that? We're two consenting adults."

"No, we're not. I told you before, but I don't think you believed me. Don't make the mistake of thinking I'm like the women I play in the movies. I'm not. I'm not the *angel with the bedroom eyes*—"

"I never thought you were!"

"Didn't you? Don't worry, you wouldn't be the first man to make that mistake," she said with a trace of bitterness. "With all the stories in the tabloids, most people find it difficult to separate the real me from the characters I play on the screen. Which is why you have to believe me when I tell you that in spite of what just happened here, I'm not looking for a romp in the hay or in your bed or anywhere else.

"I can't deny that I'm attracted to you," she continued, the blush heating her cheeks deepening, "but I have no intention of giving in to that. I can't. It would be a mistake for both of us. And to be perfectly honest, I can't afford the distraction. Emma is my only priority right now—nothing else matters but keeping her safe."

Standing there in the darkened hall, his body still humming from the feel of her in his arms, Joe couldn't summon up a single argument in his own defense. Because she was right. She shouldn't have had to remind him why, for his own sake, he had no business touching her. She was trouble tied up with a pretty bow. The kind of trouble he only had to kiss to make him forget reason. He knew that, dammit, and still he'd lost his head.

Unless he wanted to find himself with more trouble than he was prepared to deal with, he'd make damn sure he kept his hands—and his kisses—to himself.

"I agree," he said stiffly. "It won't happen again."

Chapter 6

When her alarm went off the next morning, Angel jerked out of a sound sleep and quickly slapped at the clock on the nightstand before it could wake Emma, sighing in relief when silence fell immediately. It couldn't be five yet, she thought with a quiet groan as she pushed up to frown at the clock. She'd just gone to bed. There had to be a mistake.

But when her eyes finally focused on the digital readout, there was no mistake. Like it or not, it was time to get up. If she was still tired, she had nobody to blame but herself, her conscience taunted. If she hadn't let Joe kiss her, if she hadn't kissed him back without a thought to the consequences, she wouldn't have spent most of the night crawling all over the bed dreaming about him.

I agree. It won't happen again.

All too easily, she could see the stiff set of his jaw as he'd promised her that she didn't have to worry about him touching her again. He was a man of his word. He would do everything in his power to make sure that what happened between them last night outside her bedroom door wouldn't be repeated. And although she was thankful for the fact that he was a man of principles, deep in her heart, she ached for something she couldn't even put a name to, something that had been lost to her long before she'd ever arrived in Liberty Hill.

She could have cried then, could have buried her face in her pillow and given in to the mix of emotions that swirled inside her like a maelstrom. But she had to be on the set early because of the time she'd taken off yesterday afternoon, and the director would have a fit if she arrived with red-rimmed eyes and a blotchy face. So she fought back tears and with a heavy heart, rolled out of bed.

A shower helped raise her spirits, and when she soundlessly stuck her head back in her bedroom door to check on Emma, Angel couldn't help but smile. Sprawled across the bed with her teddy bear cuddled close, her daughter was out cold and looked as innocent as a lamb. It wouldn't last, of course. Five minutes after she woke up, she'd be overflowing with energy and going strong. Especially today. She and Laura were driving to Colorado Springs to buy a birthday present for Kelsey, Emma's best friend at play school back in L.A.

Not for the first time, Angel worried if she should cancel the trip. Yesterday's horror was still sickeningly fresh, the image of yellow roses in her trailer one she wouldn't soon forget. If she listened to her fear, she'd keep Emma locked up tight in the house and never let her out of her sight. But she knew that's just what the stalker would expect her to do. And by being so predictable, she might place Emma in even more danger.

So after discussing it with Laura, she'd decided that the best way to keep Emma safe was to have no established routine and do the unexpected. And the last thing her tormentor would expect her to do was let Emma go shopping less than twenty-four hours after he'd terrorized her again. The guards provided by the studio would accompany them and make sure they weren't followed. The trip was only decided upon last night, so the stalker couldn't possibly know where they were going and try to beat them there. For the day at least, they'd be safe.

Satisfied that all was well, Angel shut the bedroom door, then quietly started down the stairs, her thoughts already jumping ahead to the first scene of the morning. In spite of the fact that she'd fallen asleep last night while she was studying the script, she had her lines down pat. She just hoped Garrett wasn't in one of his moods. If he got a chance to make her miserable, he'd do it in a heartbeat and wouldn't care that he was costing the studio money while he did it. Another actor would have never gotten away with that, but he was one of the best actors in Hollywood and he knew it. Short of committing murder, there wasn't a lot he couldn't get away with.

Shaking her head over him, she reached the bottom of the stairs, only to frown in surprise when she saw the light was on in Joe's study. The rest of the ground floor was bathed in darkness and silent as a tomb. Listening, she thought she heard the sound of papers rustling and tried to shrug it off as her imagination. Then she heard it again— the quiet whisper of papers moving—and froze.

Someone was in Joe's study.

She told herself she was being ridiculous. The alarm was on, and Buster and the security guards were still on duty outside. No one could get inside without causing a huge ruckus first. If papers were moving around in the study, Joe must have left a window open and an early morning breeze was stirring things up.

Knowing that, however, did nothing to eliminate the sudden hollow feeling in her stomach as she stepped toward the study. She'd just shut the window…

"Angel?" Joe called out, appearing without warning in the study doorway. "Is that you?"

She'd thought she was fine—until her knees went weak at the sight of him. "Joe! What are you doing up this early?"

"I'm going to drive you to work," he said simply. "You do have to be on the set early today, don't you?"

Had he made the offer at any other time, she would have been touched and gladly accepted it. But after last night and the drugging kisses they'd shared, she couldn't be alone with him in the intimacy of his truck. It was too soon. For the sake of the agreement they'd made, it was better for both of them if they didn't tempt fate by being alone together.

"I appreciate the offer, but the studio's sending a car."

"Fine. Then I'll follow you to make sure you get there okay."

"But it's only five miles and we never have to leave the ranch!"

"It wouldn't matter if it was two," he retorted. "Nick said you and Emma shouldn't go anywhere alone—even here on the ranch."

"But I won't be alone. The driver will be with me."

"But you've already instructed the guards to stay here with Emma, haven't you? Aha, I knew it!" he said when she couldn't deny it. "You'll put yourself at risk to keep your daughter safe. And I can't blame you for that. But for my own peace of mind, I'll follow you."

She started to point out that they didn't even know for sure if her stalker was in Colorado, only to shut her mouth with a snap. His jaw was set at that stubborn John Wayne angle, the one that warned her he was going to protect the little woman whether she needed it or not, and there was no point in arguing further.

"Fine," she sighed, giving in gracefully. "Have it your way."

Without a word, he strode over to the alarm box and deactivated it so it wouldn't go off when he opened the front door.

The limo the studio was supposed to send never arrived. Already late by the time they realized it wasn't coming, Joe drove Angel to the set himself. They arrived just as the sun was peaking over the horizon, and already the place was crawling with people. Crew members set up cameras and lights and strung what looked like miles of cable, while extras milled about in period costumes, waiting for the day's shooting to begin. In the open pasture where filming would soon take place, wranglers corralled a herd of horses that would later be let loose in a controlled stampede, then tried to soothe them as the animals huddled together, their ears twitching nervously as they watched the madness around them.

Studying the Hollywood cowboys with a practiced eye, Joe was relieved to see that they appeared to know what they were doing. They were, however, wasting their time trying to gentle the horses. They'd never settle down as long as there was so much shouting and yelling and people rushing about.

He had work of his own to do, but first he meant to see that Angel was safely settled. Cutting the engine, he pushed open his door and came around to open hers. Surprised, she said, "You don't have to stay. I'm sure I'll be fine."

Joe wasn't sure of any such thing, not after her limo driver couldn't even arrive on time to see that she got to the set safely. Granted, with so many people around, he doubted that even her stalker was brazen enough to try to grab her there, but he wasn't taking any chances. "I'll just walk you to your trailer and make sure the studio posted a guard outside your door," he said stubbornly.

She didn't give him an argument, but Joe didn't fool himself into thinking it was because she actually agreed that the added security was necessary right there on the set. She truly believed that she was safe in a crowd and that had him worried. If her stalker was as diabolical as he sounded, every man, woman and child in Colorado could stand between him and Angel, and he'd still find a way to claim her as his own. And the day he did that was the day Joe made him regret he'd ever been born.

The light of battle glinting in his eyes, he followed her through the mass of humanity it took to make a movie, his narrowed gaze missing nothing as they pushed their way through the crowd. If anyone was watching them or pressing suspiciously close, he didn't see them. Still, he stayed one step behind her and was ready to pull her behind him if there was the slightest sign of trouble, but no one paid them the least heed. Within moments, they reached her trailer without mishap.

There should have been a guard on duty already outside the motor home. There wasn't. Opening the door for her, Joe swore when he glanced inside and saw that the vehicle was deserted. "Dammit to hell! First your driver never shows, and now your guard's missing!"

"I'm sure he's around here someplace," she replied. "He's probably gone to get coffee."

"He should have damn well done that before you got here," he retorted. His jaw granite hard, he motioned for her to proceed him up the steps. "Go on inside and lock the door. I'm going to go find Sutton and find out what the hell's going on."

"But the guard should be back any minute—"

"Lock the door, Angel. Now."

Her eyes flashed at his autocratic tone, and too late, he realized he'd gone too far. Protecting her was one thing, treating her like a child something else entirely. "Look, I'm sorry," he said with a sigh. "I didn't mean to growl at you that way. You're a grown woman. You don't need me to tell you what to do. But I don't like leaving you here alone without a guard—even if he is gong to be back any moment. It only takes a second for someone to grab you."

"Trust me, no one knows that better than I do," she replied, softening. "I'm not discounting the danger—I've lived with it for two months now. And that's given me a lot of time to get to know this jerk. He doesn't do anything in plain sight, Joe. He likes playing with my mind by leaving little gifts for me in places he shouldn't be able to get to. He wants me to worry, to look for him in the faces of strangers, to think about *him* and nothing else. He loves torturing me, which is why I know he's not going to grab me anytime soon. That would end the game he's playing, and he's enjoying it too much to call it quits now."

She had it all figured out, and Joe had to admit, she made perfect sense. The problem was she was assuming her stalker was capable of that kind of logic. From what Joe had heard of him, he was far too unstable to be considered anything close to predictable.

The security guard arrived then and immediately started apologizing the second he saw Angel waiting for him. "I'm sorry, Ms. Wiley! There must have been a mix-up. I got a call that I was supposed to work the front gate this morning, but when I got there, Larry Anderson was already there and scheduled to work, too. By the time I realized I was supposed to pick you up, then got to Mr. McBride's place, you were already gone. You didn't have any trouble getting to the set, did you?"

Giving him a reassuring smile, Angel noted the name on

his name tag and said, "Not at all, William. Mistakes happen. No harm done. Mr. McBride drove me over."

"What about this evening?" Joe asked him. "Who's driving her home then?"

"I'm not sure, sir," he replied. "But I can check, if you like."

That was something Joe intended to do for himself. "That's all right. I need to talk to the director, anyway. But you can do something else for me, William. Make sure Ms. Wiley doesn't go anywhere alone."

Indignant, Angel bristled like a porcupine, but neither man spared her the least attention. Exchanging a knowing look with Joe, the guard nodded. "I'll do it, sir. Nothing will happen to her as long as I'm around."

That was good enough for Joe. Shooting Angel a smug grin, he turned and walked away.

He found Charles Sutton with the director of photography, discussing the camera angles and lighting he wanted for the filming of the stampede scene. "Sorry to interrupt," he said curtly, "but I need to talk to you, Sutton."

"In a minute." Not sparing Joe a glance, he gave his full attention to his associate. "When the horses start down the hill, I want the camera down low—"

"It's about Angel."

That's all Joe had to say to get the director's full attention. His head snapped up, his black eyes pinning Joe to the ground in front of him. "What about her? She's all right, isn't she?"

"Yes, but she might not have been if I hadn't been there when the limo didn't arrive to pick her up. She would have driven herself."

"What?! Dammit to hell, what do you mean the limo didn't arrive? She has a driver—"

"Who got a call that he was assigned to the front gate

this morning," Joe cut in smoothly. "By the time he realized someone had gotten their wires crossed and drove to the house, we'd already left for the set."

Muttering curses, Charles mumbled, "I don't know how the hell anyone expects me to bring this film in under budget. Yesterday we had to shut down because of a bunch of damn roses—today my star tries to get herself kidnapped." With a shake of his head, he sighed in disgust and told the photographer, "It looks like I've got another crisis on my hands, George. I'll get back to you as soon as I can."

Dismissing the other man, he met Joe's stern gaze head-on. "Don't look at me like that, McBride. I'm just as worried about this damn stalker as you are. He's been damn cunning. Do you think he had something to do with the driver not getting the message that he was supposed to pick up Angel this morning?"

Joe couldn't deny that the thought hadn't crossed his mind. "At this point, I wouldn't put anything past the bastard," he retorted. "It certainly would have been an ideal time for him to grab her. And it wouldn't have been all that difficult to find out who her driver was, then call and send him to the wrong place."

"Well, it's damn well going to be difficult from now on," he promised grimly. "The studio's paying a hell of a lot for security—too much for this kind of foul-up to be tolerated. There should have been safeguards put into place that would prevent this from happening."

Joe didn't doubt that starting from today, there would be. For Angel's sake, he wanted to believe it was because Sutton and the studio bosses cared about her as a person. But the bottom line was that moviemaking was a business, and she was worth a hell of a lot of money to the studio. She was the star of the film, with a bigger fan base than all of her costars put together. If something happened to her before the picture was completed, it could cost the studio millions.

"I've notified all my ranch hands of the situation," he said, "and they'll be on the lookout for the bastard. The problem is, nobody knows who this jerk is. He could have pretended to be Angel's driver this morning when the real one didn't show, and no one would have known the difference until it was too late."

"Then she needs to have the same two drivers all the time—one to pick her up in the morning and the other to bring her home. I'll introduce them to her myself and make it clear that she's not to get in the car with anyone else."

"And if something happens to one of them and a sub has to take their place?"

"Either I or the head of security will call to notify her of the change and describe the new driver to her."

Joe considered the plan and nodded, satisfied. "The security guards here at the set and at my house also need to be a rotating group of regulars who are familiar with her drivers. That way, they'll spot an intruder immediately."

"I agree." Relieved, the director offered his hand and shook Joe's firmly in thanks. "I appreciate your input on this, McBride. I'll meet with the head of security this morning and get this all taken care of. By the time Angel's driver brings her home this afternoon, she'll know everything there is to know about him and every other member of her security team. With so many watchdogs hovering over her, we should have no problem keeping her safe."

There'd been a time when Joe would have thought that outsmarting a nutcase was just that easy. But this wasn't the first time he'd had to deal with someone whose feet weren't firmly grounded in reality. When his sister-in-law, Elizabeth, moved to town three years ago to reintroduce wolves to the region, she and Zeke found themselves dealing with a man who was so violently opposed to the government project that he was willing to do just about anything to stop it—including kill Lizzie if he had to. Outraged, the townspeople turned out in droves to protect her, but in the end, it hadn't mattered that she was in a safe place. He'd still managed to get his hands on her and almost kill her.

Just thinking about it made his gut knot in a fist. Because Angel's stalker was far more clever than the drunken mechanic who'd wanted Lizzie dead. "I wouldn't go that far, if I were you," Joe warned. "Any man smart enough to override her security system won't be put off by a few guards. Right now, he's only toying with her. When he tires of that game, she could be surrounded by an army of guards and still be in serious trouble."

He told him about Elizabeth then and how the man who had wanted her dead had lived right there in Liberty Hill all his life and no one had thought to suspect him until it was almost too late. It wasn't what he wanted to hear, and Joe couldn't blame him. Sutton had the weight of the movie on his shoulders and was the man everyone turned to when there was a problem. But he had to know that when they were dealing with someone this diabolical, it was going to take more than increased security to keep Angel safe.

His square-cut face carved in somber lines, the director said, "You made your point, McBride. We'll do everything we have to to make sure this bastard doesn't get his hands on her. She's not just a commodity to us, you know. She's a good kid and we care about her. There isn't a person in the crew or cast that wasn't concerned yesterday when I told them about her stalker."

Joe was glad to hear it. Because Angel had never needed friends more in her life.

Satisfied that she was safe for now at least, Joe had problems of his own to deal with, not the least of which was a drought that seemed to have no end in sight. As he drove away from the pasture where the studio had constructed its current set, he scowled at the dry, parched land that was usually still green at this time of the year. But it had been a particularly hot, dry summer, and the spring rains had been nonexistent due to unusual, persistent winds out of Mexico. The cattle tanks were low, and the creeks that were fed by the high mountains' snows were down to just a trickle. If there wasn't a major change in the weather patterns sometime soon, he would either have to haul water in for the cattle or start downsizing the herd. Either way, it was going to cost the ranch a sizable amount of money.

Just as he had once a week every week for the last six months, he spent the morning and half the afternoon inspecting the ranch's water holes. And what he saw wasn't good. With no rain over the course of the last seven days to help fill the tanks in the more arid areas of the ranch, several of the tanks had dried up.

He didn't, however, expect that to be the case in Dry Creek Canyon. The creek itself was seasonal and had been dry as dust for months, but a windmill in the middle of the canyon provided a good supply of water to the livestock and wildlife in the area. A natural draw, the canyon was always windy. With a steady breeze blowing out of the southeast to turn the pump, the nearby stock tank should have been full to overflowing.

But when he turned into the canyon and made his way deeper into the heart of it, the cattle that usually collected under the trees surrounding the stock tank were noticeably absent, and the tank itself was nothing but a mudhole. And one look at the windmill told him why. In spite of the steady wind that swept down through the draw, it was still as a post, its blades unmoving.

"Dammit to hell!"

He couldn't believe it. He'd just repaired the darn thing

three weeks ago, and now it was broken again. Muttering curses, he pulled up next to the stock tank, grabbed his tool belt from the bed of his pickup, and strapped it on.

It was the hottest part of the day, and a smart man would have waited until early morning, when it was cooler and the sun wasn't beating down on him, to work on the windmill since it was made of metal. But Joe didn't want to have to come back in the morning for what was probably a fifteen minute job. Irritated, he yanked on his work gloves and started climbing up the windmill's tower.

He found the problem almost immediately—a frozen gear—but correcting it wasn't nearly as easy. He had to disassemble half the motor to get to it while balanced thirty feet off the ground. And he couldn't do it with his gloves on—they were too bulky. Spitting out an oath, he stripped them off and stuffed them in the back pocket of his jeans, then went back to work.

There wasn't a cloud in the sky to block the bright glare of the sun, and within minutes, sweat was beading on his forehead and sliding down into his eyes, blurring his vision. Absently, he wiped his brow with his forearm, but it did little good. The temperature had to be ninety-five degrees in the shade and seemed to be getting hotter with every passing minute.

"Get on with it," he growled to himself, and tested the blades to see if they would turn. With a groan, they did, but not as freely as they should have. He made an adjustment with a screwdriver, and with ridiculous ease, the damn thing was fixed.

Later, he couldn't believe he was so careless. Relieved that the job hadn't taken much more than the fifteen minutes he'd thought it would, he was reassembling the casing on the motor and thinking about the cold beer he was going to have when he got home when a wind gust that blew down through the canyon caught him by surprise and almost knocked him off the tower. His guard relaxed, he grabbed for a handhold and scraped the palm of his hand on one of the windmill's sharp metal blades.

"Son of a bitch!"

If the angle had been right, he could have sliced his hand open to the bone, but a quick glance reassured him that he hadn't cut through the skin. It was just a scrape. That didn't make it any less painful. Throbbing, it was raw and red and covered most of the palm of his hand. Just moving his fingers hurt like hell.

"Idiot!" he chastised himself. "Now what are you going to do? There's no way in hell you're climbing down this damn tower with just one hand."

A quick survey of the situation confirmed that unless he intended to spend the rest of the afternoon stuck on the side of the tower, he had no choice but to ignore the pain and finish the job. His jaw clenched on an oath, he tightened the screws in the motor casing, then began the slow, painful process of climbing down the tower. By the time he reached the ground, a cold sweat covered his brow and his hand was burning, his fingers stiff. Pulling a handkerchief from his pocket, he wrapped it around his palm, then climbed in his truck and headed home.

It was going on four when he got home. Deactivating the alarm, he found the house deserted, just as he'd expected. Laura and Emma weren't back from their shopping trip to Colorado Springs, and after taking yesterday afternoon off, shooting would probably run long for Angel. Which meant he had the place to himself for another few hours, and that was fine with him. He was hot and dirty and a dull ache had settled in his hand. He wanted a bath and a beer in that order and then some time in front of the television just to relax before Angel got home. Because he knew that once she walked through the front door, tension would crawl into his belly and he wouldn't be able to think of anything but the hot, heated moments he'd shared with her outside her bedroom door last night.

Don't go there, he warned himself, but it was too late. For most of the day, he'd pushed her from his thoughts by concentrating on the drought and what it was doing to the ranch, but there were no distractions there in the house. Everywhere he looked were memories of her—cooking breakfast in the kitchen, sleeping in his chair in the family room, the feel of her in his arms as he'd carried her upstairs to bed, kisses in the hall upstairs....

Like a butterfly unable to resist the sweet nectar of a rose, his thoughts zeroed back to last night, irritating him no end. Dammit to hell, this had to stop! There was one room in the house she hadn't invaded yet except in his dreams, and by God, he dared her to try!

His face set in harsh lines, he climbed the stairs and strode into his bedroom—only to nearly drop his teeth at the sight of Angel pulling back the sheets on his bed. "What the hell are you doing?"

She jumped and whirled to face him, her blue eyes huge in a face that had gone ivory white. "Joe! I didn't hear you come in. I thought you were working."

"Funny, I could say the same thing about you," he growled, not at all pleased to see her there. "What are you doing here? I didn't think you'd be home until after six."

"Garrett got some kind of stomach virus, so we had to knock off early."

"What about your guards? Where the hell are they? I didn't see either one of them when I drove up."

"I believe one of them's checking out the barn and the other the trees to the east. They already searched the house to make sure no one was able to get in while we were gone."

Well, that at least, was something. Knowing she was

being protected by two conscientious men gave him one less reason to think about her. But she still hadn't explained what she was doing in his room. Glancing pointedly at his unmade bed, he arched a brow at her. "Now that we've got that cleared up, why don't you tell me what you're doing in here, Goldilocks? Or do I have to ask? From the looks of things, I'd say you were just about to try out my bed."

"I was not!" she gasped, flushing. "I would never—I can't believe you think I would—"

He'd never seen her quite so flustered, and he had to admit, he enjoyed seeing her rattled. His brown eyes glinting with sudden humor, he teased, "Don't stop now. You would never...what?"

It was only then she saw the grin he made no attempt to hide, and she couldn't help but laugh herself. "Go ahead. Have your fun. I was going to wash your sheets for you since I was doing mine, but now you can do them yourself. And it's no more than you deserve."

Sniffing haughtily, she lifted her nose in the air and started to sweep past him as he stood in the doorway. But just as she drew even with him, her gaze dropped to the handkerchief wrapped around his hand. "You're hurt!"

"It's nothing, just a scrape," he began.

That was as far as he got. Grasping his injured hand above the wrist, she hustled him into the bathroom next door and with quick, efficient fingers began to untie the bandage. At the sight of the wound on his palm, she clicked her tongue, her frown fierce. "How in the world did you do that? It must hurt like hell. Sit down while I find something to clean it with." And without so much as a by-your-leave, she flipped down the lid on the commode, pushed him down, then turned away to search his linen closet and medicine chest for everything she needed to doctor the wound.

"Angel, it's not that bad."

"Have you had a tetanus shot lately?" she demanded, glancing over her shoulder to scowl at him. "Good. Then we don't have to worry about that. Do you have any peroxide? Never mind, here it is. All right, brace yourself. This could sting."

That was putting it mildly. He sucked in a sharp breath, but she was quick and efficient and used to dealing with a three-year-old who didn't sit still for much. Before he could draw his next breath, she soothed on a cool, antiseptic cream with a gentle touch. A bandage was taped into place, and less than two minutes after she'd taken his hand in hers to clean it, she was finished.

Pleased with herself, she patted the back of his hand and smiled down into his eyes. "There, that wasn't so bad, was it?"

"That depends on which end of the peroxide you're on," he retorted wryly, and pushed to his feet. "Thanks." And before she could begin to guess his intentions, he leaned down and kissed her on the cheek.

It wasn't planned—she only had to look into his suddenly somber eyes to know that he was as surprised by the innocent kiss as she was—and she should have accepted it in the spirit in which it was given. All she had to do was smile, say, "You're welcome," and turn away to return his things to his medicine cabinet, and the sudden awareness between them would have died as quickly as it had thundered to life. It was that simple.

But her heart was tripping over itself, and her feet refused to move. She knew she needed to walk away from him—it was the only smart thing to do—but she couldn't. There was a longing in her heart that made her want to weep, a need unlike anything she'd ever felt for another man. Literally aching for the feel of his arms around her, she wanted nothing so much as the heat and taste and hunger of his mouth on hers.

Helplessly, she lifted her eyes to his, the words trembling on her tongue, but she couldn't tell him what she needed. Somehow, though, he knew. She saw an answering longing in eyes that had suddenly gone nearly black with desire, felt it in the tenderness of the callused hand that cupped her cheek like she was more precious than the most fragile porcelain. With a groan that was her name, he pulled her into his arms and kissed her with a pent-up frustration that stole the air right out of her lungs.

Dizzy, she clung to him, welcoming the heady invasion of his tongue in her mouth with a passion that stunned her. How long had she wanted him this badly and not even known it? From the first time she'd met him? Touched him? Kissed him? It could have been days—or weeks—it didn't matter. She just knew she never wanted it to end.

"Joe...please," she whimpered against his mouth, "make love to me."

Groaning, he knew he shouldn't. There were a dozen reasons why he would regret this, but with her so soft and needy in his arms, he couldn't think of a single one. Just Angel. The taste and feel and scent of her. The sweet hunger of her kisses. She was in his blood, an ache that wouldn't go away. He'd fought it, sworn he wouldn't give in to it, to *her,* but then she took his hand, and just that simply, she made him burn for her. He had to have her—here, now—and damn the consequences. Need clawing at him, he swept her up in his arms and carried her into his bedroom without ever taking his mouth from hers.

The covers had been stripped from the bed and the top sheet trailed on the floor, but he didn't care. Lowering her to the mattress, he followed her down, a groan rippling through him as her arms came around him, cradling him close, and her soft, slender body took his weight. Wrenching his mouth from hers, he reached for the buttons of the cotton blouse she wore, the need to touch her, all of her, more than he could stand.

Urgency firing his blood, he wanted her naked—now!—and was stunned to find his fingers not quite steady. Concentrate! he told himself, but found it impossible when the back of his fingers brushed the curve of her breasts. Then, somehow he had her shirt off and her bra, and he couldn't think at all. Beautiful. There was no other way to describe her. Lying like a pagan goddess in the late afternoon sunshine that streamed in through the open curtains of the window, her breasts bare and creamy, her eyes slumberous with passion, she was the most beautiful woman he'd ever seen in his life.

With a rough sound of need, he leaned down and closed his mouth over her beaded nipple, caressing her with tongue and teeth and lips, and Angel thought she would die right there. Pleasure streaked through her like summer lightning, and with a strangled cry, she arched under him, lost to everything but the desperate need for more.

Frantic to touch him, she fumbled with the buttons of his shirt and finally managed to undo them. Then her hands were pushing it off his broad shoulders and her breath caught in her throat at the sight of him. She'd seen her share of buffed bodies in Hollywood that were the sole result of too many narcissistic hours at the gym. They had nothing on Joe.

His skin was bronzed from years in the sun rather than a tanning booth, his body rock-hard from a lifetime of physical labor. Unlike the pretty boys of Tinseltown, his muscles weren't overblown and sculpted, but as tough as tempered steel, without an ounce of fat. Suddenly, quite desperately, she needed to touch more than she needed her next breath. With a murmur of approval, she lifted her hands to him to stroke, to tease, to caress.

Up until then, he'd thought he was in control. No woman had ever taken that from him, not even Belinda. But with nothing more than a touch, Angel stirred something savage in him, something wild and primitive that refused to be leashed. Even as he fought it and tried to regain control of the need that threatened to take on a life of its own, he tugged off her shoes, then his, with fingers that were anything but steady. Within seconds, he'd stripped them both of their jeans.

Bare skin met bare skin, and his mind blurred. Nothing had ever felt so good, so damn right. And he needed more. A hell of a lot more. His hands raced over her, then his mouth, heating her skin, tasting every sweet inch of her, driving them both crazy. He kissed his way down her body and very nearly shattered her. She cried out, arching under him, her nails biting into his shoulders.

The world could have stopped then and he never would have noticed. She was all that mattered, pleasuring her, driving her over the edge, making her come undone in his arms. He moved against her and she gasped, parted her thighs and she shuddered. Then she was opening to him, lifting her hips to him, taking him inside her, and the fire in his blood heated to flash point. He surged into her, and then they were moving in a rhythm as old as time, their hips circling, rolling, driving toward release.

Her breath tearing through her lungs, her eyes locked with his, Angel felt the tension clawing at her tighten unbearably. Blindly, her fingers sought his. She wanted to tell him that no man had ever brought her to this, driven her to the very edge of sanity, but she couldn't find the words. Her mind clouded over, need fisted deep inside her, and then, with a suddenness that stunned her, she cried out as her senses exploded.

She was still shuddering when a low groan was ripped from Joe's throat and he followed her over the edge into a pleasure so intense it bordered on madness.

Chapter 7

Outside, the sun slipped lower in the sky, casting long shadows, and one of the guards outside called to Buster as he made his hourly rounds around the perimeter of the house and barn. Her head cradled against Joe's shoulder, the reassuring beat of his heart pounding in her ears, Angel drifted back to her senses slowly, too content to move, let alone think. Given the opportunity, she could have lain just there, with Joe's arms snug around her, for hours.

But reality had a way of forcing its way into even the most magical of moments. As her pulse steadied and her head cleared, images of their loving flashed before her eyes—hot, breathless kisses that took her outside herself, touches of tenderness that melted her heart and brought the sting of tears to her eyes. Despite the outrageous stories in the tabloids, she wasn't a woman who slept around. There'd only been one other man in her life, and that was Kurt Austin, Emma's father; and she'd never felt for him a tenth of the emotions Joe had pulled from her with just a touch. And she'd thought she loved Kurt with all her heart.

So what did that say about her feelings for Joe?

The question came straight from her heart and stunned her. No, she thought, shaken. She wasn't going to play that game with herself. She was attracted to Joe, that was all. Her feelings for him had nothing to do with affection or caring or any of the varied emotions that could, if nurtured properly, lead to love. It was just chemistry, a physical reaction brought on by loneliness and the physical needs that any healthy woman experienced after being too long by herself.

That had to be it, she thought in relief. It was the only explanation. Because she couldn't, under any circumstances, allow herself to consider, even for a second, what it might be like to fall in love with Joe McBride. She'd done that once—given her heart to the wrong man. She wouldn't do it again.

And in spite of the passion they'd just shared, there was no question that Joe could never be anything but wrong for her. Oh, he was a good man, but he had a steel barrier around his heart that no woman was ever going to get past. He could give her tenderness and desire, even affection, but he was never going to be able to give her love. And if he couldn't give her that, then she wanted nothing else from him. Because she knew what it felt like to love someone who didn't love you back, and she'd never put herself through that kind of heartache again.

Lying on his side, cradling her close, Joe felt her stiffen, and swept his hands down her naked back in a reassuring caress. Already, he wanted her again—he couldn't be this close to her and not—but he had a feeling that the sudden tension in her had nothing to do with renewed desire. "Are you all right?"

Frowning, he pulled back to get a good look at her face, but she turned away, avoiding his gaze, and slipped from his arms. "Laura and Emma will be here soon," she said

How To Play:

No Risk!

1. With a coin, carefully scratch off the 3 gold areas on your Lucky Carnival Wheel. By doing so you have qualified to receive everything revealed — 2 FREE books and a surprise gift — ABSOLUTELY FREE!

2. Send back this card and you'll receive brand-new Silhouette Intimate Moments® novels. These books have a cover price of $4.50 each in the U.S. and $5.25 each in Canada, but they are yours TOTALLY FREE!

3. There's no catch! You're under no obligation to buy anything. We charge nothing — ZERO — for your first shipment. And you don't have to make any minimum number of purchases—not even one!

4. The fact is thousands of readers enjoy receiving books by mail from the Silhouette Reader Service™. They enjoy the convenience of home delivery...they like getting the best new novels at discount prices, BEFORE they're available in stores...and they love their *Heart to Heart* subscriber newsletter featuring author news, horoscopes, recipes, book reviews and much more!

5. We hope that after receiving your free books you'll want to remain a subscriber. But the choice is yours — to continue or cancel, anytime at all! So why not take us up on our invitation, with no risk of any kind. You'll be glad you did.

No Cost!

LUCK
Car
Scratch-

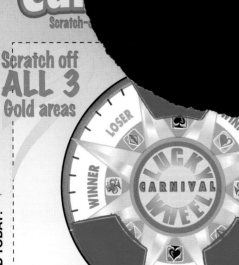

YES! I have scratched off the 3 Gold Areas above. Please send me the 2 FREE books and gift for which I qualify! I understand I am under no obligation to purchase any books, as explained on the back and on the opposite page.

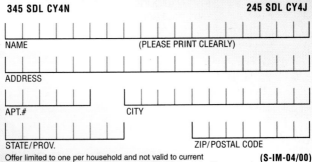

345 SDL CY4N   **245 SDL CY4J**

| | | | | | | | | | | | | | | | | | | |
NAME   (PLEASE PRINT CLEARLY)

| | | | | | | | | | | | | | | | | | | |
ADDRESS

| | | | | | | | | | | | | | | | |
APT.#   CITY

| | | | | | | | | | | | | |
STATE/PROV.   ZIP/POSTAL CODE

▶ DETACH AND MAIL CARD TODAY!

works:

...y keep the books and gift and
...'ll send you 6 additional novels
... and applicable taxes if any.*
...5.25 each in Canada — it's quite
... you 6 more books, which you

...an residents will be charged

If offer card is missing write to: Silhouette Reader Service, 3010 Walden Ave., P.O. Box 1867, Buffalo, NY 14240-1867

BUSINESS REPLY MAIL

FIRST-CLASS MAIL   PERMIT NO. 717   BUFFALO, NY

POSTAGE WILL BE PAID BY ADDRESSEE

SILHOUETTE READER SERVICE
3010 WALDEN AVE
PO BOX 1867
BUFFALO NY 14240-9952

NO POSTAGE
NECESSARY
IF MAILED
IN THE
UNITED STATES

huskily, reaching for her clothes. "I need to finish washing the sheets and start dinner. Emma will be tired. She's had a long day and I'd like to get her in bed early tonight."

She was making excuses and they both knew it. His brow knit in a scowl, Joe watched her pull on her clothes with an unconscious grace that made his mouth water and had to fight the need to pull her back down into bed with him again. Dammit, what the hell was going on? He liked to think he wasn't an insensitive man, but something had definitely upset her and he didn't have a clue what it was. It couldn't have been the loving they'd just shared—she'd been right with him every step of the way and as caught up in the moment as he was. So what the devil was wrong?

Frustrated, he was tempted to lie there until she gave him an answer, but one look at her closed expression and he knew she wasn't going to talk about whatever was bothering her. And he couldn't insist—not when Laura and Emma could return at any second.

Silently cursing the lack of time and privacy, he reached for his own clothes and tugged them on, unconscious of his nudity until she blushed and hurriedly looked away. Still frustrated, he couldn't help but be fascinated by her. Did she know what a contradiction in terms she was? She was an experienced woman, a beautiful, single movie star who had, no doubt, been exposed to any number of racy things in Hollywood that would shock the good people of Liberty Hill. Not ten minutes ago, she'd come undone in his arms when they made love, yet he only had to climb from his bed naked to turn her cheeks rosy.

Given the chance, he would have teased her then, taken her back in his arms until she softened and told him what was bothering her, but she was already stripping the bed down to the bare mattress. All business, she remade it with clean sheets, then gathered up the dirty ones and walked out without saying a single word.

"Well, hell," he growled, and strode into the bathroom for a shower.

The load of sheets was already in the washing machine and agitating when Angel walked into the kitchen to start supper. If she just kept busy, she told herself, she wouldn't have to think about Joe and the look on his face when she'd all but run out of his bedroom. He'd let her go but she didn't fool herself into thinking that he wouldn't demand an explanation when the opportunity presented itself. After the intimacy they'd shared, he had a right to know why she'd suddenly jumped from his bed like a scalded cat. And she would tell him. But not when she felt like she was going to shatter at the least provocation. She needed some time to get her emotions under control, to rebuild her defenses so that she wouldn't give in to the need to go back into his arms the second he touched her again. And he would touch her again—she didn't doubt it for a minute. It was just a question of when.

Her heart lurching at the thought, she started to turn to the refrigerator to retrieve the chicken tenders she intended to cook for Emma, only to stop at the sight of the small pile of mail on the kitchen table. Normally, she wouldn't have given it a second glance—Joe had been hurting when he came in and must have dropped it there before coming upstairs to bandage his hand—but the letter on top looked distinctly familiar.

Stepping over to the table, she felt her heart squeeze painfully as she recognized her own handwriting on an envelope that looked a little the worse for wear. It was the same letter she'd sent to her father just last week.

Had he moved without bothering to notify her or the post office? she wondered. She'd sent it to the café—he should have gotten it. Then her eyes fell on the big red letters scrawled across the bottom of the envelope in her father's precise handwriting.

RETURN TO SENDER.

Pale, she fumbled for a chair at the table and dropped into it, pain squeezing her heart as she picked up the letter. He hadn't even read it, hadn't even bothered to give her a chance to tell him about his granddaughter. She'd hoped that with time, he'd let go of the past; but with three little words, he'd told her nothing had changed. He was still a hard, unforgiving man, still judgmental to a fault, still condemning of anyone who didn't believe the way he did. He wasn't interested in why she had made the choices she had, didn't want explanations of any kind. The bottom line was that he hadn't wanted anything to do with her when she'd left home the day after she graduated from high school, and he didn't now.

Heartsick, she crumbled the letter but couldn't bring herself to throw it in the trash. Damn him, why did he have to be so hard? All she wanted to do was make peace, but he fought her at every turn. Did he even love her? she wondered as tears flooded her eyes. How could he if he could cut her out of his life so effortlessly?

She wanted to cry then, to lay her head down on the table and give in to the pain that tore at her with razor-sharp claws. But if she started to cry now, she didn't think she'd be able to stop. And then she heard Joe's step on the stairs. Hurriedly wiping at her damp eyes, she jumped up and turned to the refrigerator. By the time he stepped into the kitchen, she was at the stove, heating oil in a skillet to fry the tenders.

The crumbled letter was forgotten on the table. Glancing from it to where Angel stood at the stove with her back to him, her shoulders stiff and unyielding, Joe frowned. "Are you all right?"

"Of course," she said coolly, never taking her eyes from the skillet in front of her. "Why wouldn't I be?"

Joe could think of several reasons, not the least of which was the letter lying on the table. Who the hell was James Wiley, anyway? A brother? A father? She'd never said anything about her family, but whoever James was, he obviously wanted nothing to do with her. And for reasons he couldn't explain, that irritated the hell out of Joe. Returning a letter like that was downright cruel and totally unnecessary. If the bastard hadn't wanted any correspondence from her, he should have just pitched it in the trash and she never would have known the difference.

Which was, he thought grimly, noting the New Mexico address on the letter, why the jerk sent the letter back. He wanted her to know that not only had he not read it, but that he wanted no part of her, not even a letter.

And she'd gotten the message—there was no doubt of that. She was hurting, dammit, and he didn't like it. But he didn't have the right to help her unless she asked, and she wasn't asking. Which wasn't surprising. She might look as fragile as spun glass, but the lady was tough. Any other woman being stalked by a madman who wanted her daughter dead would have found a safe place to lie low and retreated from life like a turtle drawing into its shell until the bastard was caught. But not Angel. There was no question that the bastard had scared her, especially with his threats against Emma, but she had refused to hide out like a criminal on the run. She defiantly continued to work, and by doing so, just dared the jerk to come after her or Emma.

Considering all that, he'd thought it took a hell of a lot to get the lady down. But something had knocked her legs out from under her and drained the fight out of her, and it had to be that damn letter. And James Wiley. He started to ask her who the man was and what he meant to her, only to shut his mouth with a snap. No, dammit, this wasn't any of his business or his problem to solve. If he wanted to do himself a favor, he'd leave it alone.

The problem was he couldn't leave *her* alone. He hadn't from the beginning. He'd sworn he wanted nothing to do with her, but every passing day made it harder to keep his hands to himself. She was a fever in his blood, and after the loving they'd just shared, a woman he needed to avoid like the plague before he found himself up to his neck in something he wanted no part of. But instead of finding excuses to stay out of her way, all he could think of was that he wanted to cheer her up.

"The town always has a big parade and street dance on the night of Midsummer's Eve," he told her, "and that's this Thursday. I was wondering if you'd like to go?"

That got her attention. "You mean with you? Like a date?"

He should have said no, he didn't mean anything of the kind. But that was exactly what he meant, and he couldn't help but be struck by the ludicrousness of the situation. He lived with her, he'd slept with her, and now he was asking her *out?*

Backtracking, he said casually, "It's one of those things that the whole town goes to. Though after living in L.A., it'll probably seem pretty tame to you. I just thought you and Emma might enjoy it. And Laura, too," he quickly added. "Everyone brings their kids, but if you want to pass, it's no big deal. It might not be all that safe, anyway. The streets'll be crawling with strangers."

He expected her to turn him down flat. It would have been for the best. If he showed up with her and Emma and the nanny like a family unit, he could hear the gossips now. They'd add one plus one and come up with a fairy tale that was never going to happen. And then there were the reporters crawling out of the woodwork every time you turned around. They were bound to get wind of the story.

By the day after the festival, it would be all over the country that Angel Wiley had a new man in her life—*him*.

"Maybe you'd better not go," he began.

That was as far as he got. "No," she said quickly, a slow smile breaking across her face as she thought about it. "It sounds like fun. And Emma will love it. We'd love to go."

The night of the Midsummer's Eve Festival promised to be warm and clear and perfect for a parade. As the sun sank behind the mountains to the west and twilight gradually deepened, the stars peaked out of the heavens overhead one by one. And on the light breeze that whispered through the crowds that lined Main Street, the scent of grilled hamburgers and smoked turkey legs and roasted corn mixed with the infectious sound of laughter on the air.

Because of mechanical problems with the fire truck that would lead the parade, the start time had been set back for at least thirty minutes, but no one seemed to care. Gathered in groups and bunches along the parade route, the good citizens of Liberty Hill took advantage of the delay to stuff themselves with greasy foods and cotton candy and visit with people they'd probably seen just that afternoon.

It was so small townish—and so reminiscent of her childhood—that Angel couldn't help but smile mistily as memories swamped her. Her father closing the café on the Fourth of July and dressing up like Uncle Sam, fireworks and sparklers, riding the Ferris wheel at the carnival and sucking on big dill pickles like they were the best thing she'd ever tasted.

She'd forgotten how much fun she'd had...and how wholesome it had all been. Living in L.A., far from the world she'd grown up in, that kind of innocence was reserved for movies and Disneyland. She was glad to know it still existed.

"When's the parade going to start, Mommy?" Emma asked excitedly. Barely able to stand still, she stood between Angel and Joe, holding each of their hands, and hopped from one foot to the other. "Will they have clowns? With balloons? I want a balloon, Mommy. A great *big* one!" she said enthusiastically, spreading her arms wide in spite of the fact that her hands weren't free. "Can I have one? Please? Please? A red one—like the fire truck. Is it still broke? Why don't they fix it? Can I drive a fire truck in a parade when I grow up, Mommy?"

Her head spinning, Angel grabbed it with her free hand and laughed. "Whoa, sweetheart! Slow down and catch your breath. Mommy's had a hard week, and my brain's moving in slow motion. I can't keep up with you."

She was teasing—and spoke nothing less than the truth. Hard didn't begin to describe the week she'd had. Because they were behind in the shooting schedule, Charles had tried to make up for lost time by working the cast and crew from sunrise to midnight or longer over the course of the last three days, and the pace had been exhausting. When she hadn't been in front of the camera, she'd been studying her lines, and what meals she'd eaten had been gulped down on the run. By the time she'd finally got home each night, she'd been so tired, she'd fallen into bed and hadn't moved until her alarm went off at five-thirty, when the routine started all over again.

Exhausted, she'd only had one afternoon off, and should have used that time to rest or catch up on the chores she'd let slide because of work. But she'd promised Elizabeth McBride that she and Emma and Laura would pay a visit when she had some time off, so the three of them had spent yesterday afternoon with her and Cassie.

She'd had a wonderful time, but she still hadn't managed to catch up on her sleep. And tomorrow was another long day of shooting. Considering that, she'd actually considered staying home for the evening and turning in early. But she hadn't wanted to disappoint Emma or Laura—or deny herself the opportunity to spend some time with Joe. That, she knew, wasn't wise, but she couldn't forget those heated moments in his bed, couldn't push the sensuous images from her head. Her common sense warned her not to make more of it than it was—sex was sex, and if she let herself start to think it could ever be anything more than that, she was going to be in serious trouble.

But she was confident that wasn't what she was doing. She had her head on straight and her heart locked up tight. And it wasn't as if Joe had asked her out for a romantic dinner. It was a parade, for God's sake! What could happen when they were accompanied by two security guards, not to mention Laura and Emma, and surrounded by a crowd of hundreds?

So she'd made the decision to come, and she was glad now that she had. Just being out and about among people who had nothing to do with the movie business was like a breath of fresh air. Oh, she still had to contend with fans who wanted autographs and their pictures taken with her, but for the most part, people were respectful and, thankfully, far more interested in the festivities than her.

Turning her attention back to Emma, she grinned and patiently answered her questions. "Yes, you can have a balloon—when we start for home. I don't know when the parade's going to begin—it all depends on how long it takes to repair the fire truck. And yes, you can drive a fire truck when you grow up…if you're a firefighter. Any more questions?"

"Yeah," Joe growled. "Why don't we eat before the parade starts? I'm starving!"

"A hamburger sounds good."

"Mommy, can I have a turkey leg?"

"The roasted corn smells delicious. I could eat just that."

There were a dozen or more food booths to choose from along the parade route, and the scents that drifted from them were mouthwatering. Not surprisingly, everyone changed their mind two or three times before they finally decided what they wanted, but that was part of the fun. Before the evening was over, they'd probably eat again anyway and go through the process all over again. Enjoying himself, Joe pulled out his wallet and treated his three dates to whatever culinary delights their hearts desired.

Considering how health-conscious Californians were, he half expected Angel to limit herself to the corn since it was just about the only choice available that wasn't loaded down with fat and cholesterol, but she surprised him by going for a nice big greasy hamburger, then thoroughly devouring it. Amazed, he watched her daintily touch her napkin to her mouth when she was finished and couldn't help but grin.

"What?" she asked when she caught him watching her. "Have I got something stuck in my teeth or what?"

"No," he chuckled. "You just look like you're having a good time, and the parade hasn't even started yet."

"And that surprises you? I love things like this!"

Her mouth still half-full of the hot dog she'd polished off with every bit as much enthusiasm as her mother, Emma tugged on the cuff of Angel's shorts. "I'm done, Mommy," she announced around the food in her mouth. "Can I have some cotton candy now? You said I could when I finished eating."

Laura and Joe both choked on a laugh and grinned at Angel, waiting to see what she would do. To keep Emma from filling up on sweets, Angel had promised her she could have the special treat if she ate supper. Who could have known that the little girl could manage to eat half her hot dog without swallowing?

Solemn as a nun, Angel studied her knowingly. "What's that in your mouth?"

Caught red-handed, Emma looked up at her guiltily. "Uh—"

"That's what I thought," she said dryly, amused. "Why don't you chew that up before you choke on it? Then you can have your cotton candy."

Her eyes lighting up, Emma chewed very quickly, her little jaw working like a piston, then swallowed with an almost audible gulp.

Trying not to laugh, Laura quickly covered her mouth with her hand. "Oh, I'll get this," she choked when Joe grinned and started to pull out his wallet to pay for Emma's dessert. "It'll be my treat. Would anyone else like anything?"

"A candied apple," Angel said promptly. "I haven't had one in years."

Mother and daughter looked an awful lot alike at that moment, and as Emma skipped off with Laura and one of the security guards to collect the much anticipated sweet, Joe studied her in puzzled amusement. "I can't figure you out. I saw the news reports last summer when you had dinner with the President and First Lady in the White House. It was a state dinner and you charmed the hell out of some Prince from the Middle East."

"Prince Hammed Amin," she confirmed with a half smile. "He sent me two dozen roses the next day."

"And now you're eating candied apples in the middle of Nowhere, Colorado, waiting for the mayor to get our one and only fire truck running so we can start a damn parade that's going to be over in about fifteen minutes."

"And your point is?"

"Who the hell *are* you?"

"Angel Wiley," she said simply. "Mom, homemaker, actress. I live in L.A. now, but only because that's where I work. I actually grew up in New Mexico, in a town that wasn't much bigger than Liberty Hill. We didn't celebrate Midsummer's Eve, but we did have duck races in the winter."

So she wasn't a big city girl, after all. Surprised, he wondered why he hadn't guessed. She might have the sophistication of a woman born with a silver spoon in her mouth in Beverly Hills, but she walked the streets of Liberty Hill with the relaxed stride of someone who had lived there all her life. And unlike some of the other cast and crew members he'd heard complaining in town, she was totally unconcerned with the lack of city conveniences. She didn't whine because Liberty Hill had no multiplex movie theater or sprawling shopping mall or upscale restaurants with overpriced food and bad service. On the rare occasions when she was able to make it into town, she was content to eat the blue plate special at Ed's and buy her own groceries at Harrison's Market. And she didn't have a clue how the locals admired her for that. How *he* admired her for that.

Later, he was going to have to think about that, but not now, when there were more important things to talk about. His lips twitching, he arched a brow at her. "Duck races? Flying or waddling?"

"Waddling," she replied, chuckling. "And I loved it. But I love the Rose Parade, too. It doesn't matter how big or little the parade is, it's the people who make it fun. Like that man over there," she said, lowering her voice and nodding toward an old gentleman across the street. Tall and spry, with a thatch of thick white hair on top of his head, he stood head and shoulders above the people around him. And in his arms, held up so it could see what was going on, was a miniature poodle with hair as white as his.

Her face sparkling with laughter, she grinned up at Joe. "Now tell me, who would bring a dog to a parade? And why? So he can bark at the pretty girls on the floats? C'mon, Joe, that's hysterical!"

Chuckling, he had to agree. "That's old man Peabody and Hercules. You never see one without the other—even in Ed's Diner."

"Mr. Peabody takes his poodle into Ed's?"

He nodded, fighting a smile. "And orders him meat loaf every time. It's Hercules's favorite."

She laughed in delight, and Joe couldn't help but be enchanted. Every building and tree in town was decorated with tiny white lights that twinkled like stars, and in their soft glow, she was so pretty, he couldn't take his eyes off her. Staring down at her, he felt need tighten deep inside him and wondered how he was going to get through the evening without reaching for her.

Just then, Emma, Laura, and their security guard returned, their hands loaded down with sweets of all kinds. "Look, Mommy," Emma crowed. "We got enough for everybody!"

At Angel's arch look, Laura shrugged, her smile wry. "I couldn't resist. It's not a parade without cotton candy and candied apples."

Down the street, a loud horn blasted and they all turned in time to see the fire engine start down Main Street with its lights flashing. All around them, people stood on tiptoe to see as a cheer went up along the four-block parade route. Officially, Midsummer's Eve had begun.

Following the fire truck, the high school band fell into step and broke into a ragged rendition of "YMCA." Singing the well-known words, the crowd added the hand movements, and between one beat and the next, everyone was smiling and dancing.

And Angel loved it. With an apple clutched in one hand

and cotton candy in the other, she sang along with the crowd, her slender hips swaying as she made the letters of the song with her arms. Openly watching her, Joe grinned and never noticed that the people in front of them had shifted to block Emma's view until she tugged at his hand. Surprised, he looked down to find her holding her arms up to him.

"I can't see, Mr. Joe."

Dressed in a yellow sundress that was as bright as her bouncing curls, her eyes full of mischief, her dimples flashing and her mouth smeared red from her candied apple, she was as impossible to resist as her mother. Chuckling, Joe swept her up and lifted her onto his shoulders. "All right, little bit, up you go. Try not to get the gooey stuff in my hair, okay?"

Totally at ease letting him hold her, she grinned, pleased with the world. "Okay, Mr. Joe. I'll try."

The parade lasted fifteen minutes, just as Joe had known it would, but no one seemed to mind that it was over almost before it had begun. The crowd surged out into the street as Nick drove by in his patrol car, signaling the end of the parade, but the evening was far from over. There were arts and crafts booths to visit on the square, not to mention face-painting and fortune-telling booths and a petting zoo for the little ones. Later, there'd be a street dance that would last until well after midnight.

Thanks to the movie cast and crew's presence, the crowd was bigger than it had been in the past and there were a lot of strangers in town. If it hadn't been for their two security guards, Joe would have suggested to Angel that they call it an evening and return to the ranch. But the guards were big and burly and watched the crowd with sharp eyes that saw everything. Reassured, he strolled to-

ward the square with Angel and Laura at his side and
Emma resting comfortably in his arms.

Not surprisingly, Emma was the one who spied the petting zoo first. With a squeal of delight, she cried, "Look,
Mommy. Baby pigs! And bunnies! I wanna pet them. Put
me down, Mr. Joe."

Chuckling, he set her on her feet…and looked up to find
himself face-to-face with his mother and his sister, Merry,
who were running the petting zoo together. A veterinarian
with her own clinic on the ranch, Merry brought baby animals into town every year for the festival for the kids to
play with.

"Hello, dear." Her blue eyes sparkling with good humor, his mother glanced from him to Emma, who just then
worked up the nerve to touch the squirming baby pig that
Merry held out to her. Squeaking in surprise, she jumped
back, drawing a laugh from the grown-ups. "Who's your
date?" she teased, nodding at Emma.

"Emma Wiley," he replied with a grin, and turned to
introduce his houseguests to her and Merry. "Angel, Laura,
this is my mother, Sara McBride, and my sister, Merry."

Stunned, Angel greeted both women with a smile, unable
to believe they were mother and daughter. She couldn't
begin to guess how old Sara McBride was, but time had
been good to her. She was, Angel knew, the mother of four
grown children, yet her oval face was virtually unlined, her
skin as young and smooth as her daughter's, who had to
be somewhere in her early thirties. In fact, if there hadn't
been a touch of gray in her sable brown hair, she and Merry
could have been mistaken for sisters.

Not that Merry looked old, Angel quickly assured herself. Far from it. The woman was drop-dead gorgeous, and
that wasn't a description Angel used lightly, not when there
were beautiful women on every street corner in L.A. Not
a one of them could have held a candle to Merry McBride.

She was striking. Tall and graceful, with a cloud of dark hair she'd secured at the nape of her neck with a clip, she had the delicately sculptured features of a model and a smile that had, no doubt, slain many a man where he stood when the force of it and her sapphire eyes were turned his way.

"You have a beautiful daughter," Sara told Angel, her smile softening as it fell on Emma. "She must bring you a lot of joy."

She couldn't have said anything that could have touched Angel's heart more. "Yes, she does. I can't even remember what my life was like without her."

"Bring her over to the clinic the next time you have some time off and she can play with the puppies," Merry said as Emma scooped up a squirming Labrador pup that was half as big as she was and kissed it on the top of the head. "We've always got a litter or two running around, tearing up the place."

"I'll do that," Angel promised. "Thank you. She'd love that."

"Where's Janey?" Joe asked. "Manning the first-aid booth?"

Merry nodded. "I tried to talk her into going to the dance with me later, but you know how she is. She's going to shut down the booth at ten, then run by the nursing home and check on Mrs. Goodman."

"Maybe I'll stop by and see if I can talk some sense into her," Joe said with a frown. "She already spends too much time working as it is. She needs to go out and have some fun."

"Said the pot to the kettle," his mother retorted with an arch look, her lips curling in a teasing grin. "If I remember correctly, we used to say the same thing about you. Janey will be all right. She just does things at a different pace than the rest of you."

A flock of preschoolers rushed up then to see the animals, and Sara and Merry had to get back to work. "Stop by the house sometime," Sara told Angel as she snatched up a rabbit before a little boy could step on it. "We'll have lunch."

Thanking her for the invitation, Angel promised to do that, then grabbed a protesting Emma. "But, Mommy, I want to give the rabbit a kiss!"

"I know you do, sweetheart, but you can kiss him later. How would you like to get your face painted?"

"Aha," Joe teased, taking the squirming Emma out of her arms to toss her into the air until she giggled. "So now we're resorting to bribery."

"Hey, you do whatever works," Angel replied without apology. "God help us if they're out of glitter."

Emma got her face painted with enough glitter to satisfy even the most demanding three-year-old, only to run out of energy and fall asleep in Joe's arms as they made their way through the crowd. It was barely nine o'clock, but long past her bedtime, and with a trust that stole Joe's heart right out of his chest, she laid her cheek against his shoulder and went limp.

Touched, he cradled her close, delighted with her little girl scent of cotton candy and candied apples. "Maybe we should take her home," he told Angel. "She's a whipped puppy."

"I'll take her if you like," Laura volunteered. "Then you two can stay for the street dance."

Surprised, Joe glanced at Angel, leaving the decision up to her. He hadn't touched her since they'd made love—he hadn't dared—but he knew he would tonight if he got the chance. Right or wrong, there were some things a man just couldn't resist. And holding her again, even if it was at a public dance, was one of those things. "It's your call," he said roughly.

She wanted to say yes, he could see it in her eyes, but she hesitated uncertainly. "We came in one car. How will we get back to the ranch?"

"Janey probably came here straight from work. I'll borrow her car and she can ride back to the ranch with Mom and Merry."

Still not sure, she frowned. "What about the guards? Will they have to split up? I don't want to take any chances with Emma."

"They can both go home with her and Laura," he assured her.

"But, sir," the older of the two security guards protested. "The studio wants Ms. Wiley protected at all times."

"She will be—by me. I won't let her out of my sight." Not giving him a chance to argue, Joe looked pointedly at Angel. "She's your daughter and I would never expect you to do anything that would put her in danger or make you feel uncomfortable. Whatever you decide will be fine by me."

In the end, the choice was easy. Not because she ached to be back in Joe's arms—though she did—but because there wasn't a doubt in her mind that Emma would be safer back at the ranch. There, away from the strangers that filled the streets of Liberty Hill, she would be locked inside the house with the security system activated and Buster and the night guards on duty to protect her and see that nothing happened to her.

"I think it would be safer for Emma to return to the ranch with Laura and the guards. *If,*" she added quickly, "we can borrow your sister's car so they can take your truck."

"Then let's go find Janey," he said, and headed for the first-aid booth at the far end of the square.

* * *

Dressed in her nurse's uniform, her dark brown hair pulled back from her face and twisted up into a serviceable bun, Janey was cleaning a freckle-faced little hellion's scraped knee when Joe strode up with Emma still asleep on his shoulder and his small entourage of women and security guards trailing behind him. When Angel came to a stop beside him as they waited for his sister to finish patching up her ten-year-old patient, he didn't have to read Angel's mind to know what she thinking.

While Merry had the kind of beauty that could literally stop traffic, Janey was as ordinary as apple pie. Like Merry, she, too, had inherited their mother's flawless skin, but that was as far as the family resemblance went. While Merry's face was oval, Janey's was slightly rounder, her cheeks less sculptured. She wasn't the kind of woman who would ever walk through a room and leave men panting after her, but if anyone needed help, she was the first one to offer aid. And in her brown eyes was the kind of caring and kindness that went soul deep. Her beauty might not fit traditional standards, but it only took a smile to light up her face.

Giving her patient a sucker, she sent him on his way. When she looked up to greet her next casualty victim, her slow smile bloomed at the sight of Joe waiting for her. "Hey, big brother, I didn't expect to see you tonight. Last time you came to the festival, Roosevelt was in office, wasn't he?"

"Cute, sis," he chuckled. "Real cute. At least when I come, I don't work. Why aren't you going to the dance with Merry?"

She could have made any one of a number of excuses, but she only shrugged, the half smile that curled her mouth containing little humor. "You know me—I don't do well in a crowd." Looking past him, she spied Angel and nodded shyly. "Excuse my brother for forgetting his manners.

Some people think he was raised in a barn, but he really wasn't. Hi. I'm Janey. It's nice to finally meet you.''

"You, too," Angel replied, liking her immediately. "That's my daughter, Emma, draped all over Joe. All this excitement was too much for her."

"Her nanny was going to take her home in my truck," Joe said, "but Angel and I were thinking about staying for the dance and wouldn't have a way to get home. Unless you lend us your car and ride back to the house with Mom."

He didn't exactly ask permission, but Janey wouldn't have cared if he'd outright demanded she loan him her car. She couldn't remember the last time she'd seen this much life in his eyes, and she didn't have to ask who had put it there. Angel Wiley. If Janey hadn't thought she might be overstepping the line, she would have hugged her for it. After all that Belinda had put him through, Joe deserved a little happiness.

Reaching into her purse, she drew out her keys and handed them to him with a grin. "Enjoy."

Chapter 8

The band was live, the music country-western, the dance of choice the two-step. And the minute the single young studs of the country realized America's sweetheart was there and actually going to dance, they slicked back their hair, adjusted their cowboy hats, and made a beeline straight for Angel.

Not surprised, she'd half expected to be rushed and was ready for the stampede. Smiling sweetly, she held up a hand, stopping the crowd of wanna-be suitors before they could crush her in their haste to be the first to reach her. "Sorry to disappoint you, boys, but my dance card is full for the evening."

"Aw, c'mon, Ms. Wiley, that's not fair! I saw you first."

"Did not. You were flirting with Mary Ann Jenkins when I told you she was here."

"Forget them, Angel Eyes. Just one turn around the floor—that's all I want, then I can die happy."

The latter came from a short, fresh-faced boy who

couldn't have been sixteen if he was a day. Grinning cockily, he winked at her behind the lenses of his wire-rimmed glasses, and Angel almost burst out laughing. But he was a cute kid and she wouldn't have hurt his feelings for the world.

"That's so sweet," she told him, "but I'm afraid that's impossible. I've already promised Mr. McBride every dance. Of course, if you'd like to take it up with him…"

Letting the suggestion hang in the air, she saw all male eyes shift warily to Joe and had to struggle not to grin. She didn't have to look over her shoulder to know that he stood protectively behind her with his arms crossed over his chest and a hard look in his flinty eyes that would have had the devil himself backing up a step or two.

To their credit, her suitors didn't run for cover, but more than a few of them visibly paled. The young man who'd called her Angel Eyes, however, was far from intimidated. Sniffing at her choice in dance partners, he grumbled, "Heck, we're not going to argue with some old guy. Twice around the floor and he'll run out of gas. Then it's our turn. C'mon, guys, let's go find a place to wait so we can carry him off the floor when he keels over."

"Hey, who you calling old?!" Joe called after them when they turned en masse and walked away. "I was dancing before you pip-squeaks were born!"

Her eyes sparkling, Angel grinned. "I think you just made their point. Maybe you should have had Janey take your blood pressure when you had the chance. I don't want you stroking out on me, grandpa."

"*Grandpa?* I'll show you grandpa," he growled teasingly, and grabbed her just as the band swung into the latest country swing number to hit the top of the charts.

He didn't give her time to think, to catch her breath, to do anything but laugh and fall into step. If he'd thought he was the only one who knew swing, she quickly showed him that he was wrong. Her face alight with fun, she let him swing her away from him, twirl her and draw her around his back without ever missing a step.

All around them, people stopped to watch and clap in time to the infectious beat of the music, but she never noticed. There was just Joe, his eyes locked with hers, his hand steady and strong around hers and always there to draw her inexorably back to him before twirling her away again. Breathless, her heart pounding and head light, she loved it.

Later, she couldn't have said if the song lasted only minutes or a lifetime. She just knew that she never wanted it to end. It had to, of course, and with a final triumphant blast of the band's horns, she found herself back in Joe's arms, so close her breasts brushed his chest. Startled, her eyes locked with his. Clapping wildly, the crowd shouted its approval but she couldn't hear for the roar of her blood in her veins. An inch, she thought dizzily. All she had to do was lift her chin a mere inch, and his mouth would be on hers.

She wanted to, needed to, ached to with every fiber of her being, but the band shifted gears then and slipped into a slow, dreamy number that turned the night air romantic. Without a word, Joe cradled her close and guided her into a graceful two-step that was as natural as breathing. With a sigh, she melted against him and let him lead her where he would.

Just that easy, the night turned magical. There was no yesterday or tomorrow, no past or future, just precious moments stolen out of time and theirs for the taking. Up above, the stars shone brightly in a velvet summer sky, but they had eyes only for each other as one song gave way to another, then another and they danced the night away.

Unable to stop smiling, Angel felt like she was sixteen again, out on a date for the first time in her life, and dancing on air. Intoxicated, she never wanted it to end. The band, however, needed a break, and when they stopped for a thirty-minute intermission, she had no choice but to step out of his arms.

She wouldn't have been surprised if he'd wanted to go home then—it was going on eleven, and work on a ranch started early—but when she automatically turned toward the parking lot with some of the other dancers who had decided to call it a night, he reached for her hand.

"Not so fast, young lady," he murmured roughly, one corner of his mouth crooked in a smile. "I may be an old geezer, but the night's young. Let's go check out the carnival."

Surprised, she lifted a delicately arched brow, her blue eyes alight with sudden interest. "Can we ride the Ferris wheel? It's been years since I've ridden one."

The last time he'd been on one he'd been in high school, and he hadn't had anyone like Angel at his side. Instead, he'd been stuck with Tawny Carpenter, one of the school cheerleaders who'd only gone out with him to make Hank Sommers, her ex-boyfriend, jealous. It had worked. The second they got off the Ferris wheel, Hank was waiting for her, and Joe was happy to let her go.

"Joe? Where'd you go? I lost you."

Blinking, he came back to the present to find her looking up at him with a quizzical smile. "Sorry. I was just thinking about high school—and Tawny Carpenter."

He told her then about that night and expected her to laugh. Instead, she smiled in sympathy. "My Tawny Carpenter was Danny Kitchen. We were on the Ferris wheel when he saw Juliet Marshall in the crowd below us. I thought he was going to jump off just to get to her."

"When he was out with you?" he said, shocked. "Was he an idiot or what?"

Laughter danced in her eyes. "I like to think he was."

"Trust me, the man's kicking himself today. He had his chance and he blew it. I'm not that stupid. C'mon," he coaxed. "There's a Ferris wheel calling our name."

Her hand safely tucked in his, he headed for the open field at the end of Main Street where the bright lights of the carnival beckoned in the night.

When it came time to take their seat in the swinging gondola of the Ferris wheel that the attendant held steady for her and Joe, Angel realized that a lot had changed since she was sixteen. She was older and wiser now and a mother with the responsibility of a young child. And the Ferris wheel that had once appeared as sturdy as the Eiffel Tower to her adolescent eyes now looked like something that had been constructed from an erector set. With only a thin safety bar to keep them in their seats, disaster was only a slip away.

"I don't know about this," she said, hesitating. "Maybe this isn't such a good idea after all."

Surprised, John laughed. "Is this the same woman who does all her own stunts?"

"That's different. They're on the ground."

"Scaredy cat," he teased. "Haven't you ever heard that life begins at the edge of your comfort zone?" When she just gave him a baleful look, he laughed. "All right, if it'll make you feel any better, I'll go first."

Stepping into the gondola, he held out his hand to her, his eyes sure and steady as they met hers. "Do you really think I'd take you on anything that wasn't safe?"

She didn't even have to think about that. "No, of course not."

"Then what are you waiting for? You know I won't let anything happen to you."

Put that way, she couldn't summon up a single argument. He was asking for her trust, and he already had it. Without a word, she put her hand in his and sank down onto the seat next to him.

An instant later, the safety bar snapped into place, the attendant hit the switch to start the big wheel turning, and suddenly, the world fell away beneath their feet to the beat of a happy calliope song. With a startled yelp, Angel clutched frantically for the safety bar and latched onto it with both hands.

Beside her, Joe laughed and slipped an arm around her shoulders. "This'll be a lot more fun if you relax and sit back and look at the stars. Look!" he said, pointing suddenly to the night sky to their left. "There's a shooting star! Make a wish."

"Trust me, I am. Star light, star bright, let me get off this thing in one piece. Why did I ever think this was fun?" she gasped as the wheel stopped at the top and the sudden cessation of movement made their gondola rock wildly.

Amused, Joe lifted his hand to play with her hair. "If you'd just relax..."

"I'm trying!"

"Then let's try it this way," he murmured. Leaning over, he pressed a gentle kiss to the sensitive side of her neck, just below her ear, and sent a shiver dancing over her soft skin.

Startled, Angel's eyes flew to his. "Joe—"

"See, that wasn't so difficult," he teased huskily. "You just needed a distraction. Let's try it again."

She should have objected. She was literally up in the air, her head in the clouds and her senses still humming from dancing one dance after another with him just moments ago. But he only had to touch her to make her melt, kiss her to turn her brain to mush. With a nearly silent groan, his mouth covered hers, and sanity slipped away.

Lost in the sweetness of the moment, the stars overhead could have fallen right out of the night sky, and Angel would have never noticed. Holding her as if she was made of spun sugar, he kissed her lightly, sweetly, nibbling at her bottom lip, stroking it with his tongue, teasing her until she gasped softly and clung to him, her mouth blindly seeking his, demanding more.

She forgot who she was, where she was, that there was a crowd of strangers below who were probably watching everything she did. It didn't matter. Nothing mattered but Joe and the way he made her feel. He was all she wanted, all she could think of, and even though she knew this could only lead to heartache, for tonight, she couldn't deny herself these moments stolen out of time. Her body aching for his touch, she melted against him, sighing his name. "Joe…"

The Ferris wheel jolted back into motion at that moment, bringing them both back to earth with a jerk. Startled, they broke apart with a laugh just as they made a dizzy descent toward the ground. Then, just as they ascended toward the stars again, Angel's cell phone rang.

Surprised, she frowned. "That must be Laura. I hope Emma's not sick from all the cotton candy she ate." Pulling the phone from her purse, she quickly flipped it open. "Laura? What's wrong?"

"You bitch!"

Stunned, Angel blanched. She didn't have to ask who her caller was. She knew. She'd have recognized her stalker's voice in the bowels of hell. "How did you get this number?"

"Two-timing whore! Harlot!" Spewing vile curses at her, he didn't hear her, let alone bother to answer her. "How dare you kiss that dirtbag in front of the whole town! You're mine. Do you hear me? Mine!"

"No!"

"Oh, yes, you are. And you're going to pay for this. You just wait!"

He screeched at her like a madman, telling her all the ways he was going to punish her, but Angel hardly heard his crazy promises. She'd just gotten a new cell phone the day before she left L.A. And he already had the new number. How? she wondered wildly. How had he managed to discover what the number was when she'd been so careful to make sure that only she, Laura and Will Douglas, her producer, had it?

Shaken, she would have dropped the phone then if Joe's reflexes hadn't been lightning quick. "What the hell!" he growled, snatching up the phone before it could slip through her fingers. "Dammit, Angel, what's wrong?"

"It's him," she said faintly. "My stalker. He's got my number."

Snarling an oath, Joe jerked the flip phone up to his ear, only to find the line dead. The bastard had hung up. "What did he say to you?" he demanded.

Chilled to the bone in spite of the warmth of the night, she wrapped her arms around herself. "He called me a bitch for kissing you in front of the whole town."

"He's *here?!*"

Angel looked at him blankly, his words not yet registering. Then it hit her. She'd been so shocked that he had her number that she hadn't stopped to think that in order for him to know she was kissing Joe, he had to be there, somewhere in the crowd down below.

"Oh, God!"

What little color there was left in her cheeks drained away as her eyes flew to the crowd below as the Ferris wheel began its rapid descent toward the ground. A blurred sea of faces stared back at her. Which one was he? she wondered wildly. The tall man with the black cowboy hat who couldn't seem to take his eyes off her? Or maybe the heavyset man standing in the shadows with a sour look on his face? Then again what about the nasty-looking punk with the earring in his nose and tattoos all over his arms and chest? What kind of violence was a man like that capable of?

"He said I would have to be punished," she whispered hoarsely. Her eyes wide with horror, she clutched at his arm. "Emma! Dear God, what if he meant he was going to hurt Emma? If he knows where we're staying, he could be on his way there right now."

Already dialing the ranch, Joe waited impatiently for Laura to answer the phone. The second she did, he didn't give her time to say anything but hello before he started throwing orders at her. "Laura, this is Joe. Contact the guards and let them know Angel's stalker is in town and has been making threats on her cell phone. Then double-check the alarm to make sure it's set and check the locks on all the windows and doors, even upstairs. And don't let Emma out of your sight."

"No, sir, I won't," she promised quickly. "I'll notify the guards right now."

Joe hung up just as their gondola swept by the attendant at the controls. "Hey!" he yelled. "Stop! We need to get off this damn thing!"

The old man never even looked at them and let the big wheel continue to turn. Swept up to the top again, there was nothing Joe could do but swear.

"I think he must be hard of hearing," Angel said, glancing over the side of their gondola to peer worriedly down at the elderly man. Stooped and wrinkled, he had to be eighty if he was a day. "Look—someone else is trying to get his attention, and he's just ignoring them."

"I'd be deaf, too, if I had to listen to this damn music all the time," Joe muttered in disgust. The calliope music that had been romantic and fun before was now irritatingly loud. "C'mon, you're going to have to yell with me if we're ever going to get this guy to stop this thing. Ready? Now!''

They yelled and waved their arms and did everything but throw something as they swept by the attendant, but they still had to go by twice more before they were able to make the man understand they wanted off. Finally cranking the machine to a stop, he stepped forward to release the safety bar and scowled at them irritably. "You didn't have to yell at me. I ain't deaf, you know."

In no mood to try to make the man understand, Joe mumbled an apology, tucked Angel's hand in his, and pulled her after him down the ride's exit ramp. "Keep your eyes open and stick close," he said in a low voice that didn't carry past her ears. "If anyone even looks like they're going to give you trouble, scream your head off. Understand?"

Her heart in her throat, she nodded and inched closer to him. "Do you think he's still here?"

"I don't know," he said grimly. "But I'm getting you out of here."

He stepped into the crowd like a wild mustang scenting the air for danger, his eyes sharp and narrowed, searching the faces of the crowd. Here and there, he spotted a neighbor or friend, but most of the people who pressed in on them were strangers, either there for the festival or drawn to Liberty Hill in the hopes of catching sight of a movie star. And any one of the men could have been Angel's stalker.

Fury raged in him at the thought. How dare the bastard think he could come into town and start terrorizing her again! He might be able to get away with it in L.A., where he could disappear into the city's rat-infested sewers and alleys with the rest of his kind, but this wasn't L.A. There was no place for him to hide in Liberty Hill, and if he didn't know that yet, he soon would.

"Hey, there's Angel Wiley!"

The cry went up from somewhere off to their right, and the news went through the crowd like wildfire. Suddenly, people were pressing close, shoving and pushing to get a better look at Angel, until she and Joe were surrounded.

Joe felt Angel stiffen in panic and tightened his hand around hers. "It's all right," he assured her.

But it wasn't. Crying out for autographs and pictures, the mob clutched at Angel, trying to touch her, to get a piece of her. Snarling an oath, Joe shouldered a path for them, pushing people out of the way when he had to, knocking away the hands of anyone who dared to try to touch her.

"Get back!" he growled. "Let us through!"

Her heart slamming against her ribs, Angel ducked her head and blindly followed behind him, cringing as strangers grabbed at her like she was some kind of prize for the taking. But it was the hands stroking her hair, her arms, tugging at her sundress that made her skin crawl. Shivering in revulsion at the thought of a stranger touching her, she pushed closer to Joe's back and didn't see the rock half-buried in the ground underfoot. With a startled cry, she tripped.

Joe whirled at her first cry, but hands were already there to catch her from behind before she could fall and to help her regain her footing. In the next instant, Joe swept his arm protectively around her shoulders and pulled her snug against his side, fury etched in every line of his face as together, they fought their way through the crowd and finally broke free.

He took one look at her pale face and started swearing. "Dammit to hell, this is all my fault. Are you all right? God, you're shaking! And your dress is torn!" He cursed again, a short, pithy curse aimed solely at himself. "I never should have brought you here. I should have known it could get out of hand."

''Until you've experienced it first-hand, it's hard to imagine people acting like such idiots,'' she sniffed, tugging at the torn strap of her sundress.

He looked at her in horror. ''You mean this has happened to you before? God almighty! This is nuts!''

''Every job has its drawbacks. And it only happened once before.''

''Then tonight makes twice,'' he retorted, ''and that's two times too many.''

His eyes roamed over her, narrowing at the sight of the scrapes on her arms, her ashen face and tousled hair. She looked like she'd been in a catfight. Fury rising in him again at the thought of how easily she could have been trampled, he started to turn her around so he could check out her back, only to stop at the sight of something tangled in her hair. ''What's this?''

''What?''

His jaw granite hard, he gently drew a crushed yellow rose from her hair and held it out to her. ''This,'' he said flatly.

Angel took one look at it and stumbled back a step in horror. ''Oh, God!''

Neither of them had to ask where it had come from—they knew. And just thinking about it made Joe's blood cold. What an arrogant fool he was! He'd been so sure he could protect her, so sure that nothing was going to happen to her while he was there beside her and his hand was securely wrapped around hers. And all the time, her stalker had been right there, within touching distance, and he hadn't even known it.

Sick at the thought, he took her hand again, this time glancing around to make sure no one was near. ''C'mon. We've got to find Nick.''

With so many people in town and beer flowing freely for those old enough to buy it, Nick and his three deputies had their hands full keeping people in line. A man and his wife started yelling at each other at the dance, while over at the carnival, some of the festival-goers chased down a pickpocket who made the mistake of helping himself to the wrong pocket. Then there were the teenagers passing fake IDs in order to buy beer—just keeping track of them was a full-time job.

Every year he promised himself he was going to hire some part-time help for the festival. And every year the city council vetoed the idea with the excuse that they just didn't have the funds. Yeah, right, he fumed. If they had the money to hire the mayor's deadbeat brother to mow the city park every week, even when it didn't need it in the winter, then they had the money to hire some extra deputies once a year. And he was damn sure going to tell them that at the next city council meeting.

The sound of muffled grunts and fists hitting flesh snapped him out of his musings as he walked around the bandstand to check out the dark end of the park and the local teenagers' favorite necking spot. A fight, he thought with a groan. Great! Just what he needed. Cursing under his breath, he switched on his flashlight and shot the bright beam directly into the dark, concealing shadows under the trees on the edge of the park. And there, as expected, a ring of teenagers surrounded two boys who were trying to pound each other's brains out.

Not surprisingly, the spectators took off the second he hit them with the beam of his flashlight. The two young pugilists, however, were too caught up in their fury to notice anything but each other. They were still swinging at each other when Nick waded in to break it up.

"All right, that's enough!" he snapped, shaking them both by the scruff of the neck. "Keep this up and I'll have to throw you in jail and call your parents. Is that what you want?''

Since one of them was the preacher's son and the other the only offspring of a prominent city councilman, he felt sure that it wasn't. Hanging their heads, they both mumbled, ''No, sir.''

''Then I suggest you find another way to solve whatever your problem is,'' he said tersely. ''Now get the hell out of here before I forget my good intentions and run you both in.''

He didn't have to tell them twice. Scowling at each other like two junkyard dogs, they sulked off in opposite directions. They would, Nick knew, meet somewhere else later and exchange blows again, but the odds were slim that it would be tonight. The crowd was already starting to thin, and within another hour, the carnival would start shutting down. And it wouldn't be a minute too soon for him. It had been a long evening and he was ready to call it a night.

But when he turned back to the dance and saw Joe bearing down on him with Angel held protectively close, he only had to take one look at Joe's set face and Angel's torn dress to know that he had a hell of a bigger problem on his hands than a couple of kids fighting. ''What's wrong?''

''He's here,'' Joe said flatly.

Nick didn't have to ask who *he* was. From what he'd seen of Angel Wiley, there was only one person who could put that stark look of fear in her blue eyes, and that was her stalker. ''What do you mean *he's here?*'' he demanded, his dark brows snapping together in a scowl as he looked Angel up and down. ''Are you saying he did this to you?''

''No. At least I don't think it was him, but I can't be sure. We were caught in a mob of fans—''

''*What?!*''

''It got a little out of hand,'' she tried to explain.

''A *little?*'' Joe echoed incredulously. ''It was a feeding frenzy. Somebody recognized her, and the next thing I knew, people were pushing and shoving and grabbing at her, and we were surrounded.''

"When we were finally able to break free, Joe found this in my hair," she told Nick and held out the crushed rose.

She didn't have to remind Nick of the significance of the yellow flower. She saw from the sudden tightening of his angled jaw that he recognized it immediately for what it was—a sign from her stalker. Just thinking about how close the monster had been to her, how he'd actually reached out and slipped a rose in her hair, sickened her. Had he chosen, he could have just as easily slipped a knife between her ribs.

"He saw Joe kissing me on the Ferris wheel and called me on my cell phone," she said huskily, the first hint of color coming back into her cheeks. "He was furious. He started screaming at me—"

"He threatened her," Joe snarled, correcting her. "The slimeball said he was going to punish her. That's why he put that damn rose in her hair. He wanted her to know he could get close enough to crush her if he wanted to."

Nick swore. "We knew it was only a matter of time before the jackass showed up here, but I was hoping that it would be later rather than sooner." Taking a clean handkerchief from his back pocket, he carefully wrapped the rose in it. "I doubt that the lab will be able to pick up any latent fingerprints off this, but it's the only evidence we've got. I'll send it off to Colorado Springs first thing in the morning."

That taken care of, he turned his attention back to Angel. "Tell me about this mob again. Since I don't believe in coincidence, and it wasn't just dumb luck that someone chose to put a yellow rose in your hair, then we're going to assume your stalker was in the crowd. Considering that and all the pushing and shoving going on, you had to be scared. But of what? The mob itself and the fact that it seemed to be out of control or one person in particular?''

With no effort whatsoever, she remembered the exact moment she'd felt revulsion threaten to choke her. "Someone stroked me," she said thickly. "It was right before I started to fall. I felt someone's hand on me, stroking my hair and arm and tugging at my dress, and I just wanted to gag."

Horrified, Joe said, "My God, why didn't you say something? I'd have taken him apart."

"There wasn't time," she said simply. "It all happened so fast. The next thing I knew, I was falling and someone caught me and set me back on my feet."

"Was it the same person who'd been touching you?" Nick asked sharply. "Did you get a look at his face or even his hands?"

Regretfully, she shook her head. "No. He released me almost immediately, and then Joe pulled me up beside him and we were finally able to break free of the crowd. Do you think it was him?"

"Probably," he said bluntly, not pulling any punches. "In his twisted mind, he was probably proving to himself and you that he had the right to put his hands on you—especially after he saw you kissing Joe."

"It's none of his damn business who she kisses," Joe snarled.

For the first time in what seemed like hours, Nick had to fight the need to smile. Who would have thought it? Woman-hater Joe McBride kissing movie star Angel Wiley on the Ferris wheel. God, what he wouldn't have given to have seen that!

"No, you're right," he said, sobering. "She can kiss anyone she pleases, but I'd be careful about doing it in public until this jerk's caught. In fact, now that we know he's here, I'd keep a low profile if I were you," he told

Angel. "He's already gotten to you once. The more you're out and about, the better chance he has of doing it again. And next time, he might do a hell of a lot more than run his hands over you and stick a flower in your hair."

He knew that had to gall her—it would anyone. She was the victim here. She hadn't asked for any of this to happen to her, yet she was the one being forced to give up her freedom. To her credit, however, she didn't fuss. "I don't have a problem with that. I feel safer at the ranch, anyway."

Joe and Nick exchanged a look, and it hit her then. "But that's not going to be very safe after this, is it? He's bound to know already that I'm staying there. It's just a matter of time before he comes after me."

"The security at the house is rock-solid," Joe assured her. "As soon as we get back to the ranch, I'll let everyone know the bastard was in town tonight. He won't get his hands on you again."

"And I'll ask around at the different booths and see if anyone showed an undue interest in you tonight and where you're staying," Nick added. "Oh, and give me your cell phone number and I'll see if we can trace the call the jackass made to you. It's a long shot, but I'm not ruling anything out."

He jotted it down when she rattled it off, wishing he could be more encouraging. But lying to her wouldn't keep her or her daughter safe, and she had to know what she was facing. "I don't have to tell you that you're in a hell of a lot more danger now than you were last week. Don't trust anybody you don't already know. That means fans, caterers, flower delivery people, the cleaning crew—anybody you don't recognize instantly. Because it would be just like this bastard to infiltrate the set by pretending to be some kind of worker or something. He thinks you're his, and he's going to do whatever he has to to get close to you.''

Angel promised to be careful—she wouldn't step out of the house or her trailer on the set without first checking to make sure she recognized her security guards—but as she and Joe drove back to the ranch in Janey's car, it wasn't herself she was worried about.

How dare you kiss that dirtbag in front of the whole town.... You're going to pay for this!

The harsh words, screamed at her in a voice that even now made her wince, echoed over and over again in her head. And all she could think of was Emma. What better way to punish her than to go after her daughter? It was what he'd promised to do all along, and tonight, she'd given him a reason to carry through on his threat. God, how could she have been so stupid?

"She's all right," Joe said quietly, reading her mind as security waved him through the entrance to the ranch. "Laura and the guards aren't going to let anything happen to her."

"I know," she said, "but he's going to do something awful, I can feel it in my bones, and it's all my fault."

His eyes on the road ahead, Joe shot her a sharp look. "How do you figure that?"

"I knew that there was always a possibility that he could be somewhere nearby, watching me. I shouldn't have done anything to push him over the edge."

"Are you saying you shouldn't have kissed me?"

She should have said yes. It would have been the wise thing to do. She was starting to feel too much for him and he couldn't let go of the past. In spite of that, however, she knew that if she could have turned the clock back and re-lived that ride on the Ferris wheel all over again, she would have done things exactly the same.

"No," she said softly. "I just wish that it hadn't resulted in this."

Joe hadn't realized just how important her answer was to him until then. He wanted to tell her that he didn't regret it, either, but he couldn't find the words. Then the house came into view and the moment was lost.

Not surprisingly, the compound was lit up with lights, and several of his ranch hands' pickups were parked out front. Once Laura had notified the guards that Angel's stalker was at the festival, security would have notified his men and they'd have come running. They'd stay as long as they had to to make sure Emma was safe.

As he pulled up before the house, Buster shot out from the barn with a happy bark of recognition, and two of his ranch hands as well as the security guards came from different parts of the grounds to check out the new arrival. Angel, heeding Nick's warning, waited until she was sure she recognized everyone before she unlocked the passenger door and pushed it open. A split second later, she was running up the steps to the porch, where Laura was waiting for her at the front door.

"She's all right," the older woman told her quickly. "She's sound asleep in her bed and doesn't have a clue that anything's wrong. I haven't left her side since Joe called from the festival."

Relieved, Angel still had to see for herself that Emma was okay. Hurrying up the stairs, she quietly let herself into her bedroom and approached the bed on soundless feet. Tears flooded her eyes at the sight of Emma sprawled on her tummy with Miss Annabelle, her favorite doll, cuddled close. Lord, she was precious! And so little. If anything happened to her—

Angel stiffened at the thought. No, she silently told herself. She wasn't going there; she wouldn't even consider the possibility. Nothing was going to happen to her baby because she was going to do whatever she had to to keep her safe. Even if that meant sending her away to a place her stalker would never think to look for her.

Her mind made up, she softly kissed her good night, then marched downstairs to Joe's office to make a private call. She didn't need to call information—she knew the number by heart—and quickly punched it in. It was late and he would be asleep, but this wasn't something that could be put off.

"H'llo?"

His voice was gruff with sleep, and not surprisingly, he was less than pleased at being woke up, but Angel didn't apologize. "Dad, this is Angel. I need your help—"

That was as far as she got before he hung up on her. Once, that would have intimidated her and she wouldn't have bothered to call back, but not this time. Not when her daughter was in danger.

Her jaw set, she quickly redialed the number and wasn't surprised when she got the answering machine. "You have a three-year-old granddaughter who's being threatened by a stalker," she said curtly. "She needs a place to stay until he's caught, and I know she'll be safe with you. Please don't take your hostility with me out on her. She doesn't deserve that." Reciting Joe's phone number, she said, "I'll be waiting for your call."

Hanging up, she sat back in Joe's chair and stared at the phone, willing it to ring. Her only response, however, was silence, and it broke her heart.

Chapter 9

Standing in the open doorway to his study, blatantly eavesdropping, Joe watched Angel's shoulders sag in defeat and wished he could give her old man a piece of his mind. He didn't know what had caused the rift between the two of them, but a child's life was in danger, dammit! Nothing else mattered. If James Wiley was any kind of man at all, he would put his feelings aside for now and do what he had to to assure his granddaughter's safety.

But the phone remained coldly, obstinately silent.

Why didn't the old goat just stab her in the heart and be done with it? Joe thought furiously. She was hurting, fighting tears, and it was all he could do not to go to her. But her pain was personal, and she was entitled to her privacy.

Stepping back, he started to turn and leave her alone, but he'd waited too long. She glanced up and saw him, and with a quick apology, rose to her feet. "I'm sorry," she said huskily, looking anywhere but at him as she swiped at her wet cheeks. "I had to make a call, but I'm finished. I'll get out of your way—"

"I'm in no hurry. I was just going to call Nick."

"Why?" she asked in alarm. "Did something happen here while we were gone?"

"Buster hasn't barked all evening," he assured her. "How about Emma? How is she?"

"Out like a light." A weak smile curled the corners of her mouth. "I know Laura would have called if there'd been a problem, but I had to see for myself that she was okay."

"That's perfectly understandable. After everything that happened tonight, you had a right to be worried about her." His brown eyes swept over her, noting her still-pale face and the pain clouding her blue eyes. "And what about you? How are you doing?"

He half expected her to lie and claim she was just fine now that she was sure Emma was safe, but she couldn't quite manage the words. Tears spilled over her lashes, and with a muttered curse, she once again brushed them away. "I've been better," she said thickly. "I guess you heard, huh?"

"You calling your father? Yeah. I'm sorry if I intruded. I didn't realize you were in here until it was too late."

She shrugged off his apology with a wave of her hand. "It's okay. *I* was the one who made the mistake of calling in the first place. I actually thought my father might care that his granddaughter was in danger. Looks like I was wrong."

"He still could call," Joe said. "Give him some time."

Angel would have loved to, but she knew her father too well. Regretfully, she shook her head. "It won't do any good. Once he makes his mind up about something, he doesn't change it. And he decided a long time ago that he wanted nothing more to do with me. I should have known better than to think he might have a change of heart just because I have a daughter who needs his help."

She hadn't planned to unload on him—she didn't normally speak about her past to anyone. But it had been a roller coaster of an evening, and if she didn't talk to someone, her emotions were going to tear her apart.

Sinking back into the chair behind Joe's back, she stared blindly at the phone that remained hurtfully silent. "He was always a stern man," she said half to herself. "As stubborn as a brick wall. It was his way or no way, black or white, with no gray in between. You toed the line according to his rules, or you got out. I got out the day I graduated from high school."

"That's awfully young to go out on your own," Joe said with a frown as he propped a shoulder against the door jamb. "That couldn't have been easy."

"It wasn't, but I couldn't stay there any longer. For as long as I could remember, I wanted to go to Hollywood and act. And he hated that. He couldn't believe I would choose the decadent life-style of L.A. over the decent, God-fearing one in which I was raised. He wanted me to go to college and become a teacher like my mother."

"And what did your mother have to say about that?"

"She died when I was eight," she replied. "My father's hated the world ever since."

And that was what hurt the most. She'd lost her mother and the loving father of her childhood all in the same day. Life hadn't been the same since.

Her eyes stark with pain, she could do nothing to stop the tears that spilled over her lashes. "He never forgave me for leaving. And I was stupid enough to think he would. All I had to do was give him some time. Then I got the role in *Heart's Desire*. It was my first big break, and I was so excited. I didn't even think. I picked up the phone and called him. He hung up on me.

"And you know the crazy thing about all of this?" she laughed without humor. "I understood. He'd lost my mother, and he couldn't stand the thought of losing anyone else that he loved. So he tried to control me and ended up doing the one thing he feared the most. He drove me away. It's not me he can't forgive for that, but himself.''

''Yet you thought he would take Emma.''

Swallowing the lump in her throat, she nodded. ''It's crazy, isn't it? I couldn't wait to get away from him, but now I want him to take my daughter. And that's something else he probably won't forgive me for. Getting pregnant and having a baby out of wedlock,'' she explained when he lifted a brow. ''And not telling him until now that he has a granddaughter.''

She saw his shock and could make no excuses for her behavior. ''I thought it was for the best at the time.''

Because she hadn't wanted to hear *I told you so's* or condemnations of her life-style. She had a baby that she adored, and the how, when, and whys of her conception hadn't mattered. As far as Angel was concerned, she was a blessing, and she hadn't been able to bear the thought of her father finding fault with that. So she'd kept Emma to herself.

Now she had to doubt the wisdom of that. If she'd gone home for a visit after Emma was born and insisted her father get to know his granddaughter, he wouldn't have been able to harden his heart against her baby charm. He'd have fallen in love with her just like Angel had, and the second he'd heard she was in trouble, he'd have come running to her rescue.

Hindsight was twenty-twenty, however, and did nothing to change the present. The phone didn't ring. Pain lancing her heart, Angel reluctantly accepted the fact that it wasn't likely to. Not tonight or tomorrow, maybe not ever. And there was nothing she could do about it. If it was more important to her father to cling to his hurt and anger than let her back into his life, he couldn't love her as much as she thought he did.

Resigned, she forced a stiff smile and pushed to her feet. "I guess there's no use beating a dead horse, is there? He's not going to call, so I might as well go to bed."

She looked so forlorn that he couldn't resist the urge to help her. "I have a cousin who owns a day care in Omaha. If you like, I can call her first thing in the morning and see if she'd be willing to take Emma until this all blows over. She's a good woman, and her husband's a police officer. They'd take good care of her."

It wasn't the ideal solution—it would be best for Emma to be with family—but it was an option if her father didn't come through for her. "You don't have to decide tonight," he said when she hesitated. "Just think about it."

"I will," she said softly. "Thank you."

Murmuring a husky good-night, she eased past him and went upstairs to bed. Standing at the foot of the stairs, he watched her go up and knew there was no point in going up himself. He wouldn't sleep. Not when she and Emma were still in danger.

Grabbing a rifle from the locked gun cabinet in his office, he stepped outside and dead-bolted the front door behind him. With his ranch hands and the security guards patrolling the area, Joe knew the house was secure. Still, he had to check for himself. Whistling for Buster, who was snoozing on the front porch, he strode out into the night.

When the studio limo arrived at the house the next morning to drive Angel to the set, she ached to take Emma with her. She knew Laura and the men watching the house would do their best to keep her safe, but they weren't her mother. No one could watch over her like she could.

"She'll be all right," Laura promised her as she hesitated in the hallway. "We'll stay inside. And with four guards and Buster on duty at all times, no one's going to get anywhere near the house without someone seeing them. Especially in broad daylight.''

Angel knew she was right, but that didn't make it any easier to leave her. It had been hard enough before, when she'd thought her stalker was still in L.A. But now that she knew he was somewhere in the vicinity, it was impossible. She felt like she was abandoning her when she was in danger, and it tore her apart. If something happened while she was gone, she'd never forgive herself.

''I want you to call the set every thirty minutes and let me know she's okay,'' she told the older woman as her gaze lingered on Emma and the sweet innocence of her expression as she played with her bunny angel and other stuffed animals in the living room. ''And if anything unusual happens, don't hang around to check it out. Grab one of the security guards and get Emma out of here immediately. I mean it, Laura. Don't take any chances.''

''I won't,'' she said solemnly. ''You have my word, Angel. I'll guard her like she was my own.''

Suddenly realizing how she sounded, as if she didn't have any faith in Laura's ability to take care of her, Angel hugged her, blinking back tears. ''I'm sorry to be so paranoid. Of course you will. It isn't that I don't trust you. It's that...*monster* out there I don't trust. I don't know what he's going to do next.''

''Don't let him rattle you,'' Laura replied. ''Joe and his men and the studio security guards have done everything they can to keep you both safe. You're going to be fine.''

Angel wanted desperately to believe her, but her stomach was knotted with fear as she kissed Emma on the top of the head, then approached the front door. Remembering Nick's advice, she glanced out the sidelight next to the front door and sighed in relief when she recognized her driver,

William, talking to Joe as he waited patiently for her beside the limo. Only then did she open the door.

Straightening, William greeted her with a somber nod. "Good morning, Ms. Wiley. I heard you had a rough evening last night."

"It was a nightmare," she admitted. "I can't remember the last time I was so scared."

"I'm pretty sure the jerk didn't follow us home," Joe told her. "Nothing moved all night."

He sounded so confident that she assumed his men had already given him a thorough report. Then she noticed how tired he looked. "You were up all night?" she asked, surprised.

"I couldn't ask my hands to do something I wasn't willing to do," he said with a shrug, and deliberately changed the subject. "William is armed and more than capable of protecting you, but one of my men is going to follow you to the set just to make sure you don't run into any trouble."

He motioned to Tommy, one of the older ranch hands, to ride shotgun, but Angel couldn't let him do that. Every time she'd closed her eyes last night and tried to sleep, she'd been haunted with images of her stalker touching her, stroking her, breathing down her neck. Just the thought of him getting that close to her again scared the hell out of her. But Emma was the one he saw as a threat, the one he wanted to get rid of, the one he wanted to hurt.

"No," she said quickly. "I'd rather Tommy stay here with the others and protect Emma."

She might as well have saved her breath. Joe had that stubborn set to his jaw, the one that warned her nothing short of an earthquake was going to move him. "Emma's well protected," he retorted. "You're the one who's not. Tommy's going with you." The matter settled as far as he was concerned, he opened the rear door of the limo for her as Tommy slid into his truck and started it up. Whether she liked it or not, she had an escort. Frowning at him, she slipped into the back seat of the limo.

Fifteen minutes later, William arrived at the set and braked to a stop at a security entrance that hadn't been there yesterday. Tommy waved and turned around to return to Joe's house, but Angel never noticed. Because lined up in front of the new security entrance was most of the cast and crew.

Stunned, Angel blinked. "Good Lord, what's going on?"

"The sheriff talked to Mr. Sutton and Mr. Douglas last night and told them about your trouble," William said as he opened her door for her and helped her out of the car. "They closed the set and shut down filming for the morning so that everyone can have picture IDs made. Starting at noon today, no one gets on the set without their ID, not even the stars."

Angel had known that the studio had too much invested in her to let anything happen to her on the set, but she hadn't expected the suits to go to such extremes to keep her safe. Photo IDing everyone from the lowest caterer's helper to the producer himself was a huge undertaking that had to be costing the studio a small fortune.

"You don't have to wait in line like the rest of the cast," William informed her. "Mr. Sutton said it was too dangerous. So we'll just cut to the front and get you all taken care of, then I'm escorting you to your trailer. Taylor, my replacement, is already waiting there for you and will keep you safe until I come back for you when filming shuts down at five this afternoon."

Angel would have preferred to wait her turn like the rest of the cast, but William had his orders and he was diligent about carrying them out. Quickly and competently, he hustled her to the front of the line. There was some grumbling and hostile glares, but for the most part, people were understanding, and within minutes, she and William both had their new IDs and were allowed on the set.

"There, that wasn't so bad," he said with a grin as they headed for her trailer. "Once I get you settled, I'll stop by the caterer's truck and get you some coffee and doughnuts and bring them back to you. How do you take your coffee?"

"With cream and sugar," she said as her trailer came into sight then. As promised, her guard for the day was already there and waiting for her. "But you don't have to make a special trip. I can get it later—"

That was as far as she got. Garrett, whose trailer was next to hers, intercepted her path then, smoothly cutting her off. His handsome face twisted with dislike, he glowered at her like a spoiled little boy. "You're some piece of work, you know that? This entire set gets shut down for most of the day because of you, and you're not the least bit concerned. And why should you be? You're Angel Wiley, superstar."

Embarrassed and all too aware of the interested eyes they were drawing, Angel cringed. "Garrett, please don't do this."

"Don't do what?" he threw back at her. "Tell you what I think of you and your little power plays, Miss High-and-Mighty? Why the hell shouldn't I? Because that's all they are—little power plays you concoct to hog the limelight. *Poor Angel, she's got a stalker*," he mimicked sarcastically. "Yeah, right. Tell another one. Couldn't you come up with something more original than that to get noticed?"

Raging at her, he blasted her with one jealous accusation after another, but Angel didn't say a word to defend herself. What was the point? She couldn't control what he thought of her and wouldn't even try.

"You've had your say," she said when he finally ran out of steam and just glared at her with hate-filled eyes.

"Now if you'll excuse me, I was on my way to my trailer. I'm sure you'll understand why I have no desire to continue this conversation."

As regal as a queen, she swept around him and continued on toward her trailer with William at her side. He hadn't said a single word during the exchange, but she'd been aware of his presence as he'd stood at full alert beside her. If Garrett had made a move toward her, there wasn't a doubt in her mind that he would have intervened in a heartbeat.

"I'm sorry you had to overhear that," she said quietly. "Mr. Elliot can be quite a jackass at times."

He snorted. "Jackass doesn't begin to describe the jerk, but I'm not as nice as you. He's really got it in for you. What'd you do, tell him to take a hike when he asked you out?"

"Something like that," she chuckled. "Obviously, getting turned down was a new experience for him. He's never forgiven me."

Her trailer was fifty feet away, her guard dutifully watching everyone who walked by. "You don't have to walk me the rest of the way," she said with a smile and nodded toward the younger man patiently waiting for her. "That's Taylor, isn't it?"

"Yes, ma'am, but I've got orders to walk you all the way. Mr. Douglas said to make sure I didn't take any chances with your safety."

Taylor, however, started toward them and was halfway across the clearing that separated them when, without warning, the motor home that served as Angel's dressing room suddenly exploded. Jagged pieces of metal went flying, while fire shot into the sky with a loud roar, rocking the very ground itself.

It all happened so fast, Taylor never knew what hit him. The force of the blast slammed into him from behind, throwing him up against another trailer a hundred feet away. Shouting a warning, William stepped in front of Angel to protect her from the flying debris, but they both seemed to be moving in slow motion. Suddenly, a piece of the motor home's roof plummeted from the sky, aiming right for them. Horrified, Angel screamed and tried to shove William out of the way. He was too big, however, and they'd just run out of time. A split second later, the metal slammed into both of them, knocking them to the ground.

Pain exploded in Angel's head as William groaned and went still beside her. She tried to call out for help, but she couldn't manage so much as a whimper. Blackness descended on her like a dark cloud, weighing her down, dragging her under a wave of hurt. Without a sound, she gave herself up to it.

"Angel!"

From thirty feet away, Garrett watched in horror as Angel and her driver lay unmoving on the ground underneath a burning piece of metal that had to weigh twenty pounds. He didn't consider himself a heroic man—in the face of danger, it was every man for himself—but his feet moved with a will of their own and he stumbled toward Angel. Suddenly, he was running, his heart in his throat and his handsome face white with fear. "No!"

The metal singed his hands, but he never noticed as he grabbed it and threw it aside while more debris rained down from the sky. Angel's driver moaned, but she never moved. Pale as a ghost, the back of her head matted with blood, she lay flat on her stomach and didn't even appear to be breathing. And all Garrett could think of was how, not five minutes ago, he'd mocked her about her stalker.

"Dear God, dear God, dear God," he mumbled, praying for the first time in his adult life. "Let her be okay."

He didn't know a thing about first aid or CPR, and when he carefully turned her over, his hands were visibly shaking. Behind him, he heard shouts and people running, but he couldn't take his eyes from Angel's bruised, colorless face. "Help!" he cried, feeling for the pulse in her neck and panicking when he couldn't find it. "Dammit, I need some help over here!"

The words were hardly out of his mouth when there were people there to help. "It's okay, Garrett," somebody said behind him. "Janey McBride is here. She's a nurse. She'll take care of Angel until the ambulance gets here. You can let her go."

"I think she's dead," he said half to himself, still feeling for a pulse. "It's my fault. I should have been able to do something for her. But I didn't know how."

The woman who dropped down to her knees across from him had the kindest voice he'd ever heard in his life. "You did just fine," she said quietly. "She's not dead. See— here's her pulse." And taking his hand, she pressed his fingers to the correct spot on Angel's neck so he could feel the steady, reassuring beat of her heart.

Relief washed over him, and when he looked up at Janey McBride, he could have hugged her. She wasn't a woman who stood out in a crowd—if the truth were told, she was almost plain. Dressed in a stark white nurse's uniform, she wore only a minimum of makeup and had her dark brown hair scraped back in a schoolmarmish bun that wasn't the least bit attractive. But at that moment, he thought she was the prettiest woman he'd ever seen in his life.

"Thank you," he said huskily. "We haven't always been the best of friends, but I don't want anything to happen to her."

"She's going to be fine," she assured him. "Let me take care of her and the others, then I'll take a look at your hands. You look like you've got a couple of nasty burns there."

Surprised, he barely spared a glance at his hands. "Others? Who else was hurt besides Angel and her driver?"

Standing behind Janey, watching her every move as she quickly and efficiently worked over Angel, Charles Sutton, the director, said grimly. "At least fifteen people were hit by shattered glass and flying debris. Taylor, however, Angel's guard today, took most of the brunt of the explosion. He's in pretty bad shape."

Sirens screamed in the distance, and within minutes, the sheriff arrived with Liberty Hill's only fire truck and ambulance right behind him. Almost immediately, paramedics and firemen were spilling from their vehicles to take charge of the disaster. Hoses were run from the fire truck to put out the still blazing trailer, while the medical personnel set up a quick triage to take care of the injured before rushing them to the hospital.

And in the chaos, no one noticed the short, slender man who moved through the crowd like he had every right to be there. He wore no ID, but less than half the cast and crew had procured IDs when the explosion ripped through the set, so security didn't spare him a glance. And he wasn't stupid enough to draw attention to himself by acting guilty. An unobtrusive man, he knew how to hide in plain sight.

The sheriff had everyone move back from the sight of the now extinguished fire, and without a word, the man joined the cast and crew as they silently watched the fire marshall examine the burned-out motor home for signs of arson. The valve that controlled the recreational vehicle's propane tank had been sabotaged, but the marshall would never find the damage. He'd made sure of it, the watcher in the crowd thought with a smug smile. Early that morning, while two security guards patrolled the huge set, he'd slipped in and out of the set and engineered a little surprise for the star of the movie. And no one had suspected a thing until Angel's trailer literally blew up in her face.

.Damn, he was good! The only thing that would have made it better was if Angel had been in the motor home when it blew. The two-timing bitch deserved nothing less. Oh, well. Better luck next time.

And there would be a next time, he promised himself confidently. He could all but guarantee it. It was just a matter of setting the wheels in motion.

It was one of those mornings when the wind was out of the southwest and the temperature was already well into the mid eighties before ten o'clock. By noon, it'd be hotter than hell.

Already sweating like a pig, Joe pulled off his damp shirt and hung it on the tailgate of his pickup, then grabbed the thermos of ice water he'd brought with him. Tempted to douse his head, he took a long swig, while overhead, the sun glared down at him, baking his bronzed skin even darker.

And he loved it. The heat of summer, the icy cold of winter, working in the elements, all alone in the field with nothing but the cattle and the whisper of the wind for company. As a boy, he'd grown up helping his father run the place, and it was at times like this, when he was doing everyday normal chores like repairing a downed cross fence, that he felt closest to him.

Remembering the last time they'd worked on a fence together and his father cursed the amorous bull that had knocked it down in order to get to a pasture full of heifers, Joe grinned and tugged his work gloves back on. He'd never seen the old man so mad.

He was still chuckling over the inventive way his father had cursed that damn bull when what sounded like an explosion far off to the south rocked the silence of the morning. Surprised, he pulled off his cowboy hat and wiped his brow, his narrowed eyes sharpening on the thick forest of trees on the southern horizon. Five miles past the trees, the studio had set up its newest set, and it was from there that it sounded like the explosion had come.

Frowning, he reminded himself that there were several scenes in the movie that required special effects. He didn't have a problem with that. But the contract he had with the studio required the director to give him two days' notice of any activity that might spook the cattle so that he would have time to move them. And Sutton hadn't notified him of anything.

So it was just an oversight, he decided. Sutton had a lot on his plate right now. From what Joe had heard, filming was behind schedule. And then there was the worry and logistics of keeping the studio's number one star safe from an unpredictable headcase. With so much responsibility on his shoulders, it was a wonder the man had any time to sleep. He'd probably ordered some underling to pass on the message that dynamite or some other type of explosive was going to be used on the set today, and somehow it had never reached him.

But when Joe picked up the wire puller to go back to work, something clawed at his gut, something that sank its claws deep and wouldn't let go. He tried to tell himself he was overreacting, but that sixth sense that had never let him down in the past wasn't buying it. If he was going to get any work done today, he was going to have to make a run over to the set first and check out what was going on.

It would only take a few minutes, he reasoned as he drew on his shirt, then tossed his tools in the back of his pickup and climbed into the cab. He needed to meet with Sutton anyway and remind him of the terms of their contract. He'd let it slide this time, but from now on, he damn well wanted to be notified *before* explosives were used.

Heading south on the ranch road that led to the set, he kept his foot steady on the accelerator, the speed hovering around thirty. Still, the gravel road was pitted from the rough winter and he found himself bouncing along and fighting the wheel just to stay on the road. Then he saw the black column of smoke rising silently into the clear morning sky like a crooked finger of doom.

He heard the sirens almost immediately, a long, low wail in the distance that seemed to go on and on like a never-ending scream. His blood turned cold just at the sound of it. Muttering a curse, he pressed the gas pedal to the floor and raced toward the trees on the horizon at a speed that would have horrified his mother.

He never remembered the rest of the drive to the set. The countryside whizzed by in a blur. All he saw was that dark column of smoke rising into the sky. And he knew. He couldn't explain how or why, but just that easily, he knew Angel was in trouble.

The set looked like a war zone when Joe finally reached it. Jagged, smoldering pieces of metal lay everywhere, along with the injured. If Joe hadn't known better, he would have sworn the place had been hit by a bomb. Then he saw the motor home that had once been Angel's dressing room. It was now nothing but a charred, still-smoking shell.

Stunned, his heart stopped dead in his chest. All around him, chaos reigned. Firemen from the volunteer fire department rushed to put out hotspots while paramedics from Liberty Hill and two neighboring counties hurried to answer the painful calls of the wounded. It seemed like the entire cast and crew was standing about, but he didn't see Angel anywhere.

Panic tearing at him, he fought his way through the crowd, ready to rip somebody apart if he didn't find her soon. Then he saw his sister. ''Janey! What are you doing here?''

Her nurse's uniform smudged with dirt and blood, and her hair slipping free of its confining bun, Janey turned from the man whose shoulder she'd just bandaged. "Joe, thank God you're here! I was on my way to work when I heard the sirens. Angel—"

"Where is she? Is she okay? What the hell happened here?"

"Her motor home blew up, but she wasn't in it," she assured him quickly. "She was lucky. She got hit by some flying debris and was knocked out for a while—"

"*Knocked out!* Dammit, Janey—"

"But she's going to be fine," she continued firmly. "Her injuries don't appear to be serious, but she took a pretty good blow to the head. She really should go to the hospital for a CAT scan just to be sure everything's okay."

"Fine. Then what's the problem? Are the ambulances already full? I can take her. Where is she?"

"It isn't that easy," she said dryly, a smile curling her mouth as she nodded to the line of stretchers awaiting transport to the hospital. "See for yourself."

Following Janey's gaze, he immediately found Angel sitting on a stretcher at the front of the line. Less than two hours ago, she'd left for work looking cool and feminine in a pink gauzy sheath dress and strappy sandals designed to make a man's mouth go dry. She still wore the dress and one of the sandals, but the woman on the stretcher was a far cry from the Angel Wiley he knew. The back of her head was bandaged and her right cheek bruised. Dirt and soot soiled her skin and clothes, and the only color in her face was the blue of her eyes. She looked so fragile that a good stiff wind would have blown her away.

But she still had her fighting spirit, he noted with relief. Even as he watched, she jutted her chin out when a paramedic leaned down to talk to her and stubbornly shook her head. "I don't need to go to the hospital," she said firmly. "Take someone who's really hurt."

Struggling to hold on to his patience, the paramedic

smiled thinly. "We don't know that you're not hurt, Ms. Wiley. That's why we want to take you to the hospital. You were knocked cold for quite a while. In all likelihood, you've got a concussion. You need to have a doctor take a look at you—"

"Take William instead. He was out longer than I was. And the wardrobe girl—Shirley. She lost a lot of blood from that gash on her arm. There could be muscle damage."

"But you have a head injury!"

"So I'll take some aspirin and take it easy for the rest of the afternoon," she said obstinately. "I'll be fine."

To his credit, the paramedic hung on to his temper in spite of the fact that he wanted to throw something. Sympathizing with him, Janey couldn't help but smile. "See what I mean," she told Joe. "If she doesn't want medical treatment, we can't force it on her, but she's in no shape to make this kind of decision, Joe. She needs to see a doctor."

"Then she will," he retorted, and headed straight for Angel.

Chapter 10

Rubbing at her pounding temple, Angel listened to the paramedic drone on about why she needed to go to the hospital, and all she wanted to do was go home—to Joe's. To check on Emma, then rest and try to forget that her stalker had just tried to kill her. Oh, Nick and the fire marshall were still investigating the remains of what had been her trailer, but she knew the explosion was no accident. The monster had promised her he was going to make her pay for betraying him with Joe, and he'd succeeded. Every bone in her body ached, and the back of her head felt like someone had taken a hammer to it. With every beat of her heart, her head throbbed.

Lost in her misery, she didn't see Joe striding toward her until he was two steps away. "Joe!" With a startled cry, she jumped to her feet, only to gasp as pain shot through her like a bolt of lightning.

He was beside her in a heartbeat, gently sweeping her up into his arms when her knees buckled. "Whoa, there, sweetheart. Easy. Not so fast. Let me lay you down here—''

"No!" she cried, clutching him around the neck when he lowered her back down to the stretcher. "I want to go home."

"You will—*after* you're checked out by a doctor at the hospital."

"But I'm fine!"

"Oh, really? So why are you pale as a ghost? Look at yourself, honey. You can't even stand up. I bet your head feels like someone got loose with a jackhammer in there, doesn't it? If you go home looking like this, what do you think Emma's going to think?"

She hadn't thought of that, hadn't considered how frightening it might be for her to see her like this. "I'm sorry," she choked. "You're right. I can't let her see me like this. I'm just so worried about her."

"I'll call Laura on the way to the hospital and make sure she's all right," he promised, and gently unlocked her arms from around his neck.

The paramedic, seeing his chance, quickly strapped her onto the stretcher, and within minutes, she was in the ambulance and on her way to the hospital.

Pacing the hall outside the waiting room at the county hospital, Joe just barely resisted the urge to throw something. Over an hour had passed since Angel had been wheeled into the emergency room, and he hadn't seen hide nor hair of her since. What the hell was taking so long?

Normally, he wouldn't have worried—Janey had been pretty confident that she was fine, and he trusted his sister's opinion. But a head injury wasn't anything to play around with. What if she had a blood clot? Or some type of internal bleeding that wasn't easily detected by X rays? She could need surgery—

The emergency room doors swung open and a nurse hurried out, but she didn't spare him a glance. Swearing, he reminded himself that he had to be patient. Angel wasn't the only one who was injured in the explosion. The ER was flooded with cast and crew members who'd been hurt by flying glass and metal, and the Falls County Hospital wasn't equipped to handle such an influx at one time. The ER was so small, in fact, that some of the wounded were lined up on gurneys in the hall in order of the seriousness of their injuries, waiting for their turn to see a doctor. It could be hours yet before they were all examined and treated.

Outside, the ambulance drove up with its siren blazing, and he wondered with a frown if he should call Laura again. As promised, he called her from his mobile on the way to the hospital to tell her of Angel's injuries and make sure Emma was safe and sound. Everything at the house had been quiet and calm, thankfully, but if this morning had proven anything, it was that that could change in a heartbeat.

A harried nurse with a clipboard stepped through the double doors of the emergency room right then, calling his name and brusquely directed him to the examining cubicle where Angel was. "The doctor would like to speak to you."

Alarmed, he asked sharply, "Is Miss Wiley all right?"

Already consulting the next name on her list, she didn't spare him so much as a glance. "She's scheduled to be released. Is there anyone here for Frank Johnson?" she called out and turned her attention back to the crowd waiting for news of friends and family.

The emergency room was still a madhouse, but all Joe saw was Angel. The curtain to the examining cubicle the nurse had directed him to had been pushed aside, and he could see her sitting on the gurney she'd been wheeled in on. Her shoulders were slumped, her gaze focused on nothing in particular, her arms crossed over her breasts as if she was cold. A smaller, neater bandage had been applied to the back of her head, but she was still pale and wan and looked so damn small that he just wanted to scoop her up and hold her until the hurt went away.

Something tugged at his heart then, something he hadn't come close to letting himself feel for a very long time. Stunned, he just stood there, taken aback. Where the devil had this come from? His heart had turned to stone the day Belinda walked out on him, and he'd sworn then that he'd never again let any woman get close enough to make him feel anything ever again. And no one had—until Miss Hollywood had arrived on his doorstep and dared him to try to throw her out.

Alarm bells clanging in his head, he should have gotten the hell out of there right then. He needed to think, to pull back and regroup. But Angel looked up then and saw him, and her fragile smile made it impossible for him to go anywhere but to her side. Dear God, what was he going to do with this woman?

He hadn't meant to touch her, but her hand was cradled in his before he could stop himself from reaching for her. "I hear they're letting you out of here," he said gruffly.

She started to nod, only to freeze and suck in a sharp breath. When she finally released it, she was careful not to move. "I need to get home and check on Emma. Did you talk to Laura?"

"Everything's fine at the house," he assured her. "All you have to worry about right now is you. How's the head?"

"Much better," she said. "It hardly hurts at all now."

Joe couldn't believe she said that with a straight face. She couldn't even move because her head felt like it was going to fall off her shoulders, and she expected him to believe it didn't hurt? Who did the stubborn woman think she was fooling?

"Oh, really?" he said dryly. "Would you care to say that again and this time sound like you mean it?"

"I'm fine—"

"And I'm Howdy Doody."

"The doctor said I could go home—"

"Only if you behave yourself," said the doctor himself. Tall and distinguished, the white-haired gentleman who stepped over to the gurney greeted Joe with a grin. "Long time no see, Joe. How's your mother? I missed her at the last church social."

"Just fine, Dr. Michaels." Shaking his hand, Joe couldn't help but smile. Dan Michaels had been trying to get his mother to go out with him for the last year, to no avail. By now, he must have figured out that he was wasting his time—in spite of the fact that his father had died nearly eighteen years ago, there'd always been only one man for his mother and that was Gus McBride—but Dan was nothing if not persistent. "She's been pretty busy the last couple of weeks with her houseguests."

"So I heard. I ran into Janey at the nursing home and she told me some of the female cast members were staying with her and your mother. She never said anything about Miss Wiley staying with you, though."

"The studio was trying to keep it under wraps," Angel told him. "For security reasons."

His gaze narrowed thoughtfully on her pale face and bandaged head. "I see. And just how much did today's explosion have to do with security—or lack of it?"

"Nick is trying to discover that right now," Joe replied. "In the meantime, I'll make sure there are no more *accidents*."

"Good. And while you're at it, make sure she takes it easy for the next couple of days," the older man said. "She took quite a blow to the back of her head. Normally, I'd keep her here at least overnight, but this place is a zoo because of the explosion; and she'll get more rest at home. And I mean rest. I don't want her doing anything more strenuous than lifting a fork to her mouth when she eats dinner. Understand?''

He spoke to Joe, but his eyes were trained on Angel, and she got the message. If she didn't follow doctor's orders, she would find herself back in the hospital, this time to stay. "Understood," she promised. "I'll stay in bed for the rest of the day."

"I'll put her there myself," Joe added huskily. "And tomorrow, too, if I have to."

His eyes were dark with a glint that set her heart pounding, but if the doctor noticed, he made no comment. Satisfied, the older man smiled and patted Angel's hand. "Then you're free to go, young lady. It's been a pleasure taking care of you."

Her head still throbbing, Angel said wryly, "I can't say it's been the best experience of my life, but you've been very kind. Thank you, Dr. Michaels. I hope you won't take offense when I say that I'll consider myself lucky if I never have to see you again."

"I understand perfectly," he said, chuckling as he gave her hand one last squeeze, then released her and stepped back. "If we do meet again, hopefully it'll be under better circumstances. Now, go on and get out of here while you still can," he said as an orderly produced a wheelchair. "Here's your ride."

Normally, the orderly would have personally wheeled her to the front door himself, but with so many unexpected patients to deal with, he was needed elsewhere. So Joe did the honors and rolled Angel out of the emergency room and into the corridor. When she saw the injured cast members still waiting to see a doctor, she suddenly remembered William and Taylor. She'd forgotten all about them in the mad confusion of the emergency room.

"What about Taylor—the guard at my trailer? And William?" she asked Joe with a frown. "I saw him right after I regained consciousness, but I don't remember what happened to Taylor. Are they okay?"

Joe hesitated, but there was no way he could avoid telling her the truth. "William had a concussion and a bad cut across his shoulder. He had to have surgery."

"Oh, my God! Is he going to be all right?"

He nodded. "The doctor expects a full recovery, but he's not going to be driving anywhere for a while."

"And Taylor?"

"The explosion threw him into another trailer," he replied. "He has internal injuries and cuts on his face from the shattered glass."

Stricken, she gasped. "Oh, no!"

"I know it doesn't sound like it, but he was lucky. Some of the witnesses said they saw him waiting by your trailer for you just before the explosion."

"Yes, that's right. Then he saw me and William and started walking toward us."

"And that saved his life," he pronounced solemnly. "If he'd still been standing right by that trailer when it blew, there would have been nothing left of him to pick up, honey. So don't beat yourself up over this. Nobody died, and the studio's bringing in a plastic surgeon from Denver to treat Taylor. With time, he'll be fine, and so will everyone else."

She was blaming herself for the entire incident—he could see the guilt in her eyes—but before he could convince her she had nothing to feel guilty about, they reached the hospital entrance and the double doors parted to reveal

Garrett. The second Angel's costar saw her, relief washed over his face and he headed straight for her.

Scowling, Joe didn't like the man, never had. Especially after that day on the set when he'd watched him blow one take after another so Angel would have to kiss him over and over. The bastard had known he was humiliating her, and he'd enjoyed every second of it.

"What do you want, Elliot?" he growled.

He didn't, as Joe expected, answer him with some smart-ass remark. Instead, his attitude was gone, his expression unusually humble. "I just wanted to talk to Angel for a minute."

"I'm taking her home," he said before Angel could open her mouth. "She needs to rest."

"It won't take long," he insisted. "I just want to apologize for the way I treated her."

Her eyes wide, Angel made no attempt to hide her surprise. "You mean this morning? When you didn't believe me when I told you I really was in danger?"

"Yeah." His voice gruff, he nodded. "I thought you were just being paranoid. I'm sorry."

"The sheriff doesn't know yet that Angel's stalker caused the explosion," Joe pointed out. "He and the fire inspector are still investigating."

"It doesn't matter what the cause was," the other man replied. "She was scared and I should have been more sympathetic."

In honor of fairness, Angel pointed out, "You aren't the only one who thought I was exaggerating."

"No, but that doesn't excuse my behavior. And I'm not just talking about this morning. I owe you an apology for all the times I was so nasty to you. I acted like a jerk," he said stiffly, "because you refused to go out with me. But I guess you know that already."

If she'd been a cynical woman, Angel might have wondered if he was acting. There was no question that he was one of the best actors she'd ever worked with. When he chose to, he could go from laughter to tears in the blink of an eye and make you think he'd just lost his best friend.

But he'd just humbled himself, not only in front of her and Joe, but other members of the cast and crew within listening distance. And a man with his kind of pride didn't do that lightly. She'd never seen anyone look more miserable in her life, and she had to believe he was sincere.

"I guess I wasn't as tactful as I could have been, either," she admitted. "So we both could have handled it differently. Considering that, I'm willing to let bygones be bygones if you are. What do you say?"

If he'd expected her to make it more difficult for him, she surprised him. Relieved, he laughed, the grin that had slain millions of women's hearts curling one side of his mouth. "Yeah, I think I can manage that. Thanks."

While Joe retrieved his truck from the parking lot and brought it around to the hospital's front entrance, Garrett waited with Angel and made sure no one bothered her. Thankful for his help, she tried to keep up her end of the conversation as he talked to her, but the adrenaline from the accident had worn off, leaving her exhausted. She could barely keep her eyes open.

"I'm sorry, Garrett," she said as Joe drove up and he wheeled her out to the truck. "I'm not very good company right now."

"Hey, don't worry about it. You've had a rough day." Hovering close, he watched Joe help her into the cab of the truck. "Go home and get some sleep."

He didn't have to tell her twice. Safely buckled in, she turned in the seat slightly so that she could rest her cheek against the headrest, and before Joe drove out of the hospital parking lot, she was asleep.

It was the rough gravel road of the ranch that woke her. Joe tried to avoid the worst of it, but at times, it was like driving over a washboard. Every bone in her body protesting the sudden jostling, Angel woke with a groan.

Shooting her a quick glance of concern, Joe grimaced. "Sorry. I didn't realize this road had so many damn potholes in it. Hold on. It's only a couple of more miles."

He slowed down to almost a crawl, but that only dragged out the torture. By the time he finally reached the house and pulled into the front drive, Angel was pale and drawn and gritting her teeth to keep from crying out in pain.

"Just sit right where you are," Joe ordered roughly with a frown when she reached for her door handle. "I'll carry you in."

"No, I can walk," she insisted. "Emma's going to be upset when she sees the bandage on my head. If you carry me, it'll only frighten her more."

He didn't like it, but she didn't give him time to argue. Stubbornly setting her chin, she carefully pushed open the passenger door and eased out of the truck. Her feet barely touched the ground and Joe was at her side, muttering under his breath about damn fool women who where too bull-headed to accept help when they needed it.

"Mommy!"

At the first sound of the key in the front door, Emma cried out in joy and darted into the foyer two steps ahead of Laura, only to hesitate when Angel carefully walked inside with Joe hovering close behind her. At the sight of Angel's pale face and bandaged head, the smile lightening her eyes died and her bottom lip began to tremble. "Mommy? You look funny. Do you have a boo-boo on your head?"

"Something like that, sweetheart," she said, forcing a smile. "But I'm going to be okay. I just need to rest for a while."

"Why don't you go upstairs to your room and finish the card you were making for Mommy?" Laura suggested. "I'm sure she'd love to see it."

Emma didn't have to be told twice. Happily distracted, she ran up the stairs, leaving the adults still standing in the foyer. The second she was out of sight, Laura said grimly, "I hate to be the bearer of bad news, especially after what happened this morning, but a floral delivery was made this afternoon that you need to know about."

Surprised, Angel stiffened. "Floral? But I asked the florist to hold all deliveries."

"I know. I don't know what happened. There must have been some kind of mix-up. I didn't call you at the hospital because I didn't want to worry you, but it can't be put off any longer. It was for Emma."

The color drained from Angel's cheeks. "Emma? He sent Emma something?"

Wishing she didn't have to tell her, Laura nodded. "Yes. A funeral wreath."

"A funeral wreath?" she repeated in confusion. Then she understood. "For my death," she whispered, horrified. What little color there was in her cheeks drained away. Suddenly light-headed, she seemed to have lost all the starch in her knees.

Swearing, Joe swept her up into his arms the second her knees started to buckle and carried her into the family room. "She could use some hot tea, Laura," he threw over his shoulder. "As strong as you can make it. And put plenty of sugar in it."

"Of course. It won't take me a minute."

She hurried into the kitchen and was back within a matter of moments, carrying a tray loaded down with tea and cookies. "I'm so sorry," she said in a rush as she set the tray on the coffee table and quickly prepared a steaming cup for Angel. "I shouldn't have told you—"

"No, I needed to know." Seated on the couch with Joe hovering close, waiting to help her if she so much as blinked wrong, she looked around. "Where is it?"

"Out on the back porch. I didn't want Emma to start asking questions."

"Was there a card?" Joe asked as the older woman handed Angel her tea.

She nodded. "I didn't read it. It's on your desk in your study."

Turning on his heel, he strode into his office and returned with a small white florist envelope. Angel took one look at the fury in Joe's brown eyes and felt her stomach turn over. She'd never seen him quite so livid. Whatever message was in the card had to be awful.

Setting down her tea, she held out her hand. "Let me see it."

His jaw rock-hard, he crumbled the card in his fist. "No."

"You can't protect me from this, Joe. Not if it involves Emma. I have a right to know."

She was right and they both knew it. Still, he didn't give in graciously. "Dammit, there's no reason for you to read it. It's just going to hurt you. Let me call Nick and he can deal with it."

Wordlessly, she held out her hand.

"All right!" he growled, striding over to her and dropping the message in her hand. "Have it your way. But don't blame me when you get more than you bargained for!"

"Thank you," she said huskily, and carefully smoothed out the balled-up missive.

After all the hell her stalker had put her through and all the times he'd terrorized her, she'd thought there was nothing new he could do to frighten her. She'd thought wrong. Staring down at the typed message that was delivered with the wreath, she felt as if he'd somehow reached inside her and ripped her heart right out of her chest.

Dear Emma,
I would like to express my deepest sorrow over the death of your mother. If she had just listened to me, she would be alive today.

                                                        Sincerely,
                    A man who loved her more than life itself.

"He's a fiend," she whispered hoarsely, unable to drag her eyes away from the sinister message. "A lunatic who delights in finding new ways to torment me. He's going to kill me."

"The hell he is!" Joe rasped. "He's not coming anywhere near you."

"He didn't get near me this morning and look what he was able to do," she argued. "If the studio hadn't decided today of all days to require everyone to have a picture ID made, I'd have walked into my trailer when I arrived on the set and I'd be dead right now. The timing was off. Next time it won't be."

Her eerie confidence unnerved Joe—and infuriated him. Dammit, did she think he was going to stand by and let the bastard hurt her again? He'd kill him himself before he let that happen. "There isn't going to be a next time," he said coldly.

He would have said more, but Emma had finished making her card and came running down the stairs. Her round, dimpled face alight with excitement, she burst into the family room with it clutched tightly in her hand. "Look, Mommy! Auntie Laura showed me how to drawed the flowers. It says *I love you just because.*"

She took it with hands that weren't quite steady, her smile tremulous. "I know, sweetheart," she whispered thickly, and pulled her into her arms for a desperate hug. "It's beautiful. I'll keep it always."

Over the top of Emma's head, Angel's eyes met Joe's, and the stark despair in them shook him to the core. She really thought she didn't have an always, that her days were numbered and quickly running out. And she had no idea how that terrified him. She couldn't give up. If she was going to beat the bastard who was doing this to her, she had to keep fighting.

"I'm calling Nick," he told her tersely. "He needs to know about this."

Nick, however, was already on his way. Stopping by Joe's after leaving the site of the explosion, he arrived just minutes after Joe called his office in town. "Harold Bailey and I just finished our investigation of the scene," he said as he strode inside. "Where's Angel? The hospital notified my office that she'd been sent home. She'll want to hear this."

"In the family room with Emma and Laura," Joe replied, shutting the door behind him. "Did you get my message?"

"Yeah. So the son of a bitch sent Angel flowers again, did he? I've got to give him credit—his timing couldn't have been better if he'd planned the whole damn thing."

Surprised, Joe frowned. "What the hell are you talking about? He did plan it."

"No, he didn't." And with that cryptic remark, he headed straight for the family room, where he found Angel on the couch, leaning against some pillows propped behind her back, looking like death warmed over.

Laura spied him first and rose to her feet as Joe joined Nick in the arched doorway. "Emma and I are going to go upstairs. She's been wanting to watch the new Rugrats video, and I think now would be a good time."

Eager to watch her favorite cartoon, Emma left without

a word of complaint, and within seconds, the three of them were alone. Struggling to sit up straighter, Angel forced a grimace of a smile. "Thank you for coming so quickly, Nick."

"Don't move," he said quickly, moving to one of the overstuffed chairs flanking the couch. "You're fine right where you are. How are you feeling?"

"Better now that I'm back home." For a brief moment, weak humor sparkled in her eyes. "I have a harder head than I thought."

"Thank God you do," he said with a grin. "That's probably what saved your neck. If it's any consolation, though, you'll be happy to know that there's no evidence of arson. Harold Bailey, the fire marshall, went over the scene, and the only cause of the explosion he could find was a rust spot on the propane tank that must have been leaking for some time."

"Then Harold needs to get his glasses checked," Joe retorted, "because he missed something. Dammit, Nick, I told you about the flowers. The son of a bitch sent Emma a funeral wreath today!"

"What?!"

"And a card with his condolences over my death," Angel added, handing it to him. "It was delivered earlier this afternoon while I was still at the hospital."

Without a word, Nick took the card and opened it, his angular face turning hard as granite as he read the short message. "He's a cold son of a bitch, I'll give him that," he muttered. "And damn clever if he orchestrated that fire without leaving any clues behind."

"What do you mean *if?*" Joe demanded. "You read the damn card. Are you saying its just *coincidence* that the jerk sent Emma a funeral wreath the same day as Angel's almost killed in an explosion? C'mon, Nick, you know better than that! The jackass planned the whole thing."

"Or he heard about the explosion and wants to take credit for it," he argued. "For all we know, he ordered the flowers from Becca Ryan this morning, after the explosion. The man's into head games, Joe. I wouldn't put anything past him, but I'll call Becca just to make sure."

"Good. Because I want to know why she allowed flowers to be delivered here when Angel specifically asked her not to."

"I'll find out," he promised grimly, and strode out.

He placed the call from Joe's office, only to return to the family room a few minutes later, swearing like a sailor, yet at the same time, practically rubbing his hands together in satisfaction. "You were right, Joe. The son of a bitch came in first thing this morning—*before* the explosion—and ordered the wreath."

On her second cup of tea, Angel nearly dropped her cup. "He *came in?*"

"Yeah. Becca was sick this morning, so her nephew, Randy, opened up for her—which was why the flowers were delivered here. He didn't know he was supposed to hold all deliveries. Your stalker was waiting for him when he got to the shop. Apparently, he was quite agitated and in a hell of a hurry."

"Son of a bitch!" Joe swore. "I knew it!"

Somber, Nick said, "I don't know how he managed it, but he did something to those gas lines that Harold and I missed. I'm going to call in someone from Colorado Springs to check them out, but first I'm going to meet Victor Hughes at Becca's shop and see if he can draw a composite sketch of our boy from Randy's description.

"Victor's the high school art teacher and the closest thing we have to a police artist," he told Angel. "If we're lucky, by this time tomorrow, we'll have posters of the bastard plastered all over the county. Then the calls will start coming in. Because somebody's seen him—they just didn't know it at the time.''

He was more optimistic than Angel had ever seen him, and before he headed back to town with the card and wreath stowed in evidence bags in the trunk of his patrol car, she didn't have the heart to tell him that capturing her stalker wasn't going to be that easy. She, more than anyone, knew just how elusive the man was. Time and again, he'd managed to evade capture, slipping through security systems and past guards and the police like a ghost, always somehow staying just out of reach. It was unnerving—and horribly frightening. Because there seemed to be no rules where he was concerned, no boundaries. He did whatever he wanted to do, just daring the authorities to try and catch him.

And he wanted her dead. He'd just missed blowing her to bits this morning, and there wasn't a doubt in her head that he'd try it again. When he decided to make his move, no one—not Joe or Nick or an army of security guards— was going to stop him from doing whatever he wanted to her.

And that shook her to the core. All this time, with so many people watching over her, she'd thought she was at least safe on the set and at Joe's. But she wasn't. And neither was Emma.

''You need to be in bed,'' Joe reminded her as he picked up the tea things to return them to the kitchen. ''Let me put this stuff in the kitchen and I'll help you up the stairs.''

But she was already pushing to her feet, her decision made. ''I have to call my father first.''

''The hell you do,'' he growled, setting the tray back down with a bang to scowl at her when she wavered unsteadily on her feet. ''Sit back down before you fall down. Whatever you have to say to your old man can wait until tomorrow.''

"Tomorrow may be too late," she argued. "I have to get Emma out of here today. Before she gets hurt, too."

He wanted to assure her that she was worrying need-lessly, but how could he when she sat there with a bandage around her aching head and she was so stiff she could hardly move? She'd just barely escaped with her life this morning. She had every right to be worried about her daughter's safety. He was worried himself.

"You're in no shape to be traipsing all over the house," he said gruffly. "If you want to use the phone in my study, I'll carry you in there." And with no other warning than that, he bent and gently lifted her into his arms.

The tears came out of nowhere. Hot and quick, they filled her eyes before she could blink them away. Willing them not to spill over her lashes, she wondered if the man had a clue what his unexpected thoughtfulness did to her. Just when she was prepared to argue with him, he understood what she was going through, and it just destroyed her.

Given the chance, she would have buried her face against his neck and cried her heart out in the safety of his arms. But they'd reached his study by then and she didn't have the time to give into her emotions. If her father turned his back on her again, she would have to find someplace else for Emma to stay, and that would take time.

So she choked back the lump in her throat and hastily wiped at the tears that trailed down her cheeks as he gently deposited her in the chair behind his desk. "This probably won't take very long," she said thickly when he started to leave so she could make her call in private. "I'd like for you to stay."

Without a word, he took the chair across the desk from her. Only then did she reach for the phone and punch in the number.

"Someone blew up my trailer on the set and tried to kill me this morning," she told her father the second he said hello. "Emma could be next. I know you may not care about me, but I would hope that you would care about an innocent child who's never done anything to hurt anyone."

For one long, heart-wrenching moment, she thought he wasn't going to say anything, just hang up on her as he had before. Silence stretched between them, tearing her apart. Then, just when she thought she couldn't stand another second of the torment, he said gruffly, "Send the child to me. She'll be safe here."

She cried then because she couldn't help herself. Because for the first time in over six years, her father was actually speaking to her. Because he cared, whether he wanted to admit it or not. Because her daughter, whom she loved more than life itself, was finally going to be out of her stalker's reach and safe. But most of all, she cried for herself and all the years that had been lost between them. They could never be regained, but at least maybe now, the two of them could make peace and try to go on as a family.

"She and her nanny will arrive there later this evening," she said huskily. "Thank you, Dad."

"You don't have to thank me," he grumbled irritably just before hanging up. "She's my granddaughter."

An hour later, Emma and Laura's bags were packed, the travel arrangements made. The studio had sent a limo to convey them to Colorado Springs, where they would take a private jet to Albuquerque. From there, another limo would be waiting to drive them the forty miles to Thomasville, the small town where Angel had grown up and her father still lived. The entire way, they would be accompanied by two security guards who would protect them until Angel's stalker was caught.

"I don't want to go," Emma pouted as the last of the luggage was put in the limo and Angel carried her outside. "I want to stay here with you," she told Angel. "And Mr.

Joe and Spotty. Mr. Joe said when he was big, I could ride him. Please, Mommy, can I?''

Her heart aching just at the thought of letting her out of her sight, Angel forced a smile. ''It's just for a little while, sweetheart. Just until Mommy finishes this movie. Then we'll see about buying our own ranch. Some place just like Mr. Joe's, where you can have your own baby horse and anything else you want. How does that sound? Would you like that?''

It was an out-and-out bribe, one that even at three, Emma recognized for what it was—one of those rare moments when she was in the driver's seat and could get just about anything she wanted if she played her cards right. Cocking her curly head, she eyed Angel speculatively. ''Can I have a real pig? Like Babe?''

Angel's lips twitched. ''I don't see why not. Though he really doesn't talk, honey. Except in your imagination.''

''Can he sleep with me?''

Chuckling, Angel nuzzled her neck, making her giggle. ''We'll see, Miss Wheeler-Dealer. In the meantime, you're going to get to stay with your grandfather and sleep in the bed that Mommy slept in when she was a little girl. And I'll write you every day, and Auntie Laura will help you write me back. Okay? It'll be fun.''

Safe and secure in her mother's arms, she arched a delicate brow at Joe, who was helping the limo driver load the last of the luggage into the trunk. ''Will Mr. Joe write me, too?''

''Every chance I get, little bit,'' he told her solemnly, his brown eyes twinkling. ''I'll even send you some stickers. I already gave Laura some for you to play with in the car.''

Her face lit up at that. ''Okay, Mommy, I'm ready to go now.''

Fighting tears, Angel laughed and kissed her, then

handed her over to Joe, who tickled her until she giggled and went limp in his arms. She was still laughing when he placed her in the car.

"Don't let her out of your sight," she told Laura as she hugged her. "And call me when you get there."

"I'll call you every step of the way," Laura assured her, giving her one last hug. "Don't worry, she's going to be fine. You just take care of you."

"I will," she promised huskily. "Hopefully, this will all be over soon."

There was no reason to linger after that. After a last wave from Laura and Emma, the limo headed back to town, and Angel was left alone with Joe and the knowledge that she'd done the right thing.

Chapter 11

"She'll be all right," Joe said gruffly, breaking the silence that had fallen in the wake of their leave-taking. "The guards won't let her out of their sight, and neither will your father or Laura. Between the four of them, they're going to make sure nothing happens to her."

Dragging her gaze from the spot where the limo had disappeared from view in the distance, Angel could manage only a halfhearted smile. "I know. I just miss her already. The house is going to seem so empty without her."

Joe couldn't argue with that. Emma might have been only three, but the little shrimp had a way of making her presence known. In the relatively short time she'd been there, she'd staked out a place for herself in his home and his heart, and for the life of him, he didn't know how she'd done it. Maybe it was the way she called him Mr. Joe with that twinkle in her eye. Or her pert grin when she climbed uninvited into his lap and demanded he tell her a story. She was a sweetheart, one of those fascinating females who would leave a string of broken hearts behind her wherever she went, and his was the first she'd stolen. Yeah, he was going to miss her. He hadn't realized just how much until now.

"It won't be for long," he said as she turned and gingerly made her way up the steps of the porch. "I know the jerk's managed to outsmart the police so far, but he's starting to get careless. One or two more mistakes like the one he made today, and Nick'll nail him. It's just a matter of time."

Buster let out a sharp bark then, and they both turned to see a car racing down the road toward them, dragging a cloud of red dust behind it. His eyes narrowed on the vehicle in the distance, Joe frowned. "That looks like Nick now."

It was. He pulled up a few minutes later and stepped out of the car to come striding toward them, his angled jaw set purposefully. "That was quick," Joe said by way of a greeting. "What happened? Run into another dead end?"

"Maybe. Maybe not," he replied as he joined them on the porch. "On the positive side, Randy was able to give Victor a darn good description of the stalker. Unfortunately, he was obviously in disguise this morning, and that complicates things. Still, it's the best news we've had all day," he said quickly. "Especially since the lab wasn't able to do anything with the rose Angel found in her hair last night. When the phone company couldn't trace the call on her cell phone, either, I was beginning to wonder if we were ever going to get a break. It looks like we finally did.

"Here," he said, handing Angel the charcoal sketch the high school art teacher had drawn. "Take a look and tell me what you think."

Her heart thundering, she stared down at the lifelike drawing and half expected to see the familiar face of someone she'd passed on the street or in the grocery store. But the man who stared back at her was a stranger, someone she would have sworn she'd never laid eyes on in her life.

Granted, the disguise he wore was obvious, but effective. A bad wig that was too big for his head concealed the style and color of his hair, while thick, black-rimmed glasses distorted not only his eyes, but the shape of his face. Even his size was disguised by the tattered, oversized shirt he wore.

At first glance, he appeared to be a large, unkempt myopic man who needed someone to take him in hand. But a second, closer look chilled Angel to the bone. The eyes nearly hidden behind the glasses were stone-cold and filled with hate, the thin-lipped mouth a slash of anger in a narrow-jawed face. Despite the oversize shirt, he had a scrawny neck and was, in all likelihood, a small man, but no less dangerous for that. He might look harmless, but she wouldn't want to meet him in a dark alley or anywhere else. Violence emanated from him in waves.

With trembling fingers, she handed the sketch to Joe so he could look at him. "I've never seen him before," she told Nick. "I would have remembered those eyes."

Joe agreed. "Did Randy see what kind of car he was driving or get an address from him? He must have gotten some information from him when he ordered the wreath."

"Unfortunately, he paid with cash," Nick said flatly. "And he must have parked in the parking lot on the side of the shop instead of out front. Randy never saw a car."

"What about the other businesses in town? He should have stuck out like a sore thumb walking around in that getup. Someone besides Randy must have seen him."

"I've got my deputies checking on that right now and circulating copies of the sketch around town. But you've got to remember it was *barely seven o'clock* in the morning when Randy found him waiting for him at the shop," Nick reminded them. "Most of the other businesses in town, except for Ed's, were closed. In all likelihood, Randy was the only one who saw him.''

''And even if anyone else did see him, he wore a disguise that only a fool would wear again,'' Joe said in disgust.

Nick nodded. ''Exactly. And this jackass is no fool. He likes taking chances, likes thumbing his nose at us. And even when he's furious at Angel and seems out of control, he's smart enough to take precautions to make sure he can't be identified easily.''

Angel's heart sank at that. ''Then we're back to square one. What good is a sketch of him in a disguise he's never going to wear again?''

''We've got more than we had before,'' Nick replied, and counted them off for her. ''One—we know he's not a big man. Two—even the best disguise can't hide a person's height unless they're wearing stilts and he wasn't. Randy said he was about five foot seven, give or take an inch or so for the wig. Three—he's small-boned and thin, and, according to him, had well-kept, manicured hands. And last, but certainly not least, he has a narrow face with a fairly sharp chin and close-set blue eyes that are colder than hell.

''Put that all together,'' he continued with satisfaction, ''and we've got a suspect who's five foot seven, approximate weight one hundred and forty pounds, with a small build, narrow face, and close-set blue eyes. He has above-average intelligence, is controlling and possessive, and has a dominant personality. In all likelihood, he's a professional, college educated, and doesn't get along well with his co-workers. It goes without saying that he's capable of extreme violence.''

Stunned, Angel just looked at him. ''You got all that from that one sketch?''

''Not all by myself,'' he admitted. ''There are profiles on these types of creeps. And for your own protection, you need to remember where this jackass is coming from. He has a controlling personality and he thinks of you as his. So when he sees you with someone else like he did last night," he continued, shooting Joe a telling look, "he goes ballistic. This morning, he retaliated by blowing up your trailer. If there's a next time, there's no telling what he'll do. Just be careful. I know you're surrounded by security, but watch yourself. Okay?"

He didn't say the words, but Angel knew exactly what he was saying. If she was going to kiss Joe again, she'd be wise not to do it in public. Heat climbing in her cheeks, she didn't dare look at Joe. "Okay," she said huskily. "Thanks Nick."

He left soon after that to show the sketch to members of the cast and crew, then post it around town, and with his leave-taking, an awkward silence fell that neither she nor Joe seemed inclined to break. Finally, unable to bear it a second longer, she said, "Don't feel like you have to stick around here because of me. I know you have work to do. And I need to lie down. In fact, I think I'll go up now. I'm really tired."

She turned to go inside, but he was already there before her, opening the door for her. "I'll help you upstairs."

With Nick's warning hanging between them, memories of the kiss they'd shared on the Ferris wheel came rushing back, and just thinking about Joe helping her upstairs and into bed had her heart pounding in her breast.

"No!" she said quickly. Too quickly. "I...I'm f-fine. Really," she insisted when he hesitated. "I can make it by myself."

His dark brows knit in a frown, he studied her with too-sharp eyes. "You're still weak as a kitten. You've got no business climbing the stairs by yourself."

"It's my head that's hurt," she pointed out. "Not my legs. If I take it slow, I'll be fine."

He wanted to argue, but she didn't give him a chance. Stepping through the door, she headed straight for the stairs and started up them. Behind her, she heard Joe swear and hurry to catch up with her, but she kept climbing, her pace steady and her hand resting on the banister just in case she needed it. She didn't.

Standing at the bottom step, prepared to run to her rescue and catch her if she so much as hesitated, Joe watched her stubbornly climb all the way to the top and wanted to shake her. She had to be the most independent woman he'd ever met in his life! Even when she could barely move, she still insisted on doing things herself. Did she have any idea how frustrating that was for him? Or how much he admired her for her bullheaded determination? She was strong and persistent, soft and fragile, a contradiction in terms that fascinated the hell out of him. And the day was quickly coming when he would have to deal with his feelings for her.

But not today. Today, all he could think of was sticking close and making sure nothing else happened to her. Oh, she would have been safe with the guards and Buster patrolling the grounds and watching for intruders, but he couldn't bring himself to walk away from her. Not yet. Not when the smell of smoke from her burning trailer was still on his clothes. So while she slept upstairs, he puttered around the house, doing repairs and chores that he'd been too busy to do for the last six months.

She almost slept around the clock, waking only long enough to take a call from Laura when she and Emma arrived safely in New Mexico. Once she was sure her daughter was safe, she went back to bed. Worried about her, Joe lost track of the number of times he checked on her to make sure she was okay, but she was always fine, just exhausted from the trauma she'd been through. Then when she did wake up, she was still tired, still in need of rest. Because of the explosion and the injuries to much of the cast and crew, work was cancelled for the remainder of the week, and Angel took advantage of every second of it. If she wasn't sleeping, she was lying down, taking it easy, healing.

By the morning of the fourth day after the accident, Joe came down for breakfast to find her already in the kitchen eating a bowl of cereal. Surprised, he stopped in his tracks, his dark brows knit in a frown across the bridge of his nose when he saw she was already dressed despite the fact that it was barely six in the morning. Wearing a sleeveless white cotton blouse and simple yellow shorts that showed off the enticing length of her incredible legs, she appeared to be completely recovered from her ordeal earlier in the week. The color was back in her cheeks, and her blue eyes had a sparkle that had been noticeably absent since the explosion of her trailer.

She looked fresh and cool and beautiful, and just looking at her had the air backing up in Joe's lungs. For the last few days, he'd given little thought to the fact that they were alone in the house together for the first time since they'd made love. There'd been no time—he'd been too concerned about Angel's health to think about anything but getting her back on her feet.

But now she was whole and healthy and gorgeous, and Emma and Laura weren't there to keep him from doing something stupid—like give into the need that had been clawing at him from the first time he kissed her. Silently swallowing a curse, he glared at her. "What are you doing out of bed? The doctor said you're supposed to rest."

"I did," she replied, wry humor spilling in her eyes. "I slept for three days. Don't you think that's enough?"

Scowling at her, he didn't so much as crack a smidgen of a smile. "How's your head?"

She grinned and wobbled her head. "Still attached." When he still didn't smile, she said gently, "I'm fine, Joe.

Really. All the aches and pains are gone—my head doesn't even hurt anymore. And Emma's finally safe. The only way I could be better would be if Nick had my stalker in custody, and even that's within the realm of possibility now that we have a description of him.''

''That could take a while,'' he warned her. ''No one's come forward with any information on him yet, and he's been awfully quiet over the last three days.'' Glancing past her to the wall of windows that gave a sweeping view of the mountains to the west, he frowned as the first rays of the sun crept over the ranch. ''Too quiet, if you ask me. I don't like it. The bastard's up to something. I can feel it in my bones.''

''Maybe he's just lying low until all the hoopla from the explosion dies down,'' she said. ''Nick plastered that sketch of him all over town, didn't he? He's got to be nervous.''

''Are you kidding? We're talking about a man who walked right into town to order a wreath for your funeral the same day he tried to blow you to kingdom come. The Devil himself could be after him and he'd spit in his eye. No, he's not worried—he's too arrogant for that. He's planning something, and God only know what it is.''

She'd been afraid of that. Over the course of the last three days, even when she was sleeping, the knowledge that he was out there somewhere, waiting for the chance to hurt her again, had hovered just on the edge of consciousness like a dark shadow waiting to swallow her whole.

As she'd regained her strength, she'd tried to convince herself her imagination was just playing tricks with her mind—the idiot wasn't stupid enough to come after her when Nick and his deputies were turning over every rock in the county looking for him! But deep down inside, she'd known better. He was obsessed with her, and he wasn't going to stop tormenting her until he had her right where he wanted her—in his power.

Her appetite forgotten, she rose and carried her half-eaten bowl of cereal to the sink. "So what do we do now?"

"The only thing we can," he said grimly. "We wait for him to make a move and pray that we're ready when he does."

Joe didn't tell her that he'd let his own work slide in order to watch over her while she was recovering from the explosion, but he didn't have to. She'd been aware of his presence in the house every time she woke up. He hadn't hovered over her or even checked in on her that much, but she'd known he was there, somewhere nearby, within calling distance in case she needed him.

Now that she was better, though, she'd expected him to leave her with her army of guards and get back to the business of running the ranch. He didn't. After he ate a breakfast of cold cereal himself, he grabbed some tools from his workshop in the barn and returned to the kitchen to fix a leaky faucet.

Another woman might have been fooled, but she was sharper than that. She knew exactly what he was doing when she came downstairs with a load of dirty laundry and found him sprawled on the floor with his head under the kitchen sink. "You don't have to stick around because of me," she said. "I'm much better."

Grunting as he loosened a nut with a wrench, he never looked up. "Good, because I'm not. I've been meaning to do this for a long time."

She didn't believe him, but she couldn't very well argue about him hanging around his own house. "Well, then, I'll get out of your way," she told him, and stepped over his legs where they jutted out into the room. "I've got some things to do upstairs."

She retreated to her room, expecting the day to fly by. It wasn't often that she got so much time off, and besides washing her laundry, she had correspondence to catch up on and lines to study. But time seemed to drag, and regardless of what she did, she just couldn't seem to concentrate. With a will of its own, her mind kept wandering off in a dozen different directions.

Disgusted, she tried to blame it on the blow to her head. It must have scrambled her brains. Or maybe she was just groggy from too much sleep. She hadn't focused on anything since the explosion and she was just out of practice. All she had to do was be patient and guide her thoughts back to the matter at hand every time they started to drift.

It should have been that simple. But each time Joe banged on a pipe downstairs and the sound seemed to vibrate throughout the house, her attention immediately zeroed in on the kitchen. And Joe. All too easily, she could see him stretched out on the kitchen floor with his head and shoulders under the sink, muttering curses to himself as he tried to loosen the last bolt that would allow him to install a new faucet.

Irritated with herself, she grumbled, "Stop it! You've got work of your own to do, for heaven's sake! Get on with it."

For a while, she did. Using Laura's room as an office, she sat down at the small desk in the corner and began sorting through the correspondence that had accumulated over the course of the last few weeks. Every other star she knew in Hollywood had a secretary to handle such things, but she'd always preferred to do it herself. If someone took the time out of their day to sit down and write her a letter, the least she could do was sit down and write them back. So she diligently wrote out checks for her bills, then started reading her fan mail. She'd barely finished the first letter and was formulating a response when the screen door opening onto the back porch banged.

He needed something from his workshop.

The thought came out of nowhere to drag her attention back to Joe, and whatever response she'd been planning to the fan letter flew right out of her head. With her mind's eye, she pictured Joe heading for the barn, his square face lined with concentration, his long strides eating up the distance between the house and his workshop. Any second, he would return with whatever tool he needed and let the screen door once again slam behind him as he walked into the kitchen.

On the heels of that thought, the door slammed again. And just that quickly, she realized her inability to focus had nothing to do with too much sleep or the blow to her head and everything to do with Joe—his constant presence in the house, the sound of him working in the kitchen, the clean scent of his aftershave drifting upstairs to tease and distract her. As long as he was underfoot, she wasn't going to be able to concentrate worth a damn.

Stiffening at the thought, she immediately tried to reject it, but memories stirred like the embers of a fire that refused to go out, warming her deep inside and filling her with a longing that stunned her. Her heart thumping crazily, she couldn't forget the feel of his arms around her, holding her close to the hard length of his body, his mouth hot and hungry on hers as their clothes just melted away.

Shaken, she pushed to her feet to pace the confines of her room restlessly, her fan mail forgotten. When had she come to need him so much? To want him to the point that instead of concentrating on her work, she couldn't stop wondering when he was going to find something to do upstairs. This had to stop! She wouldn't, couldn't let herself start to care for Joe McBride. She'd already made the mistake of falling for one man who was all wrong for her. She wouldn't do it again.

And there was no question that he was wrong for her. Oh, he was a good man—she didn't doubt that for a second. He'd been there for her and Emma and gone out of his way to keep them safe. But he still had a chip on his shoulder where women were concerned, still didn't trust her as far as he could throw her. He'd kissed her and taken her to bed and shown her an ecstasy she'd only dreamed about, but she didn't fool herself into thinking that what he felt for her was anything more than plain, old-fashioned lust. He'd only let one woman touch his heart, only to have her rip it out by the roots. He wouldn't chance that kind of pain again. If she didn't want to end up making a fool of herself over him, she'd do well to remember that.

Her eyes glinting with resolve, she turned on the small boom box she'd brought with her from L.A. and cranked up the volume until it blocked out all the noise from downstairs. Only then was she able to work.

She couldn't, however, stay in her room indefinitely without slowly climbing the walls. So she took breaks over the course of the day, going downstairs to wash and dry another load of clothes, to eat lunch, to get something to drink. And every time she came out of her room, she found herself listening for him, looking for him, finding him. If he wasn't outside repairing a loose railing on the porch, he was in the downstairs bathroom patching a cracked piece of drywall or in the laundry room sanding a cabinet door that had an irritating tendency to stick.

And try though she might, she couldn't, to her growing frustration, ignore the man. She turned the music up until she couldn't hear herself think, but when he came upstairs to reinforce a wobbly shelf in the linen closet in the hall, she knew it immediately. It was as if she had radar where he was concerned. All her senses went on alert, her heart started to flutter in anticipation, her nerve endings to tingle. It was mortifying, annoying, exhilarating.

She couldn't, she told herself, spend another day cooped up with him in the house. So she escaped downstairs with her script and called Charles to tell him she was a hundred percent better and ready to get back to work. He was thrilled. Every day shooting was shut down the studio lost a small fortune, so the sooner they could start filming again, the better. Promising her he'd have a car for her the next morning with one of the drivers she knew, he quickly hung up so he could notify the rest of the cast and crew to report back to work the following morning.

If she still needed incentive to concentrate, that should have done it. There was no question that everyone would be tense returning to the set after the explosion, and that meant blown lines and missed cues. To make matters worse, the scene scheduled to be shot in the morning was a love scene, and she always found those awkward and nerve-racking. She hadn't looked at her script in days. If she didn't want to be the one responsible for a long day of take after take, she'd make sure she had her lines down pat. With her script in hand, she retreated to the living room to study.

Shutting the door on the linen closet, its newly secured shelf loaded down with sheets and blankets, Joe gathered up his tools and would have moved on to another project, but there weren't any more. He'd fixed every loose board in the house, changed every burned-out lightbulb, even cleaned the air-conditioning vents in every room but Angel's. There was nothing left to do except face the inevitable. He could work from sunup to sundown, until he was so tired he wanted to drop where he stood, but he still wanted her. And they were alone together in the house and would be until her stalker was caught.

Outside, the day had already slipped into evening and he hadn't even noticed. Soon it would be completely dark. A muscle clenched in his jaw at the thought of the two of them sitting around, waiting for bedtime. Maybe he'd just lock himself up in his study and reorganize all his computer files. Then tomorrow night, he'd start on his workshop in the barn. His pickup needed a tune-up, and if worse came to worse, he'd give the barn a new coat of paint. At the rate he was going, he thought irritably, by the time it was safe for Miss Hollywood to finally leave, the place would look brand new.

Scowling, he returned his tools to his workshop, then strode back inside to make himself something to eat. He'd skipped lunch and should have been hungry, but the sandwich he ate while he stood at the back door and glared out at the night could have been cardboard for all the notice he gave it. All he could think of was Angel, sitting in the living room, studying her lines and doing a damn good job of ignoring him.

He should have been pleased. She was in one part of the house, he was in another, and at the rate they were going, they could coexist alone there together for months without ever coming face-to-face. And that was just the way he wanted it. Then, when she eventually left and returned to her life in Hollywood, he wouldn't find himself looking for her everywhere he turned. All he had to do between now and then was keep his distance.

He might as well have asked the stars not to shine in the night sky.

Without saying a word, she drew him to the living room doorway, and there didn't seem to be a damn thing he could do about it. There was just something about her he couldn't resist. Standing there, he watched her frown down at her script and tried to figure out what it was, but he couldn't explain it. It wasn't as if she went around the house in a negligee and deliberately tried to seduce him. With her face free of makeup and her hair pulled back from her face with a headband, she looked like a teenager in jeans and a T-shirt.

And still, somehow, she was beautiful.

He felt need hit him hard and low and should have gotten the hell out of there right then. But she swore softly then and threw down her script in frustration, and before he could stop himself, he stepped farther into the living room. "Problems?"

Startled, she jumped. For the first time all day, she'd actually been able to put him out of her mind, and now here he was, and she hadn't even heard him walk in the room. "I'm just having trouble with my lines," she said with a dismissive shrug. "Sometimes that happens."

"Maybe it would help if I read them with you. Not that I'm any good at that kind of thing," he added quickly, "but hearing the other character's lines might help you remember yours."

The second he made the suggestion, Angel knew he wanted to take the words back. If she'd had a brain in her head, she would have let him. All she had to do was give the excuse that she'd never been able to work with someone else when she was learning lines, and he would have accepted it.

But when she opened her mouth to politely decline his offer, no one was more surprised than she when she said, "You might be right. If you're sure you don't mind."

What could he say? "No, of course not. I'm game if you are."

So without quite knowing how it happened, she found him seated close beside her on the couch, his knee and shoulder almost brushing hers as she held the script between them where he could read it, too. He didn't touch her, didn't move except to help her steady the script, but her heart was racing, her mouth suddenly desert dry. Swallowing she tried to focus on her opening line in the scene, but the words swam before her eyes.

"I like you with your hair down like that. It makes you look all soft and touchable, the way a woman's supposed to look for her man."

His voice was rough with emotion and stroked her like a lover's caress. Surprised, Angel's eyes flew to his, but his gaze was focused on the script. Heat flooded her cheeks. What an idiot she was! She should have realized he wasn't talking to her, but to her character, Grace, the woman Garrett's character, Sebastian, was in love with. This was all just an act, just words on a page to Joe, and she'd do well to remember that.

Still, her heart fluttered with emotion as she dutifully repeated her own lines. "Am I your woman, Sebastian? Or are you just looking for someone to warm your bed for a while before you move on further west? Because I want more than that from the man I give myself to. I'll have more than that."

"So what do you want?" he murmured. "My heart and soul? You've already got it."

Tearing his eyes from the script, he turned to face her, his gaze dropping to her mouth, and too late, she realized she should have told him that all they were rehearsing were the lines themselves. It wasn't necessary to act out every single detail of the scene. "Joe—"

"Sebastian," he whispered huskily, leaning close and brushing her mouth with his. "My character's name is Sebastian."

She should have protested, should have beat a hasty retreat and put the length of the room between them while she still could. But it seemed like forever since he had kissed her. Her senses spinning, the script forgotten, she lifted her mouth to his. "Joe."

That was all she could manage, just his name, then his arms came around her, cradling her close, and he was kissing her hungrily, as if he were starving for the taste of her and was afraid she would be taken from him any second. Slanting his mouth over hers, his tongue urgent and seducing, he consumed her like a man possessed.

She loved it. He was always so careful with her, his emotions kept under a tight rein, that she hadn't thought she could drive him to such wildness, such need. Burying his hands in her hair, he tore his mouth from hers, but only to change the angle of the kiss and take her mouth all over again. Dizzy, delighted, the thunder of her heart roaring in her ears, she gave herself up to him without a murmur of protest, giving him back kiss for kiss, touch for touch.

"You conniving little slut!"

From the safety of the trees a thousand yards away and downwind from the house, the furious man stood in the all-concealing darkness of the night and watched the couple in the living room with high-powered binoculars. They were all over each other, unable to keep their hands off each other. And with the blinds wide open and the guards patrolling the perimeter of the house, they didn't care who knew it.

Then, even as he watched, McBride reached over and switched out the lights. Instantly, the living room went black.

Rage burned in the watcher's gut like hot oil, and what little self-control he had snapped. Damn them! Damn them both to hell! She was his. He'd told her time and again, but she just didn't get it. And neither did McBride.

But they would, he promised himself savagely, lowering his binoculars. By the time he got through with the two of them, they would both regret that they hadn't listened to him when they had the chance.

Hatred glinting in his eyes, he turned his back on the house and slipped away in the dark. Like a shadow, he silently blended in and out of the trees until he disappeared completely into the night.

Surrounded by the darkness of the night and the strength of Joe's arms around her, Angel sank down to the cushions of the couch with him. Lying side by side, facing each other, the kisses they shared turned hotter, longer, hungrier. When he reached for the hem of her T-shirt, she knew she should have stopped him, but she couldn't. She loved him.

Shaken, she knew herself too well to question what she was feeling. It was love—there wasn't a doubt in her mind. It seemed to be her fate in life to love men who couldn't love her back. First, with Kurt, Emma's father, and now Joe. The feelings she'd had for Kurt were nothing compared to what she felt for Joe, but the result was the same. He might want her and need her, but he wasn't going to let himself love her.

And it broke her heart. He was a good man who was wonderful with children and deserved a wife and family of his own, but he'd resigned himself to living the rest of his life alone. If she just had the time, the optimist in her had to believe she could find a way to get past the wall he'd built around himself because of his ex-wife's betrayal. But she had to leave him soon, and she didn't know how she was going to find the strength to do it. Filming on the ranch would be wrapping up next week, and then they would move on to another location in southern Utah. Once she left Liberty Hill, her chances of ever seeing him again were slim to none.

Tears welled in her eyes at the thought. This time with him was all she would ever have. Her hands helping his, she pulled her T-shirt over her head. Before it hit the floor, her fingers were fumbling blindly in the dark for the buttons of his shirt as he worked at the fastener of her bra.

Breathless, her heart rolled over in her chest when he pulled her under him and his work-roughened hands finally found her breasts. Merciful heavens, what hands he had! His fingers stroked and teased and played with her until she was wild with need, then his mouth latched onto her nipple and suckled strongly. Desire, white hot and swift, shot straight from her breasts to the heart of her femininity. With a soft, strangled cry, she arched under him. "Joe...please!"

Lost to everything but the feel of his mouth at her breast, she couldn't have said what she asked for, but he knew. With a muttered curse, he pulled back, but only long enough to tear off the rest of both of their clothes. Then he was coming back down to her, his hard, lean length pressing her softer one into the cushions of the couch, and nothing had ever felt so good.

Moaning, she took his weight gladly and gloried in it, loving the differences in their bodies. If he'd done nothing else but hold her that way the rest of the night, she would have been happy.

But the fire he'd lit in her blood was hotter than ever, the flames licking at both of them, and deep inside, she ached for more. Moving under him, she slid her hands down the long length of his whipcord lean back to urge him closer. His response was immediate—and hard.

In the dark shadows, her eyes met his. "Make love to me," she said softly. "Right here. Right now."

He should have taken her upstairs to his bed. At the very least, he should have retrieved the condom in his wallet. But it was in his jeans, and he'd sent them flying when he'd finally tugged them off. He thought they'd landed somewhere by the fireplace, but there was no way on God's green earth that he was letting go of Angel long enough to look for them—not when he had her right where he'd wanted her for days.

"I won't be gentle," he warned in a low growl as his body tightened with need. "Not this time. I want you too much."

For an answer, she lifted her hips to his and gently nudged him.

Groaning, he couldn't have resisted her then if a herd of cattle had stampeded through the living room. Something in him snapped, something dark and primitive that no other woman had ever touched in him. Moving over her, he didn't give her time to think, to gasp, to do anything but moan with delight as he took her to the first peak with his hands alone. She was still shuddering when he kissed his way down the center of her body and nearly shattered her.

"Joe!"

His gut a knot of need, his body unbearably tight with tension, he went wild at her cry. Parting her legs, he surged into her and laced his fingers with hers. Then they were moving, dancing, racing toward insanity and loving every second of it.

Just as he'd promised, he was rough, too rough. But she'd long since destroyed what was left of his control, and he was helpless to do anything but take the ride with her to the end. Setting a bruising pace, he groaned as she kept up with him. Then he felt her start to come undone around him, and the madness caught him. Her name torn from his throat like a prayer, he thrust into her one last time and felt his senses explode.

Chapter 12

When the phone rang in the middle of the night, Angel came awake with a start, her heart pounding. Beside her, Joe reached for the phone on the nightstand, and memories of their wild loving on the couch in the living room came rushing back. He'd carried her upstairs afterwards to his room, his bed, only to love her again until they'd fallen asleep in each other's arms, too exhausted to move.

It had been the most wonderful night of her life, like a dream come true, but something told her the dream was over. No phone call at that hour of the night was good news.

Afraid that something had happened to Emma, Angel sat up, clutching the covers to her breasts as Joe swore and slammed down the phone. "What is it?" she asked, alarmed as he rolled out of bed and quickly reached for his jeans. "What's wrong?"

"Forest fire," he said shortly. "Near Merry's clinic. She's already called the volunteer fire department, but everything's so dry because of the drought that the trees are going up like cinder and the buffalo grass has started to burn. The wind is blowing it straight toward her house and the clinic.''

Tugging on a shirt, he stepped into his boots. ''I've got to go help. I'll be back as quick as I can.''

''Wait! I'll go with you.''

She started to throw off the sheet, but he stopped her. ''No. It's too dangerous. I'll have to take everyone but one of the guards with me—we'll need all the help we can get to keep this thing from raging out of control—but you'll be safe here with Buster and the one guard to watch over you. I'll reset the alarm on my way out,'' he promised. A split second later, he was gone.

Left alone in the dark house with nothing but apprehension for company, Angel shivered. She'd seen a forest fire once as a child and had never forgotten the horror of it. In an instant, it had taken on a life of its own and consumed everything in its path. Thousands of acres of forests had been lost; people had died. Tonight, while she was safely tucked away from the licking flames, Joe and his family would be right out there in it, fighting to stop it before it took everything they held dear. And it scared her to death.

Chilled, she pulled on one of Joe's denim shirts and hugged it to herself as she hurried toward the windows. She couldn't see Merry's house and clinic because it was too far away and trees blocked the view, but even from that distance, she could see the thick black smoke billowing into the clear, moonlit night sky. And somewhere, far off in the silent night, she heard the desperate whine of a fire truck's siren.

Just watching the smoke, she knew the fire was worse, much worse, than she'd first thought. Worried sick, she wrapped her arms tighter around herself and prayed.

She never knew how long she stood there, unable to drag

her gaze away from the view from the window. Downstairs, there was a noise at the front door, but she hardly gave it second thought. It was just the security guard checking to make sure that Joe hadn't forgotten to lock the front door on his way out. There'd been a shift change an hour ago, and the late-night guard was always very conscientious about his duties.

Outside, the wind howled around the house, fanning the flames of the fire on the horizon, and she could only imagine the heat Joe and the volunteers who had rushed to fight the fire must be feeling. Were they wearing protective gear? And what about water? There was no city water system this far from town. How did they fight a fire without water?

Chewing on her bottom lip, she stared at the glow of the fire on the horizon and knew she had to do something. If Joe didn't want her to help fight the fire, she could respect that—she wouldn't know where to begin, anyway. But the volunteers would be tired and hungry when they finally got the fire under control, and she could at least make them something to eat and drink and have it there waiting for them when they needed it. She would get the guard to help her and they'd take everything in her car.

Relieved that she'd finally come up with a way to contribute, she whirled from the window. She had to get dressed. And make a list of everything she would need so she wouldn't forget anything. There was a large ice chest on the top shelf in the laundry room. And she'd check the freezer for sandwich meat—

Caught up in her thoughts, she didn't see the man who stepped into the bedroom doorway until she was halfway across the room. She looked up and gasped, her heart in her throat. Suddenly he was just there, as if he'd appeared out of nowhere. Dressed all in black, his face smeared with something dark to conceal the paleness of his skin, he had a can of gasoline in his hand and looked like the Devil himself.

And just that quickly, Angel knew who he was. Her stalker.

Terrified, she wanted to scream, to run. But he blocked the only exit, and there was no point in screaming for help anyway, not now. The gasoline can told its own story. He'd set the forest fire near Merry's house to draw everyone on the ranch there. Then, while they were all fighting the fire, he'd somehow found a way to eliminate her guard and Buster—otherwise he would have never gotten into the house. And no one had suspected a thing.

There was no one to help her, no one to save her but herself. She was alone with her worst nightmare.

Terrified, she could have easily begged him right then for mercy, but he didn't know the meaning of the word. And she only had to see the expectation in his cold, soulless eyes to know that that was exactly what he wanted her to do. She'd be damned if she'd give him the satisfaction.

Drawing herself up to her full five foot seven inches, she faced him squarely, fearlessly, and never let him know that inside, she was shaking like a leaf. "I don't know how you got in here or who you are, but you're not welcome here. Get out!"

"Without you?" he taunted in a cruel, sinister voice that she had heard far too many times at the other end of her telephone. "I don't think so. You're mine." And with that announcement, he stepped completely into the room.

Shivers of revulsion skated down her spine, but she didn't so much as flinch. "You obviously have me confused with someone else. Leave now, or I'll call the security guard."

She was bluffing, of course, and they both knew it. "Go ahead," he goaded as a slow, evil smile transformed his face into that of a devil. "He can't help you from the grave."

Horrified, she gasped. "You're lying!" she cried, and desperately wanted to believe it. But he reeked of gasoline. What had he done? Set the poor guard on fire? Dear God, no! "You didn't kill anyone."

"No one is keeping me from you," he snarled. "No one! Not a dog or a fat old security guard or a dirty cowboy who doesn't know how to keep his hands to himself. If they all die, you have no one to blame but yourself. *You gave yourself to him!* Just like a cheap whore!"

His self-control nearly nonexistent, he shrieked the accusation at her like a madman, but there was no doubting the ring of truth in his words. Shocked, Angel realized that he knew. Somehow, some way, he'd discovered she and Joe were lovers.

Just the thought of him possibly seeing them, watching them together, made her skin crawl, but she'd be damned if she'd explain herself to him. "What I do or don't do with Joe is none of your business," she said coldly. "I'm not yours. I never have been yours. I never will be yours."

The minute she said it she knew she was waving a red flag in front of a bull, but she didn't care. She was tired of living her life in fear because of him, tired of constantly searching for him everywhere she went, tired of dreading the day when she finally came face-to-face with him. That day was here, and by God, she wasn't going to cower before him!

And he didn't like it. He wanted her on her knees before him, begging for mercy. "Bitch!" Screaming at her, he threw the gasoline can in the corner, where it slammed against the wall and fell on its side on the floor. Jarred by the blow, the lid fell off and gasoline silently pooled on the carpet.

"You're mine!" he roared. "Do you hear me? You're

mine and no man is ever going to take you away from me again. I'll make sure of it!'' Lightning quick, he stepped toward the corner where the gas can lay and struck a match.

''No!'' Angel screamed, but it was too late. The gasoline caught fire with a horrifying whoosh, and flames raced like quicksilver across the carpet. Before Angel could do anything but gasp with horror, the room was ablaze.

The heat was like something out of the bowels of hell. Incredibly intense, mind-numbing, so hot it actually singed the air itself. Out of the southwest, a strong dry wind fed the flames, whipping them into a raging inferno that consumed everything it touched. Whole trees, decades old, went up like matchsticks. Even the ground burned.

His face flushed from the incredible heat, sweat dripping from his brow to blind him, Joe wiped his arm across his stinging eyes and was forced to back up another few steps from the encroaching edge of the fire. All around him, friends and neighbors beat at the flames, trying to stomp them out, but he was afraid they were fighting a losing battle. The fire was too big, too hot, and already out of control. Merry's house and clinic stood right in the path of the grass fire that spread out from the trees, and if the fire trucks from Spring Falls and the other surrounding communities didn't arrive soon to help, there wouldn't be much point in coming. There would be nothing but ashes left by the time they got there.

His concentration focused on the raging inferno in front of him, he never saw the gust of wind that sent sparks skipping across the dry buffalo grass behind him. Like kindling doused with lighter fluid, it burst into flame, and in the time it took to blink, he was surrounded by a three-foot-wide circle of fire.

Someone shouted behind him, the sound nearly lost in the roar and crackle of the fire. Blasting heat hit him from all sides. Suddenly realizing his predicament, he spun around sharply, his lungs burning with every breath he took, only to swear. He was trapped.

"Over here!" Appearing out of the thick smoke that filled the night, Zeke beat a narrow path for him, one that would only last seconds before it was swallowed whole by the fire. "Hurry!"

He didn't have to tell him twice. There was no time to think, no time to do anything but throw himself through the wall of flames. Sucking in a searing breath, he felt the shirt on his back catch fire right before he hit the ground clear of the fire.

"Roll!" Zeke yelled hoarsely, and fell to his knees beside him to pound out the smoldering sparks on his shirt with his bare hands.

His heart hammering, Joe rolled over the rocky ground, hardly feeling the hot spots that singed his back and arms. Close, he thought, swallowing to force moisture into his parched throat. That was too damn close.

"What are you doing, you idiot?" Zeke demanded furiously as he helped him up and pulled him away from the fire. "Trying to cremate yourself?"

"It's the damn wind!" he growled, brushing himself off. "It keeps changing directions. Where the hell's it going to come from next?"

Scowling, he lifted his face to the dark, swirling wind, only to freeze as his eyes fell on the horizon to the south. The forest fire was miles from there, yet the night sky was bright with what looked like a fire…right where his house was. And Angel.

His heart stopped dead in his chest, a fear unlike anything he'd ever known clutching his heart. He must have made a sound—he didn't remember—because suddenly Zeke was swearing, his gaze, too, focused on the horizon.

"Son of a bitch! The bastard orchestrated this whole

damn thing! Go!'' he yelled, pushing Joe toward where he'd left his truck. ''I'll round up some of the others and be there as quick as we can!''

Later, Joe had no memory of the drive to his house. His hands gripping the steering wheel until his knuckles were white, the accelerator pressed all the way to the floor, all he saw was the fire in the distance, licking at the night sky.

Engulfed in flames by the time he finally reached it, the house looked like something on a Hollywood film set that had been created with special effects. But there was no director standing by, waiting to yell cut, no crew in the wings armed with retardants to douse the fire. The security guard lying on the front porch wasn't an actor playing a part, but a real guard who'd been knocked out cold. And Angel was nowhere in sight.

Bursting from his truck, Joe ran to the porch and dragged the guard to safety, all his instincts telling him that Angel couldn't be inside. No one could be in there and still be alive. She would have gotten out. She would have found a way.

But there was no sign of her anywhere.

''Angel!'' His raspy cry carried on the hot wind, but his only response was silence. A deep, deadly silence that turned his blood to ice.

Then he heard her scream.

Screaming, choking on smoke, Angel struggled with her stalker, fighting the hold he had on her arm as he tried to drag her into the flames that danced wickedly around them. He was a small man, but wiry strong, with a grip like a vise. Slowly, relentlessly, he pulled her closer to the fire.

He was going to kill her. While the house burned down around them, he was going to kill her and laugh while he did it. She knew it as surely as she knew her own name. Fighting like a wild woman, she kicked and bit, determined not to make it easy for him. Her gouging fingers raced toward his eyes, catching him off guard, and sinking deep. With a cry of outraged pain, he slung her across the room.

She hit the wall with a grunt of pain and slid to the floor, shaken, but almost immediately, she scrambled to her feet and ran toward the door.

"No!"

Too late, he recognized his mistake and charged after her with a roar of fury, but she never looked back. Sobbing, she darted into the hall. Smoke choked her, blinding her, but she knew the house well now and didn't need to see to find the stairs. Her heart thundering, she stumbled down them, her only thought to get away.

Spewing curses at her, he was so close behind her that Angel could practically feel him breathing down her neck. Sick with terror, she almost fell, only to catch herself with a whimper. She couldn't fall, couldn't miss a step or he would be on her. And if he got his hands on her a second time, he wouldn't let her outsmart him again.

Caught up in the nightmare of what he would do to her if he got the chance, her eyes focused on her feet as she took the stairs two at a time, she never noticed the heat of the banister under her hand or the thick smell of gasoline that permeated the smoky air. Her only thought was to run. If she could just get to the front door—and outside—she could lose him in the darkness.

But she never made it that far. The second she reached the lower floor, she turned toward the front door, only to gasp in horror. The entire lower floor of the house was in flames, the smell of gasoline so strong that she nearly gagged, every exit cut off by a wall of flames.

Stunned, she hesitated, and in a heartbeat, her stalker was on her. Grabbing her arm and wrenching it behind her back, he laughed when she screamed. "You didn't really think you were going to get away, did you?" he jeered in her ear. "I made sure of that before I came upstairs. We're going to burn in hell together, sweetheart. I hope you like the heat."

"No!" she choked as he forced her arm farther up her back and pain shot up to her shoulder. "I won't let you do this."

"You can't stop me—"

With no warning, the front door burst open, and through the flames that surrounded it, a dark specter charged inside like an avenging angel. Tall and dark, his face covered with soot and grime, Joe snarled, "Let her go!"

Far from alarmed, Angel's captor only laughed insanely, madness glinting in his eyes as he jerked her back against him. "Oh, no. Not in this lifetime, " he said, then laughed again at his own twisted wit. "Not in this lifetime! Get it? This lifetime's over. Look around you, cowboy. We're toast. All three of us!"

He spoke nothing less than the truth. The house blazed around them, upstairs and down. The heat was so intense that lightbulbs shattered in their sockets and the floor buckled beneath them. Smoke swelled in thick dark clouds, making it nearly impossible to breathe, let alone see.

And still the bastard laughed like a maniac. Fury raging in his eyes, Joe wanted to rush him, to jerk Angel free of his touch and drive the son of a bitch into the ground with his fists and make him pay for every time he'd hurt her. But there wasn't time. The house was on the verge of coming down around their ears any second. If he couldn't convince the madman to see reason, they really were all going to die right there because there was no way in hell he was going anywhere without Angel.

"It doesn't have to be that way," he rasped, choking on the smoke that filled his lungs. "There's still time to get out."

"And leave this nice cozy fire?" her stalker tossed back

flippantly. "I don't think so. I brought marshmallows. Wait. Where did I put them? Oh, yes, now I remember."

Truly mad, he began to pat down the pockets of the overlarge black shirt he wore. Suddenly, directly overhead, a large, burning beam groaned loudly. Startled, they all three looked up just as it started to fall in a shower of sparks right where Angel and her stalker stood.

"Look out!" Joe yelled.

His insane grin turning to a look of horror, Angel's stalker screamed and instinctively shoved her out of the way. A split second later, the beam slammed into him, cutting off his horrified cry and crushing him.

With that, the house began to fall in upon itself. The ceiling broke up in huge, burning chunks, while upstairs, the roof caved in in a crash that shook the place to its very foundation. Flames climbed the walls, the curtains at the windows, the stairs. Everywhere you looked, there was nothing but fire.

What had once been the front door was now an inferno, but there was no time to look for another way out. Dodging the debris that fell all around them, Joe swung Angel up into his arms and ran for safety. Blocking his path was a wall of fire.

"Hang on," he warned, and burst through the flames at a dead run.

They felt the heat—and the lick of fire. Then, just when they both thought they were going to burn alive, they stumbled out onto the porch and into the yard, gasping for air. Almost immediately, Zeke was there with the rest of the family, not to mention half the ranch hands.

"Son of a bitch, what the hell took you so long?" Zeke demanded furiously as he helped Joe ease Angel to the ground. "I was giving you five seconds, and then I was coming in after you! Have you got a death wish or what?"

"Don't yell at them, dear," Sara McBride scolded quietly as she and Janey settled blankets around them. "We've all just had a horrible fright."

"I had to get Angel," Joe rasped, throwing off the blanket so he could check on Angel himself when she couldn't seem to stop coughing. "God, is she all right?"

On her knees at Angel's side, Janey quickly listened to her lungs. "She's suffering from smoke inhalation, and it looks like she's got several nasty burns."

"The ambulance will be here any second," Merry said as she returned her cell phone to her pocket. "Joe, you need to be checked out, too."

"Later," he coughed, his own voice hoarse from smoke as he turned back toward the house. "The stalker's still inside. I've got to get in there."

"The hell you do!" his brother snapped. "Are you crazy? Look at the place. There's nobody in there alive."

There was no question that he was right. From fifty yards away, they could still feel the incredibly intense heat of the fire. The gusting wind swirled around the house, fanning the flames even higher as windows shattered and what was left of the walls collapsed. The porch was the next—and last—thing to go, and all they could do was stand there and watch it burn.

By three in the morning, all the fires were out, and there was nothing left to do but to assess the damage. Standing in what had once been Joe's front yard with his family and Nick, Angel couldn't seem to stop crying. Using a corner of the blanket she still clutched around her, she wiped her teary eyes. "He saved me at the last minute," she whispered in a croak. "If he hadn't pushed me out of the way at the last second, I'd be dead right now."

"If he hadn't set the fire in the first place, you never would have been in that position to begin with," Joe retorted. "Don't feel sorry for him. He wasn't joking when he said he planned for the three of us to die tonight. An attack of conscience at the last second doesn't excuse what he did.''

"He's right,'' Nick said as he watched the ranch hands hose down the last smoldering areas of the foundation that still glowed red with heat. "We found his car two miles down the road and hidden in some brush. His name was Eugene Tyler. He left a suicide note and instructions for his burial.''

"But why?'' Angel cried. "Why did he do this? Why couldn't he just leave me alone?''

"He wasn't sane, Angel. He had a history of mental illness but was released from an institution in L.A. because of a cutback in government funding. He became fixated with you and was determined to have you.''

"But he didn't even know me!''

"He knew the woman on the screen, the angel with the bedroom eyes. When you were in L.A., he actually thought he could court you with flowers and gifts and win you. When that didn't work, he got a job with the security company that monitored your home. Every time you changed your phone number or access code, he knew it almost immediately.''

"So that explains how he was able to deactivate Joe's security system and get in the house tonight,'' Zeke said. "He worked in the business.''

Nick nodded. "Then when Angel left L.A. and showed up here at Joe's, it pushed him over the edge. He couldn't stand the idea of her being involved with another man. If he couldn't have her, he intended to make sure no one else could either. So he set the fire in the woods near Merry's, then went back to Joe's and, in the excitement of everyone leaving, was able to leave some meat laced with tranquilizers for Buster. With him out of the way, all he had to do was wait until the guard checked the front door, sneak up on him from behind, and knock him out.''

Just that easily, he'd cleared the way to kill her and Joe and he hadn't cared who he'd hurt in the process, Angel thought. He'd destroyed not only Joe's house, but Merry's and her clinic, as well as hundreds of acres of forest before the fire was finally under control. And it was all her fault. If she'd never come there, never lured Eugene Tyler to the ranch and given him a reason to hate the McBrides, none of this would have ever happened.

Staring at the charred remains of what had once been Joe's home, she knew he had to hate the day she'd walked into his life. She'd brought him nothing but trouble and cost him everything he owned.

Her throat raw from the smoke she'd inhaled, she choked, ''I'm so sorry. I don't know what to say except that you won't have to worry about me causing you any more grief. We're almost finished filming here—next week we go to Utah. Then I'll be out of your hair forever.''

Standing at her side, Joe swore, but she didn't dare look at him or she would lose what little control she had left. ''Nick, if we're through here, would you mind giving me a ride to the set? The studio had another trailer brought in for me—I'll stay there tonight.''

Surprised, he said, ''Of course, if that's what you want. But wouldn't you be more comfortable at Myrtle's? She's got plenty of room and I know she'd be thrilled to have you.''

''And there's always my place,'' Sara McBride added. ''Joe's going to go to Zeke's, and Merry can double up with Janey. There's a couch in my sewing room that converts to a bed, and you can have it all to yourself.''

Angel couldn't believe her generosity. How could she be so kind to her after Joe had nearly died because of her? Impulsively hugging her, she said thickly, ''Thank you. But you've already got a full house, and I think I really need to be alone for a while. I'll be fine at the trailer.''

Left with no choice, Nick said, ''If you're sure that's what you want, I'll take you now.''

He escorted her to his car, but not before he shot Joe a silent look that demanded he do something. His jaw set in granite, Joe didn't say a word. Left with no choice, Nick helped her in the car and drove away.

Silence fell like a rock. Janey, who seldom lost her temper, surprised everyone by glaring at Joe in exasperation. ''What are you doing? Can't you see she loves you? Go after her!''

''You heard her,'' he said stiffly. ''She wants to be alone.''

Unable to believe he'd fallen for that, she rolled her eyes. ''Surely you can't be that dense. She's hurting, Joe. You just lost everything you own, and she blames herself. If you don't go talk to her, she's going to think you do, too.''

Scowling, he snapped, ''That's ridiculous! Who gives a damn about things when she could have been killed?''

Pleased, Janey grinned while the rest of the family tried to hide their smiles. ''Exactly. So why don't you go tell her that? She needs to hear it. And while you're at it, you might tell her you love her, too. She already has a reason to leave. Give her one to stay.''

How had she known he loved her? he thought irritably. He hadn't known it himself until he'd seen his house engulfed in flames and known Angel was in there. He'd come so damn close to losing her that just thinking about it, even now that he knew she was safe, scared the hell out of him. She'd stolen his heart when he would have sworn he didn't have one to steal.

And she was leaving. Just like Belinda, she was going to walk out on him and go back to the big city—and take his heart with her. Unless, as Janey suggested, he gave her a reason to stay.

"Let me clean up first and then I'll talk to her," he said in a rough voice. "Zeke, can I borrow some of your clothes? Unless I go to her in my birthday suit, I've got nothing to wear."

Delighted, his brother grinned. "I've got a new pair of jeans and a shirt at the house that I haven't worn yet. Consider them my contribution to the cause."

The trailer was small and simply furnished and stocked with everything from makeup to clothes. It could have been bigger than a palace and decked out in diamonds and gold and a wardrobe fit for a queen, and Angel wouldn't have noticed. Standing under the shower, washing the soot of the fire from her hair, she'd never been more miserable in her life. What did she care where she stayed when she'd lost Joe?

Not that she could lose something she'd never really had, she reasoned with a sob as she turned off the water and reached for a towel. He'd wanted her, but a part of her had known he was never going to chance his heart with someone like her. He'd made it clear right from the beginning that he'd wanted nothing to do with a woman like Belinda, nothing to do with a city girl like her. And it turned out, with good cause. She'd brought the wickedness of the city to his ranch, and he'd been the one who'd suffered because of it. All things considered, he'd no doubt be glad to see the last of her.

And that hurt. Because she knew that what they'd shared had been much more than desire. She'd felt it every time he touched her, kissed her, made love to her. It was there in his eyes every time he looked at her. If he'd just let go of the past and admit it—

And what about you? a voice in her head demanded.

Have you told him that you love him? Or are you going to just walk away without fighting for the man you love? When did you become such a quitter?

In the process of tugging on a nightshirt, she stopped, startled, her eyes wide as she stared at her reflection in the mirror. A quitter? she thought, stung. She'd never been a quitter in her life. She'd fought her father and the odds to become a successful actress and never thought of giving up without fighting for what she wanted.

So why are you doing any less for the man you love?

Why, indeed? she thought, stunned. Dear God, she had to find him, talk to him, *tell* him! Then if he let her walk away next week without a word to stop her, at least she'd know in the lonely years to come that she'd tried.

Scrambling around for something to wear, she knew she should have waited until later to talk to him. Sunrise was only a few hours away; he had to be as exhausted as she was. Then there was her father—she had to call him and let him know that she was okay and the nightmare was finally over.

But all she could think of was Joe. She couldn't let another hour pass without telling him how she felt about him.

Later, she couldn't have said what clothes she finally pulled on. She just grabbed the first thing that came to hand—a red knit dress—and tugged it on, then found a pair of brown loafers under the bed. She was still slipping into them when she ran to the door and pulled it open...only to gasp in surprise at the sight of Joe standing there, his hand raised to knock.

"Joe!"

He, too, had bathed and changed into clean clothes, but she hardly noticed. He was there. Nothing else mattered. Her heart expanding with love, she pulled the door wide. "How did you know I needed to talk to you? I—"

"I won't keep you long. I just wanted to tell you—"

"…know I should wait, but I can't. I've already waited days as it is—"

"…that I know you have to leave, but there's something you should know—"

"I love you!"

"I love you!"

They spoke at the same time, each talking over the other in a rush to get the words out before they lost their nerve. Then it hit them what they'd said.

For what seemed like an eternity, they just stood there, staring at each other, shock registering in their eyes. Then a slow smile curled the corners of Joe's mouth. Stepping inside, he shut the door behind him. "Why don't we back up and start over?" he suggested huskily. "This time, one at a time."

She didn't need a second prompting. "I love you." The words came so easily, straight from her heart, and setting her aglow. "I know this isn't what you wanted at the beginning, but I couldn't stop myself. You were so wonderful with Emma, and even when you tried to convince yourself that you wanted nothing to do with me, you were right there to protect me every time I needed you. How could I not love you? You touched my heart, and I had to tell you even if you didn't want to hear it."

"I love you, too," he admitted softly, lifting his hand to her hair to play with a curl by her ear. "And you're right, I didn't want to hear it. I didn't want to get hurt again, and I knew you could hurt me in a way Belinda never could. All this time, I thought I was holding my own, protecting my heart, then tonight, when I got to the house and realized you were in there—"

Unable to finish, he swallowed, forcing the tightness from his throat, and hugged her close. "Let's just say, I don't ever want to go through anything like that again. If I lost you—"

"You won't," she promised thickly, blinking back tears at the thought of how close they'd come to losing each other. "The bad's all behind us and there's nothing but happiness ahead of us."

"I want us to get married."

It was the last thing she expected, the last dream she'd dare let herself hope for. After all the heartache he'd had with Belinda, she'd have sworn he'd never want to get married again. "Are you sure?"

"I've never been more sure of anything in my life," he replied without hesitation. "I know we've got some things to work out. Your career means a lot to you, and that's in L.A. I don't care much for cities, but I can learn to tolerate anything if that means having you in my life. I'll talk to Zeke about taking over the ranch for a while—"

"No!" Horrified that he would even consider giving up something he loved so much for her, she cupped his face in her hands and kissed him gently on the mouth. "No," she said again. "I've never liked L.A., Joe. Never cared about living the life of a movie star. If I could have my dream life, it would be here, on the ranch, with you and Emma."

"But your career—"

"Doesn't require me to live in California. I can live any-where. So I choose here, where Emma can grow up like other kids, with parents who are there for her, and you can keep doing what you love. I'll continue to make movies, but only once a year so that I won't be away from the two of you any more than I have to be, and the rest of the time, I'll just be a regular wife and mother. If that's okay with you."

He didn't have to tell her that was more than okay—his broad grin said it all. They'd both found what they'd never thought they would. Drawing her close, he kissed her like he would never let her go. And when he finally let her up for air, together they spoke the words that were in both their hearts.

"I love you."

Epilogue

As the credits rolled for the premiere showing of *Beloved Stranger,* the audience clapped and cheered wildly. Delighted, Angel squeezed her husband's hand and graciously accepted the praise of the friends and family who surrounded her and Joe and Emma in the Denver theater. Critics all over the country were already predicting that this was the movie that would put her career over the top and earn her an Oscar. There'd been a time in her life, when she was just getting started and was hungry for success, that she would have sworn that that was all she needed to make her happy. She couldn't have been more wrong.

Flanking her other side, her father leaned over and kissed her cheek. "Your mother would have been proud of you."

He couldn't quite bring himself to admit that *he* was proud of her, but he was a stubborn man and Angel understood that there were some things his pride would never let him say. And that was all right. In the eight months that had passed since the fire, she and her father had come a long way in their struggle to make peace. The fact that he was there at all to celebrate her success meant more to her than any words.

Blinking back tears, she smiled. "Thanks, Dad. I'm glad you could be here."

With a sleepy Emma draped over his shoulder, Joe slipped his arm around Angel's waist and her world was complete. She had her husband, daughter, father and in-laws there and wanted to laugh aloud with joy. Whoever said that happily-ever-after only happened in the movies hadn't known what they were talking about. She was living it, and life didn't get any better than that.

*   *   *   *   *

Look Who's Celebrating Our 20ᵗʰ Anniversary:

Celebrate
20
YEARS

"Working with Silhouette has always been a privilege—I've known the nicest people, and I've been delighted by the way the books have grown and changed with time. I've had the opportunity to take chances…and I'm grateful for the books I've done with the company. Bravo! And onward, Silhouette, to the new millennium."

—*New York Times* bestselling author
Heather Graham Pozzessere

"Twenty years of laughter and love… It's not hard to imagine Silhouette Books celebrating twenty years of quality publishing, but it is hard to imagine a publishing world without it. Congratulations…"

—International bestselling author
Emilie Richards

INTIMATE MOMENTS®
™ Silhouette®

SILHOUETTE'S 20TH ANNIVERSARY CONTEST
OFFICIAL RULES
NO PURCHASE NECESSARY TO ENTER

1. To enter, follow directions published in the offer to which you are responding. Contest begins 1/1/00 and ends on 8/24/00 (the "Promotion Period"). Method of entry may vary. Mailed entries must be postmarked by 8/24/00, and received by 8/31/00.

2. During the Promotion Period, the Contest may be presented via the Internet. Entry via the Internet may be restricted to residents of certain geographic areas that are disclosed on the Web site. To enter via the Internet, if you are a resident of a geographic area in which Internet entry is permissible, follow the directions displayed on-line, including typing your essay of 100 words or fewer telling us "Where In The World Your Love Will Come Alive." On-line entries must be received by 11:59 p.m. Eastern Standard time on 8/24/00. Limit one e-mail entry per person, household and e-mail address per day, per presentation. If you are a resident of a geographic area in which entry via the Internet is permissible, you may, in lieu of submitting an entry on-line, enter by mail, by hand-printing your name, address, telephone number and contest number/name on an 8"x 11" plain piece of paper and telling us in 100 words or fewer "Where In The World Your Love Will Come Alive," and mailing via first-class mail to: Silhouette 20th Anniversary Contest, (in the U.S.) P.O. Box 9069, Buffalo, NY 14269-9069; (In Canada) P.O. Box 637, Fort Erie, Ontario, Canada L2A 5X3. Limit one 8"x 11" mailed entry per person, household and e-mail address per day. On-line and/or 8"x 11" mailed entries received from persons residing in geographic areas in which Internet entry is not permissible will be disqualified. No liability is assumed for lost, late, incomplete, inaccurate, nondelivered or misdirected mail, or misdirected e-mail, for technical, hardware or software failures of any kind, lost or unavailable network connection, or failed, incomplete, garbled or delayed computer transmission or any human error which may occur in the receipt or processing of the entries in the contest.

3. Essays will be judged by a panel of members of the Silhouette editorial and marketing staff based on the following criteria:

   Sincerity (believability, credibility)—50%

   Originality (freshness, creativity)—30%

   Aptness (appropriateness to contest ideas)—20%

   Purchase or acceptance of a product offer does not improve your chances of winning. In the event of a tie, duplicate prizes will be awarded.

4. All entries become the property of Harlequin Enterprises Ltd., and will not be returned. Winner will be determined no later than 10/31/00 and will be notified by mail. Grand Prize winner will be required to sign and return Affidavit of Eligibility within 15 days of receipt of notification. Noncompliance within the time period may result in disqualification and an alternative winner may be selected. All municipal, provincial, federal, state and local laws and regulations apply. Contest open only to residents of the U.S. and Canada who are 18 years of age or older, and is void wherever prohibited by law. Internet entry is restricted solely to residents of those geographical areas in which Internet entry is permissible. Employees of Torstar Corp., their affiliates, agents and members of their immediate families are not eligible. Taxes on the prizes are the sole responsibility of winners. Entry and acceptance of any prize offered constitutes permission to use winner's name, photograph or other likeness for the purposes of advertising, trade and promotion on behalf of Torstar Corp. without further compensation to the winner, unless prohibited by law. Torstar Corp and D.L. Blair, Inc., their parents, affiliates and subsidiaries, are not responsible for errors in printing or electronic presentation of contest or entries. In the event of printing or other errors which may result in unintended prize values or duplication of prizes, all affected contest materials or entries shall be null and void. If for any reason the Internet portion of the contest is not capable of running as planned, including infection by computer virus, bugs, tampering, unauthorized intervention, fraud, technical failures, or any other causes beyond the control of Torstar Corp. which corrupt or affect the administration, secrecy, fairness, integrity or proper conduct of the contest, Torstar Corp. reserves the right, at its sole discretion, to disqualify any individual who tampers with the entry process and to cancel, terminate, modify or suspend the contest or the Internet portion thereof. In the event of a dispute regarding an on-line entry, the entry will be deemed submitted by the authorized holder of the e-mail account submitted at the time of entry. Authorized account holder is defined as the natural person who is assigned to an e-mail address by an Internet access provider, on-line service provider or other organization that is responsible for arranging e-mail address for the domain associated with the submitted e-mail address.

5. Prizes: Grand Prize—a $10,000 vacation to anywhere in the world. Travelers (at least one must be 18 years of age or older) or parent or guardian if one traveler is a minor, must sign and return a Release of Liability prior to departure. Travel must be completed by December 31, 2001, and is subject to space and accommodations availability. Two hundred (200) Second Prizes—a two-book limited edition autographed collector set from one of the Silhouette Anniversary authors: Nora Roberts, Diana Palmer, Linda Howard or Annette Broadrick (value $10.00 each set). All prizes are valued in U.S. dollars.

6. For a list of winners (available after 10/31/00), send a self-addressed, stamped envelope to: Harlequin Silhouette 20th Anniversary Winners, P.O. Box 4200, Blair, NE 68009-4200.

Contest sponsored by Torstar Corp., P.O. Box 9042, Buffalo, NY 14269-9042.

PS20RULES

ENTER FOR
A CHANCE TO WIN*

Silhouette's 20th Anniversary Contest

Tell Us Where in the World
You Would Like *Your* Love To Come Alive...
And We'll Send the Lucky Winner There!

Silhouette wants to take you wherever
your happy ending can come true.

Here's how to enter: Tell us, in 100 words or less,
where you want to go to make your love come alive!

In addition to the grand prize, there will be 200
runner-up prizes, collector's-edition book sets
autographed by one of the Silhouette anniversary
authors: **Nora Roberts, Diana Palmer,
Linda Howard** or **Annette Broadrick**.

DON'T MISS YOUR CHANCE TO WIN!
ENTER NOW! No Purchase Necessary

Silhouette®
Where love comes alive™

Name:

Address:

City: State/Province:

Zip/Postal Code:

Mail to Harlequin Books: **In the U.S.**: P.O. Box 9069, Buffalo, NY
14269-9069; **In Canada**: P.O. Box 637, Fort Erie, Ontario, L4A 5X3